"Everything you see…happens,"

Austin said with urgency.

Shaine's thoughts jolted to the scene of her in his arms. He was right. Everything she saw in her dreams *happened*. And that was how she knew without a doubt that she would make love with Austin Allen—glorious, breathless, rapturous love.

She surveyed him and embarrassment clawed its way to the surface of her mind. She barely knew him, but she knew the taste and urgency of his kiss, and what his body would feel like cradled between her legs.

"Yes," she whispered. She didn't know whether to feel giddy or guilty to possess this disconcerting knowledge. "Everything I see happens."

And right now she didn't know whether or not she would change anything even if she could.

Dear Reader,

With the coming of fall, the days—and nights—are getting cooler, but you can heat them up again with this month's selections from Silhouette Intimate Moments. Award winner Justine Davis is back with the latest installment in her popular TRINITY STREET WEST miniseries, *A Man To Trust*. Hero Cruz Gregerson proves himself to be just that—though it takes heroine Kelsey Hall a little time to see it. Add a pregnant runaway, a mighty cute kid and an opportunely appearing snake (yes, I said "snake"!), and you have a book to cherish forever.

With *Baby by Design,* award-winning Paula Detmer Riggs concludes her MATERNITY ROW trilogy. Pregnant-with-twins Raine Paxton certainly isn't expecting a visit from her ex-husband, Morgan—and neither one of them is expecting the sensuous fireworks that come next! Miniseries madness continues with *Roarke's Wife,* the latest in Beverly Barton's THE PROTECTORS, and Maggie Shayne's *Badlands Bad Boy,* the newest in THE TEXAS BRAND. Both of these miniseries will be going on for a while—and if you haven't discovered them already, you'll certainly want to come along for the ride. Then turn to Marie Ferrarella's *Serena McKee's Back in Town* for a reunion romance with heart-stopping impact. Finally there's Cheryl St.John's second book for the line, *The Truth About Toby,* a moving story about how dreams can literally come true.

Here at Intimate Moments, we pride ourselves on bringing you books that represent the best in romance fiction, so I hope you'll enjoy every one of this month's selections, then join us again next month, when the excitement—and the passion—continue.

Yours,

Leslie J. Wainger
Senior Editor and Editorial Coordinator

Please address questions and book requests to:
Silhouette Reader Service
U.S.: 3010 Walden Ave., P.O. Box 1325, Buffalo, NY 14269
Canadian: P.O. Box 609, Fort Erie, Ont. L2A 5X3

THE TRUTH
ABOUT TOBY

CHERYL
ST.JOHN

Published by Silhouette Books

America's Publisher of Contemporary Romance

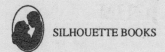 **SILHOUETTE BOOKS**

ISBN 0-373-07810-2

THE TRUTH ABOUT TOBY

Copyright © 1997 by Cheryl Ludwigs

Books by Cheryl St.John

Silhouette Intimate Moments

A Husband by Any Other Name #756
The Truth About Toby #810

Harlequin Historicals

Rain Shadow #212
Heaven Can Wait #240
Land of Dreams #265
Saint or Sinner #288
Badlands Bride #327

CHERYL ST.JOHN

is the pseudonym for Nebraska author Cheryl Ludwigs. Cheryl's first book, *Rain Shadow*, 1994, received nominations from *Romantic Times* and *Affaire de Coeur,* and was a finalist for the Romance Writers of America RITA Award.

She has been program director and vice president of her Heartland RWA chapter, and is currently a liaison for Published Authors' Network and a conference committee chairman.

Married mother of five, grandmother of three, Cheryl enjoys her family. In her "spare" time, she corresponds with dozens of writer friends from Canada to Texas, and treasures their letters. She would love to hear from you.

Send a SASE to:

Cheryl St.John
P.O. Box 12142
Florence Station
Omaha, NE 68112-0142

For their infinite patience and steadfast support,
my heartfelt thanks go to my critique group:

Ginny McBlain, Bernadette Duquette,
Maureen McKade, Barb Hunt,
Janie Jensen and Lea Pounds
(in the order only they will understand!)

Prologue

Raindrops collected like silvery dots of light on the window. A lonely man stood watching the rain. His pain was so intense, Shaine was sure that if she touched him, it would become hers. Something drew her toward him anyway, drew her to touch him, feel his pain, taste it. She had the ability to take his anguish inside herself and ease his burden. There was a way to transform his suffering to a bearable level, but the means escaped her. She searched within herself for the answer.

The sound of the rain faded away. The lightning disappeared, and enveloping clouds obliterated the moon.

Only the sound of ragged breathing remained.

Hers.

A clap of thunder jolted Shaine Richards upright in her bed. Through the sheer curtains, the streetlight cast a lacy shadow on her bedroom ceiling. The luminous red digits on her clock radio told her it had been less than an hour since her last dream.

Reaching for the phone on the nightstand, her finger hovered over the auto dial button before she clamped the receiver back in its cradle. Slipping out from under the covers, she padded into her living room, the only room of her basement apartment below the inn that had a full-length window, and gazed out at the rain.

Instead of her own likeness reflected in the panes of glass, she again saw the man in her dream. An occasional flicker of lightning had illuminated one side of his granite-hewn face, mirroring his lonely image. He had a hard, square jaw that hinted eloquently at a sober, spiritual respect for life and all its frailties. Eyes, dark and agonized, knew things the man behind them wished he didn't know.

A leaf blew against the window, clung stubbornly for seconds, then was caught up in another gale.

Without a sound, without the least warning, the man in her dream had known he was being observed, and in the slender threads of moonlight, he turned his head and unerringly found her.

Minutes passed in which the only sound was the patter of rain against the glass, and the mournful howl of the wind beneath the eaves. Lightning had momentarily sucked away the blackness in a rapid succession of flashes, as quick as a camera strobe, the light again revealing only one side of his face.

Shaine closed her eyes, the line between dream and reality dangerously blurred. Another face superimposed itself over the man's: Toby's.

She hadn't recognized him when she'd first started having the dreams. Her nephew had only been a little over eighteen months when Shaine's sister's car had gone off a bridge into the Missouri River with both Maggie and Toby in it.

In her dreams Toby was a year older, as he would be now.

"They're both so lonely," she whispered.

She should call Tom Stempson, the researcher at the institute in North Carolina who'd worked with her for the past six months. But it was late, and she knew he'd just tell her to record the dreams.

Back in her room, Shaine lay down, turned on the lamp and flipped through the pages of her journal. Each entry was marked with an *'R'* for regular dreams, or a *'K'* for knowing dreams, the way she had learned to identify them.

Dreams of Maggie were "regular" dreams, like the dreams of them doing things they had as kids. The dream of the man at the window and those of Toby were "knowing" dreams. She scanned the knowing dream entries. A woman with a white apron...a document on a wall...an Irish setter bounding through the woods...the man at the window... What did he have to do with Toby? Somehow, she knew instinctively that there was a correlation between the two dreams...and the others tied into the equation somewhere.

The therapists at University Hospital had told Shaine her mind couldn't cope with the possibilities concerning Toby's death. Maggie's body had been recovered from the river, but Toby's had never been found. The police said because he was so small, he could have become snagged below or washed up anywhere. The doctors said Shaine needed to let go.

She'd wanted to let go.

She'd tried to let go.

But the dreams wouldn't let her.

Shaine rolled over and curled into a tiny ball, wadding her knuckled fists against her eyes. She'd done her best to refuse the frightening uncertainties, but ignoring them had done no good. The dreams brought all the exhaustive questions to life. Shaine had to sleep, and when she did, the dreams took her captive.

Finally, one of the university doctors had taken her aside and given her the name of a Ph.D. at the Psychic Research Center.

Tom had taught her not to fight the dreams.

Tom had taught her how to keep them from taking over

her existence. If only Tom could help her understand and do something with them. But she'd come to depend too much on his long-distance voice, and he'd done all he could for her. She needed to get a handle on this thing herself.

She wasn't like the others he worked with. And they both knew it.

Shaine took her hands away from her eyes and breathed evenly, relaxing her body.

And then she dreamed a new dream.

Chapter 1

Shaine poured batter onto the hot waffle iron and closed the lid, turning to stick the syrup pitcher in the microwave. She always got a kick out of the fact that the Victorian Inn's customers spent the night in the authentic 1800s restored mansion with its claw-foot tubs and pull-chain toilets, sipped tea in the oak-floored lace-curtained dining room and then received electrically grilled, perked, toasted and microwaved breakfasts.

"If you'll do the beds and bathrooms again this morning, I'll do the laundry and clean up the kitchen," Audrey Pruitt said from behind her.

"Sure. Your legs still bothering you?"

Audrey, over eight months pregnant with her first baby, shuffled over with her swollen feet stuffed into a pair of fuzzy bedroom slippers. "Isn't this disgusting? Nick must feel like he's getting into bed with a circus elephant every night."

"How long?" Shaine asked. "Three or four weeks left?

That time's going to fly by, and you'll be so happy to have the baby, you'll forget all about this. I remember…''

"What?"

"Oh, I was just going to say I remember when Maggie was pregnant with Toby. She was miserable, too."

Beside her, Audrey was silent.

From the portable television atop the double-wide steel refrigerator came the morning news. "Four-year-old, Jimmy Deets has been missing from his Arlington home since yesterday afternoon," the female reporter said. "Concerned neighbors, along with the county sheriff's department, have combed the area surrounding the Deetses' farmhouse. One neighbor recalls seeing a car parked on the highway around supper time, but he said nothing seemed amiss at the time."

Shaine's hands trembled. Her heart beat so fast, its severity frightened her. Her gaze shot to the screen.

A fair-haired young woman appeared, her eyes red-rimmed, her hair gathered in a hasty ponytail. She wiped her hands on a white apron tied at her waist. "If anyone has any information at all about Jimmy, please call the police," she begged.

The child's color photograph filled the small television screen, his dimpled face smiling.

Shaine dropped a plastic spatula on the tiled floor. She pressed her hand to her quaking chest.

"Shaine, what's wrong?" Audrey asked.

She'd dreamed of Jimmy Deets last night.

She stared at the television long after the child's image was gone, replaced with a car dealership commercial. That had been the woman with the apron she'd dreamed of several weeks ago.

A scorched smell permeated the kitchen.

"Shaine!" Audrey said. "The waffles are burning. Hon?"

Ignoring everything but her consuming panic rising inside, Shaine shot out the kitchen door and stood on the wooden porch, her breath coming out in shallow pants.

She'd seen that child last night! She'd dreamed of him! But she didn't want to believe the picture she had in her mind. She couldn't accept it.

She ran back in and grabbed her purse.

"Are you all right?" Audrey asked. She'd tossed the blackened waffles in the waste bin and stood ineffectively waving a dish towel at the thick smoke.

"I have to go." Shaine turned away.

"But—"

"I'll be back to do the upstairs." She ignored Audrey's pleading words and ran for her car. She started her Topaz and shot away from the inn. Like the arrow of a compass seeking north, she drove.

She didn't think about where to turn or how far to drive. She simply steered the car toward the area that compelled her, instinctively knowing something would clue her where to turn. Twenty minutes outside the city, she pulled off the highway and followed a two-lane blacktop road until she spotted a water tower in the distance.

This was it.

She parked on the side, got out and ran across an expanse of gravel until she came to a low barbed-wire fence. The wire was loose enough to hold down with one foot while she climbed over. The ground beneath her shoes was uneven, and she stumbled several times. Neither words nor feelings could explain what compelled her forward. Some indefinable source drove her like the moon drove the tide. Crisp fall air lifted the hair at her temples, and she pulled her jacket around her more snugly.

At first she'd thought the child in her dream was Toby, but then she'd known that it wasn't. This boy had dark hair. He was older, maybe three or four. She turned her face to the right like a magnet seeking steel.

And he was here.

She stopped, unable to make herself go any farther. Dread rose up inside of her.

The child was here—at the bottom of a deep hole.

The knowledge terrified Shaine. Not suspicion. Not a hunch. *Knowledge.*

Her limbs trembled as though the morning air was colder than it really was. In the distance a few cars whizzed past on the highway. She was almost close enough to reach him...if she veered a little to the right.... No, she couldn't. *She couldn't!* With a stifled cry expanding her throat, she turned and raced back to her car. If she hurried, maybe it wouldn't be too late!

Forcing herself to take deep breaths and compose her shaking limbs, she clutched the steering wheel, drove to a pay phone and punched in 911. "I—I don't know how I know this, but you've got to believe me. That little boy— the one—the one whose mother was on the news—is... He's..." She gave explicit directions to the place she'd just returned from and slammed down the receiver.

Exhaustion washed over her in a mind-drugging wave. She drove home and collapsed on her bed.

A determined pounding hammered at her door. Groggily Shaine pushed up and oriented herself. She was fully dressed, still wearing her jacket. Her purse lay lodged beneath her.

The persistent knocking came again.

She made her way to the door, feeling like she'd had her head in a bucket of sand, her mouth dry and her eyes gritty.

Audrey stood outside, a concerned frown on her face. Her gaze took in Shaine's rumpled clothing. "You okay, hon?" she said as she came in.

Shaine shook her head, more to clear it than as a reply. She dropped her purse and groped for the remote, clicking on the TV and perching on the edge of the sofa.

"What are you looking for?"

"That little boy," she said.

"That's so sad." Standing with her hand in the small of her back, Audrey shook her head.

Shaine scanned channels, looking for the one that ran local news twenty-four hours. Audrey's words registered. She faced her. "What?"

"Well, they found him. Said they had an anonymous call. Shaine, are you all right?"

"Was he—is he...?"

"He wasn't alive. He'd fallen down a well sometime yesterday."

The news sifted through the fog of confusion in Shaine's head. "What could I have done differently? There must have been some way I could have prevented this!"

She pictured the child's mother, and tears came to her eyes.

"What are you talking about?" Audrey asked, bewilderment in her voice. "The police said it was an accident."

Shaine jumped up and paced the floor, hugging her waist with her arms. "I should have done something. I should have known what to do, but I didn't."

"Shaine, you're just upset because he was a little boy like Toby, and this was another senseless accident. Sit down and I'll get you something to drink."

"Something to drink is not going to fix this! That kid is dead!" She clapped her hand over her mouth, trapping the hysterics that threatened to pour out.

Audrey's eyes widened, and she stared.

Shaine calmed herself and dropped her arms to her sides. "I'll call Tom."

She ignored the expression on Audrey's face, more convinced than ever that she needed more help than she'd get from Tom.

Audrey watched her with a look of apprehension...and something more. Sympathy. Fear. A look Shaine couldn't acknowledge. It was the same way her mother had looked at her.

Chapter 2

Toby needed his hair washed and cut. He needed someone to pick him up and hug him, hold him. He was alone. Frightened. Hungry. So hungry, his stomach hurt.

A yellowed decal, a swan among faded water lilies, was peeling from green plastic tiles. The bird was a peach color with a black bill. A rusty metal cabinet sat on peeling linoleum.

Toby's lip hurt.

Somewhere, as if in the distance, music played. A disembodied voice blended with the music, one minute in indistinct speech, the next in weary crying. Sometimes he slept through it; sometimes the pitch changed and woke him. Sometimes he cried. If he wasn't too tired. Or too hungry.

Shaine shot straight up in bed. Thin shafts of light striped her bedcovers. She pressed the backs of her fingers against her heated cheeks. Somewhere, within the billions of cells and tissues and bits of DNA and protoplasm that made up Shaine Richards, was a place of knowing. No rationalization or scientific theory could explain away the fact that she knew what she knew at any given time. Shaine trembled with the knowledge of her dream.

Toby needed help.

She reached for the phone and hit auto dial. Though he'd officially retired from the institute, Tom Stempson still kept a hand in several of the research projects. Taking an interest in Shaine, he'd given her his home number, along with his permission to call anytime day or night. And Lord help her, she had.

"Tom," she said when he answered.

"Shaine? How are you doing?"

"Not so good." She explained the dream and what had happened with the Deets boy that day.

"That's incredible. Won't you consider coming back to the institute for a while? I could work with you full-time."

She hugged a pillow to her stomach. "I can't, Tom. I hate it there. I just don't fit in."

"But you're so gifted. We could learn so much from you—from each other."

She leaned back on the bed, weary with the weight of this burden he called a gift. "I just can't."

"If you were here, we'd have an opportunity to explore how far-reaching this thing is."

"But can you show me how to use it? Can you help me with the dreams about Toby?"

"No, Shaine. Everyone's ability is so different. It's something that takes time to define."

"I don't have time. I tried it your way once—"

"Once, and a month wasn't enough time—"

"A month was way too long for Toby. I can't do it again. We didn't get anywhere. We're still not getting anywhere. Today proved it to me. What happened with that little boy validated everything I've been going through. Tom, I saw that child."

"I know," he said softly.

"I knew exactly where he was and I told the police."

"I know," he said again.

"I can see Toby, too. And I know where he is." She covered her eyes with her hand for a minute. "I mean—I can see him—see exactly where he is and what he's doing. I just don't have the—the coordinates," she said for lack of a better explanation. "I need help figuring that out. I know it's possible, I just don't know how. I'm at the end of my rope, here, Tom."

He was silent for a long minute, and when he finally spoke, his voice held a note of apprehension. "You've gone beyond me, Shaine," he said.

"Yeah." She'd known it before he had. "I don't think anyone who hasn't experienced this himself would know how to help me," she said. "You've spared my sanity, Tom. I couldn't have survived these months without you. I appreciate that, believe me I do, but I can't come back there."

"I guess I knew that." He released a breath. "Do you have any idea how old I am?"

The odd question made her think a minute. "No. You're semiretired. Sixtyish?"

"I'll be seventy-six next month."

It was hard to believe the lean, active doctor she'd worked with at the institute was that old. "Wow."

"And in all those years I've known only a few people with an ability equal to yours."

Shaine didn't reply. In the past, whenever she'd questioned him about his other patients, he'd regretted that he couldn't share those things with her. His work was confidential. She understood, and she appreciated his integrity. That meant he wouldn't share things about her, either.

"We're at a stalemate here, Shaine."

She knew it, too, obviously having been a pretty disappointing subject. She'd bombed on the ESP tests, couldn't move objects for their psychokinesis testing and had no out-of-body experiences to report. Now that she wasn't willing 'to put herself through any more analysis, he'd run out of help for her.

"I worked with someone years ago," he said.

Her interest sparked, and she gripped the phone a little tighter.

"In the late sixties, early seventies, he helped the police solve crimes in Delaware and Pennsylvania and farther west."

Shaine's heartbeat increased with a new hope. "Why are you telling me this now?"

"He has an extraordinary ability," Tom said. "I worked with him for years, and learned something new at every turn."

"He let you poke him and prod him and pick his brain."

Tom's silence affirmed her words.

"Did he do well on the ESP tests?"

"Not outstanding."

"Better than me."

"Yes."

"Could I learn from him?"

"I think so."

"Is he still alive?" she asked, imagining him to be elderly by now.

"As far as I know."

Excitement rose in her chest. She sat up in her bed. At last! At last someone to help her find Toby! Tom wouldn't have brought it up if he didn't think this man could teach her how to use the dreams. "Will you help me find him?"

"I hope he'll forgive me. But I'll help."

This was the craziest thing she'd ever done.

Shaine handed the flannel-jacketed college student the thirty dollars they'd agreed on and watched him drive back down the rough road to Gunnison, Colorado, leaving her in the midst of her pile of bags, assorted boxes of food and supplies, a tent, a cooler and a Coleman stove.

Having found someone to help Audrey for a week or

two, she'd spent every available dime on camping equipment and used her credit card for the plane ticket. There was no turning back now.

This old man she'd come to find was the answer to her dilemma. He would know how to help her. He would understand the torment she was going through and help her use this horrible wonderful gift to find Toby.

There was no other way. She wouldn't consider anything different.

Shaine scanned the thick growth of trees and shrubs the boy had called Bentley Ridge, and observed the smoke rising against the crisp blue sky.

A log house stood in the clearing, a massive garage off to the side. An open porch stretched around two sides of the house, a door on each side. Assorted rustic furniture lined one porch wall.

Surely he'd heard the Jeep and knew someone was out here. Unless he had his television on loud and was hard of hearing.

She'd been envisioning this moment ever since she'd decided to come. She'd imagined Allen with a wife, maybe a few grown and married children. But maybe his wife had died. Living way out here, he might appreciate a visitor. Praying he would, she approached the house.

There was no doorbell, no knocker. She garnered her courage and determinedly pounded the rough wood with the side of her fist. Nothing happened.

She tried again.

Nothing.

A huge pent-up gust of air escaped her lungs. She turned and surveyed the clearing. A stump sat at one corner of the house and several chunks of tree lay nearby. Someone must chop wood for him.

No sound came from inside. Hesitantly she tried the door, and it swung inward. Her heart raced at her unexpected intrusion. She peeked at the open rough-walled room and dominating gray stone fireplace and couldn't make herself go any farther. Pulling the door shut, she walked around the house.

Again, she noted the smoke rising from the chimney, assurance that the old man was indeed here, and took comfort in the wires running to the corner of the house.

Out of breath, Shaine walked back to the porch, brushed off one of the dusty wood chairs and sat, wondering why he hadn't answered the door. The air felt chilly after a while, and she tugged her jacket around herself more snugly.

She hoped he wasn't ill. Or hurt. If he didn't show up soon, she'd go in and make sure he was okay.

The nearby woods had a life of their own, birds twittering, and small rustling sounds came from the dry grass and weeds. Shaine listened and found herself relaxing. Her eyes closed.

She didn't know how much time had passed when a rhythmic pounding startled her. The dry ground cover off to her left was being disrupted by something or someone moving fast and breathing hard. Shaine sat forward on the chair and gripped the arms, straining to see into the dense forest. Her heart pounded with apprehension.

A figure shot out into the sunny clearing fifty feet from the house. It was a dark-haired man wearing a faded Super Bowl sweatshirt with a dark trail of perspiration down the center. A pair of gray shorts exposed long muscled thighs that flexed with each step carrying him closer to the house.

At the sight of her, his steps faltered, and he walked the rest of the way to the porch, stopping with one tennis-shoed foot on the top step.

Shaine stood. "Are you here to see Mr. Allen?"

"Who are you?" The hair at his temples was damp. Breathing hard, he ran a hand through one side and splayed his long fingers on his hip.

"I'm here to see him," she went on. "I knocked, but I didn't get any answer. I was wondering if I should go in and check to see that everything's okay." She glanced back the way he'd come. "Are you a neighbor?"

The man advanced to the porch. He was head and shoulders taller than she, his broad chest and rugged frame touching her with a sense of unease. From the top of his head to the bottom of his running shoes he was a formidable example of health and male virility. He must be the one who chopped wood for Mr. Allen.

Austin Allen took stock of the girl's suede hiking boots, her long legs in faded jeans and the denim jacket that hinted at a tantalizing air of indifference about her appearance. "What do you want with him?" he countered.

"I need to talk to him. I've come a long way to find him."

"You a reporter?"

"No!" she said, obviously surprised at the question.

"A cop?"

She shook her head.

"That leaves one possibility." Austin turned, looking for her vehicle, and discovered the suspicious pile of gear several hundred feet from the house.

"What possibility is that?" she asked.

Without replying, he turned back and eyed her. "He's not here."

"When will he be back?"

Her straight hair parted on the side and fell to her shoulders in a sleek curve, bangs that the wind had becomingly arranged, complementing her topaz eyes. "What do you want him for? And how did you get here?"

Those eyes darkened to the color of maple sugar, and she licked her lips in a nervous gesture. "I got a ride. And I need to talk to him—in private."

She moved a little closer, and he realized she wasn't as small as he'd first thought. She was slender, her features fine, but she probably stood over five-six. "If you'd called ahead, you'd have learned he doesn't see any visitors."

"Isn't it an unlisted number?"

"You have it, don't you?"

Her expression didn't reveal the answer. "How do you know I didn't call?"

"Because I take all the messages."

"Do you live with him then? Work for him?"

"Something like that." Her warm rich hair and eyes, her heart-shaped face, winged brows, delicate nose and chin gave her a classic beauty all her own. A feminine appeal no man could help but notice. Especially a man unaccustomed to company of her gender. "How do you plan to get back?"

She glanced toward the woods, a barely noticeable sign of uncertainty. "I—uh, thought after Mr. Allen heard me out and let me stay awhile, I'd call for a ride."

"I'll give you a ride back right now." He moved for the door. "It'll only take me a few minutes to shower and change."

"Wait a minute!"

He stopped with his palm holding open the screen door and turned back. "What?"

She gestured with one hand, a halfhearted kind of wave that encompassed the porch, her things across the way, him. "Look."

She crossed her arms, tucking her hands under the sleeves of her jacket, and he wondered if it was more a defensive gesture than protection from the cooling air.

Austin's damp sweatshirt chilled his skin.

"I came a long way to see Mr. Allen. I'll just wait until he gets back."

"He won't be back. Hang on a minute while I change."

"He's not—" Her hand shot out and her cool fingers grasped his wrist.

Immediately he backed up all his defense mechanisms, but couldn't suppress the disturbing physical effect her touch created.

"He's not dead, is he?" she asked, her eyes rounded.

He wasn't used to being touched. He had to force his

mind to think around the sensation of her gentle fingers on his skin. The concern in her eyes was so sincere, he almost felt remorse for taking a firm stand. "No. He's not dead."

"Oh, thank goodness." She released him and sat on the chair with her arms wrapped around her. "Thank goodness. I'm waiting for him, then. If it'll be a while, I've brought enough supplies to last. I think. If you'd let me know for sure," she said, those wide eyes raising hopefully to his, "I could make better plans. If you won't tell me anything, I'll just stick with this plan."

Frustrated, he ran a hand through his damp hair. How the hell had she found this place, and exactly what did she hope to extract from him? He'd covered his tracks years ago, and only the most persistent, the ones with the most at stake or those with the most money had sought him out.

He glanced at her assortment of gear, thinking she obviously didn't fit into the money category. Which left a lot at stake and determination. He could be every bit as stubborn as she was persistent, however. "Fine. Stay out there till you rot, for all I care. But you're not going to see anyone but me around here."

He entered the house, slamming the door behind him.

Austin stood in the shower, appreciating the warmth of the flesh-tingling spray. He lathered his hair, his body, rinsed and stood under the water, wondering how long she'd last.

He could wait her out. It would get colder as the sun set and night crept down from the mountains. Unless she had a warmer coat and a kerosene heater, she'd be forced to stay in her tent and sleeping bag. And how long could she hack it without water to drink or wash with? She'd come begging him for a ride back to civilization.

He didn't want to know anything about her. He didn't care that she had a vulnerable slant to her Cupid's bow lips and a haunted look behind her weary eyes. He hadn't allowed himself to care about anything like that for too many years.

He'd developed the skill to not know. To not care, and to not feel guilty about either. No searching young woman with self-doubts and pain-dimmed features was going to get him to change.

He couldn't change.

There was too much risk involved.

Chapter 3

The sunset was spectacular; a panorama of reds and golds and ambers streaked with lavender that turned the trees and the countryside into a brilliant inferno of rustling color. The display ended much too soon, and with the sun went the afternoon's warmth.

Shaine shook the tent out of its bag, laid out the poles and stakes and searched for the instructions. Another rustling in the underbrush alerted her to the approach of something or someone else. An Irish setter bounded into the clearing and headed for the house.

Shaine stood slowly, staring in awe. She'd seen the dog before. In a dream. Much as the man before him had, the dog stalled at her presence. Any remaining doubts she'd had fled. His appearance confirmed the rightness of her being there.

The dog was obviously friendlier than the man, demonstrated in the way he came close to her camp area, his long nose sniffing the air.

"Can you smell if I'm a good guy or a bad guy?" she asked.

At that, the animal's tail brushed the leaf-strewn ground, and he crouched, laying his chin on his forepaws, luminous brown eyes imploring.

"Do you live there?" she asked.

That must have been enough of an introduction, because he bolted forward and sat at her feet.

He sniffed her palm, gave her wrist a lick, and she scratched his whiskered chin.

Shaine chuckled. "You're a lot friendlier than the last fella I met up here. I'll probably get about as much information out of you, though."

He made himself comfortable against her legs, and she brushed through his coat with her fingers, removing bits of twigs and leaves he'd picked up in the woods. After several minutes, he roused, gave her hand a parting lick and bounded toward the house and around the side out of sight.

Shaine missed his warmth. And his company. She turned back to the flexible poles and bright blue nylon fabric. Surely she was smarter than this tent. Too bad she'd thrown the box with the color picture away; seeing the finished product would probably have helped.

It would be completely dark before long; she didn't have much time left to get in out of the night. Glancing toward the house, a movement at the window caught her attention. The dog grinned at her from behind the glass, and by the movement of his head and shoulders, she could tell his tail wagged. Though it felt a little silly, she waved.

A shiver rolled up her spine, and she scrounged through her duffel bag for a hooded sweatshirt to pull on beneath her jacket.

Okay, what was the worst thing that could happen?

She'd never get the blasted tent together, a bear would ramble down from the hills and devour her. Worse than that? That this Allen fellow didn't really live here after all.

That she'd have to go back home no closer to finding any answers.

That unfriendly fellow in there had been willing—make that *eager*—to take her back.

Why was he so opposed to merely answering her questions about the old man? The simple courtesy of a conversation would have gone a long way. His behavior struck her as curious.

A flash of light illuminated the fabric she slipped over the flexible aluminum poles, and the distant rumble of thunder followed.

Okay, rain would be a pretty depressing possibility, too. She blew on her cold fingers, staring at the tent she hadn't made any progress on in the last twenty minutes.

Maybe the guy knew more than he wanted to tell. Maybe the old man *was* in there and this man was...was what? His nurse? She chuckled to herself. More likely his bodyguard. Or...his *son?*

Most likely.

Shaine glanced up at the house, but the dog was gone. A warm glow shined through the window, leaving her with the same lonely ache she'd fought for the last year. She was alone. Completely, entirely, totally alone.

Her hands dropped to her sides and she stared off into the dark foliage. If a bear thundered out of those woods and ate her right now, the only person who'd eventually notice would be Audrey Pruitt when the time came for her to have that baby, and Shaine wasn't there to work the inn.

That jerk inside certainly wouldn't care.

Oh, right. Feel sorry for yourself. She shook off the self-pitying thoughts and glanced around. Looking on the bright side, it would be too cold out here for her to sleep sound enough to dream. And if she did dream, it would be about grizzly bears or Bigfoot or the like. Something safe.

Digging through the other bag, she found her flashlight, shone it on her watch and remembered she had some cereal bars that she could eat without any work. She dug one out and ate it. A big glass of milk would go good with it. No, she corrected the thought, a steaming mug of hot chocolate.

She was feeling a little light-headed. Out of breath, too. She hoped the snack would help.

A smattering of drops smacked against the fabric pooled on the ground. She had the poles all through the pockets; now all she had to do was figure out how to make the blasted thing stand up. Was she supposed to have brought a hammer to get those stakes in the ground?

Austin stood in the darkened living room, away from the window, and watched the blue tent fluttering and flailing in the flashlight's beam. What was the fool woman doing now?

Thunder rumbled overhead. Served her right. He resented any invasion of his privacy, and it took a lot of guts to camp out on a guy's property. Or attempt to camp out, that is.

She had definitely lost her Girl Scout manual somewhere on her way to the mountains. Granted, those five-man dome tents were tricky to assemble, but why hadn't she practiced a couple of times? And the place where she'd chosen to set it up was unprotected from the wind. A good gust would flatten it in a heartbeat.

Not to mention the water that would probably wash across that spot in a torrent.

Let her figure it out the hard way. He turned to adjust the log he'd placed on the fire earlier. The heat drew his skin tight across his cheekbones. He watched the flames lick up the sides of the slab of ash.

A clap of thunder startled him. Rain pelted the metal flue in the chimney. Memories of her slender vulnerable woman's body and her troubled, yet proud, expression came to him more as a feeling than as pictures, a feeling like a vague ache in his chest. Against his will, he was drawn to the window once more.

Don't do it, don't do it, don't do it, his levelheaded conscience cried out to him. *She's a woman, alone and unprotected,* his victorious mind argued.

Besides, it was pouring rain and the temperature was dropping. He wouldn't be much of a human being if he left her out there.

Shaine had the tent standing and was trying to use the cooler to keep one side propped up, when she caught sight of a bright beam of light coming near. She looked up and saw the inhospitable man storming toward her in a hooded orange slicker.

"Grab your clothes," he said.

"What?"

"Get your bag and come with me."

"I was doing all right," she said defensively.

"I can see that." He shone the flashlight inside the wobbling tent, its light glaring off muddy puddles shaped like the soles of her boots.

"I can dry it out."

"What about you?"

Her clothes were nearly soaked, and her hair was probably plastered to her head by now. She had packed a couple of towels. Somewhere.

He grabbed the duffel and firmly took her arm. Shaine picked up the other bag, unwilling to admit she was a little relieved at his support. She accompanied him to the house, where the dog waited on the porch, tail wagging. "What's his name?"

"*His* name's Daisy."

"Oh." She stopped to pat the animal's head and receive a few licks.

"Notice she's smart enough to stay out of the rain," he said, and opened the door. The dog bounded in ahead of them.

He removed the dripping slicker and left it on the porch, revealing a deep green sweater over a broad chest, and snug jeans encasing legs she knew were muscled and dusted with dark hair. The thought combined with his woodsy scent as she passed him, created an odd feeling in her already trembling limbs.

She stepped away and followed the dog into the warmth of the enormous firelit room. Two Navajo-patterned sofas faced one another before the stone fireplace. A welcoming fire crackled.

A counter sectioned off a kitchen area, and above, a log rail separated a loft area. He led her into a hall. "The bathroom's here. The washer and dryer are in the closet. Throw your clothes in. Hair dryer's on the wall there."

Shaine entered a room bigger than her bedroom at home, with cedar walls and a long, tiled counter with two sinks. One corner held a shower, and the other a sunken tub with whirlpool jets.

He left, pulling the door shut.

She glanced around. A rumpled towel lay on one end of the vanity. A black-bristled hair brush with a wooden handle lay beside it.

Shivering, Shaine peeled off her wet clothing, opened the double oak doors and indeed found stacked appliances.

The steaming water felt wonderful. The soap in the dish had the identical fresh woodsy smell the man did, and standing naked in the same spot he had earlier was innocently erotic. Shaine washed her hair, and enjoyed the tingling warmth of the spray over her scalp and body as she rinsed.

She dried her hair quickly, dressed in clean jeans, her Husker sweatshirt and warm socks. She wiped the vanity, hung her towels up, as well as his, and flipped off the light.

The table between the sofas, a long low slab of varnished pine, had been set with plates, cups and a platter of sandwiches.

"Sit."

Shaine turned, uncertain if the command was for her or the dog. The man motioned her to the sofa, and she lowered herself, keeping an eye on him as he sat across from her.

She glanced from the food to his sober expression. "Why did you do this?"

He handed her a plate. "Couldn't let you stay out there and catch pneumonia."

She selected a sandwich and took a bite, trying to concentrate on the chicken salad. "I'm a little dizzy."

"It's the altitude."

"Oh, sure." The steam rising from the mugs on the table met her nostrils, and she reached for one. *Hot chocolate.* She inhaled, blew across the surface and sipped.

They ate, the mannerly Daisy dozing on the carpeted floor.

"How'd you find this place?" he asked.

"Tom Stempson."

He stopped chewing for a moment, but didn't look up.

After Shaine had appeased her hunger, she sat back with her mug between her palms.

"Where are you from?" he asked.

She looked up. "Omaha."

He gave a half nod.

"Have you been there?"

"I've been through is all."

"I've never been much of anywhere else. This is the first time I've been to Colorado. It's beautiful."

"It's prettier the later in the season it gets. The aspens turn first, like they're starting to do now. For weeks all you see are shades of yellow." He clamped his mouth shut and looked away as though realizing he'd been chatting with an unwelcome visitor.

"Please. Tell me, are you Mr. Allen's son?"

His gaze came back and didn't waver. "Yes."

She leaned forward, not wishing to dampen the few friendly words they'd finally exchanged, but unwilling to wait any longer. "If he won't see me, will you talk to him for me? I know I've imposed on you, coming here like this. I wouldn't have done it if I wasn't desperate."

"Who do you want to find?"

How many hundreds of people had sought out Austin Allen for his extraordinary ability to help them find their loved ones? Why would she seem any different? But she didn't want him to find Toby for her...did she? She wanted him to help her understand her dreams. "My nephew was—"

"Ah," he said with a curt nod, interrupting as if she'd just explained it all, and it wasn't worth his attention. He reached for the empty plates.

"No. Wait a minute." Shaine leaned forward and reached toward him.

Pausing, he stared at her palm.

"I don't want your father to find my nephew." She waited for him to look up at her.

Finally he did.

Sighing, she brought her hand to the side of her face, her fingertips touching her temple. "I want his help with something personal. Something I'm going through."

Several seconds passed. A burning log snapped and hissed in the grate. "How personal?"

She lowered her hand and met his penetrating dark stare. Nothing transparent about this guy. Had he learned to guard every thought and emotion from a father with extrasensory capabilities? She shrugged halfheartedly. "Personal enough that I think he might be the only one who'd understand."

"Try me."

She studied him. "If I do...if I tell you...will you pass it along to your father?"

"I promise he'll hear it just the way you tell me."

"Well..." She glanced around the interior of the log house, not really taking note of the rough-hewn walls or the masculine furnishings. She couldn't help glancing to the loft above, where the light from the fire and the table lamps didn't penetrate. "A year ago my sister's car was found in the Missouri River. Her body was in it."

He said nothing, showing no reaction while waiting for her to continue.

"My eighteen-month-old nephew was never found."

"You want his body found?"

She turned her gaze back to his. "A few months back I started having dreams."

He listened, waiting without expression, without encouragement or assessment.

"The dreams have continued."

"What are the dreams about?"

"I dream that he's alive. That he's frightened and lonely and that he needs me." She described the dreams, ending with the one of Jimmy Deets and how she'd known where the police could find him.

"He was dead, wasn't he?" he said, his tone flat.

She gave him a grim nod.

"They're nearly always dead."

She assessed his face quickly, and for a moment she almost thought she saw something there, some obscurely familiar emotion too painful to express, but a second later she realized she must have imagined it. "What do you mean?"

Ignoring her question, he picked up the plates and the platter of remaining sandwiches and carried them behind the counter.

Shaine traced the rim of her cup with her forefinger.

"Want a refill on that?"

She nodded.

He filled both their mugs.

"How did you know I wanted hot chocolate?" she asked.

He took his cup and sat on the stone hearth. "Fall evenings in the mountains get pretty chilly," he said. "You don't have to be clairvoyant to know a cup of hot chocolate would hit the spot."

She studied his face, lit on only one side by the fire, and the familiarity of the scene unnerved her.

"What brought them on?"

"What?"

"The dreams."

Unconsciously, she frowned. "I don't know."

"A bump on the head? A mental trauma?"

She shook her head. "Nothing like that."

"Had you ever had dreams like them before?"

She hesitated a moment. "Sometimes. When I was a kid. It spooked my mom, so I quit telling her about them. After a while I quit having them."

They sat in silence for a long moment. Finally she tried once again to convince him. "I'm not here to get your father to find Toby for me. *I've* found him. I just can't get to him—yet."

"Toby being your nephew."

"Yes. My dreams have convinced me that he's alive. If I could learn how to…" She stumbled for the right words to express what she knew was possible. "Connect," she said for lack of a better word. "How to understand what's going on with me and do it myself, I think I can find him. I hope I can."

"I wouldn't be doing you any favors if I didn't warn you not to hold out false hope," he said. "I can't encourage you."

"It's not false hope. I just *know*…somehow…that he's alive."

"Was the Deets boy alive?"

"It's not the same."

"It's exactly the same. Who are you kidding here? You hoped against hope that that child was alive at the bottom of that hole. You felt every minute of his fear and his pain. You knew when the pain ended that it was over, but you hoped. You prayed his parents wouldn't have to get the awful news. You hoped he was waiting for someone to find him, hanging in there until you could tell the police where he was."

She stared at him, her heart pounding, the protracted torment of those hours painted afresh in her mind.

He stood abruptly and moved around the sofas toward the kitchen area.

Shaine followed, not caring that he hadn't invited her.

He opened a drawer, plucked out a couple of self-sealing bags and efficiently placed a sandwich in each.

He had described her feelings in exact detail. "How do you know what I hoped?" she asked softly.

"Was I wrong?"

"No."

"Then you're going to have to trust me."

"Okay, I hoped they would find that boy in time. But Toby is different. It's been a year since he disappeared, but in my dreams he's older, just as he would be today. I know he's alive."

"That's your hope speaking. You want it to be true so badly that even when there's no basis for your belief, you're clinging to it, inventing reasons why it should be so."

"I'm not inventing anything," she said, less calmly, her frustration already at a dangerous level. "Or do you think I'm crazy?"

His head snapped up and he met her eyes. "I don't think you're crazy."

"Then help me." The words came out more pleadingly than she'd intended. She quickly looked down at her hands while she composed herself. "All I want is a chance to talk to Mr. Allen about my dreams. If he's busy, I'll make it quick. If he's not well, I won't upset him. I'd hoped..."

"What had you hoped?"

She gazed at a tin baking soda sign on the wall behind the counter. "I'd hoped he was a lonely old man who'd welcome a little company."

He released a reproachful little grunt. "There you go with your groundless hope again."

She returned her gaze to his face. "He's not lonely?"

Something moved behind those flint-colored eyes, something less callous and mocking than his unsympathetic face would have her believe. "He's not old."

A gnawing suspicion that she'd refused to entertain, now blotted out all of Shaine's reasoning thoughts. "You can't be him. You're not old enough."

His uncompromising expression softened. "Old is relative."

"But all the cases solved were in the late sixties, early seventies." What was he telling her?

He nodded, uneasily.

"But you would've been only—" The realization rocked her senses. "Oh my goodness! You were only a boy!"

"Youth is subjective, too." He opened the refrigerator and stacked the bagged sandwiches on a shelf.

"I never guessed."

"No one did."

Her mind whirred with the information Tom had shared with her…and the disturbing knowledge that it hadn't been a man at all, but a *young boy* who had helped detectives with those crimes.

"The police protected me from publicity so I'd have a 'normal' childhood," he went on with unveiled sarcasm.

Shaine allowed the new data to sink in.

He turned to her, "You've used my shower and eaten my food, and you haven't even told me your name."

"Shaine," she said, forcing her brain to switch gears. "Shaine Richards."

His face had relaxed some, though his dark eyes were masked and grave. His lips were stern, but sensual. He was probably the most striking man she'd ever met, not only physically, but in another, more elemental way. She'd never met him before tonight, but something about him was so…deeply *familiar.*

A niggle of discomfort scratched at her thoughts. "Do you know what I'm thinking?"

One side of his arresting mouth actually turned up in

what could have been a grin if he'd let it happen. "I'm not a mind reader. Your thoughts are safe."

"But the hot chocolate…"

"I make it for myself every night."

"Really?"

"Really." He led her back to the seating area before the fire and hunkered down to adjust a log with the poker. "My ability is more like psychometry."

"Which is?"

"Sensing impressions stored in inanimate objects."

"But you're telepathic."

"In as much as I could sense the thought patterns of victims and killers. I never read minds."

"You say it all in the past tense."

"Because that's where it is."

"You can't do it anymore?"

"I won't do it anymore."

"Why not?"

He perched on the stone hearth again, the position stretching his jeans taut around his thighs, and Shaine forced her attention away. "Did you pick up on the Deets boy's mother?" he asked.

She could still remember the sound of the woman's voice and the expression in her eyes from the television broadcast. "No."

"Be grateful. If you had, you would have felt her pain as if it had been your own, just like you did the boy's. The families of the victims suffer as much or more than the victims themselves, and the suffering would have been yours. Did you feel what the boy felt?"

"Some of it. I don't think I had a handle on it, though. It was like a radio channel not quite tuned in."

"Be glad you didn't have to experience either person's suffering. You never want to have to go through that."

Maybe she had a shred of understanding now. A faint glimpse of why he was so unwilling to talk with her, to help her, why he had placed the experiences in his past like a best forgotten memory.

"You can just shut it all off?"

Thunder clapped, but neither of them moved.

"It took years to perfect the ability to use the gift," he said. "It took years to learn to turn it off, too."

Compelled by the all-consuming need within her to understand and use her dreams, Shaine moved to sit on the hearth only a few feet from him. The fire heated her back and the side of her face. "You said I don't want to feel those things, but in a way I am…with Toby. I need someone to show me how to use the dreams. Will you teach me?"

"I'll teach you," he said calmly.

Her heart dared to lift on those promising words.

"I'll teach you how to shut it out."

Disappointment knifed through her chest. Shut it out! Shut it out? Slowly she stood.

From her position on a braided rug, Daisy raised her head and studied Shaine expectantly.

Austin pushed himself to his feet. "Wanna go out, girl?" After he and Daisy left the cabin, Shaine paced the floor, distractedly studying the masculine surroundings. Some sort of animal's horns hung over the front door. A yawning bear's head stared at her from a furry hide on the floor.

He wanted to show her how to shut out her dreams of Toby. Why on earth would she want to do that? She needed to learn how to access them, not turn them off. She was Toby's only hope!

She stared without really seeing floor-to-ceiling bookcases shelving leather-bound classics and paperback fiction, all arranged with no attention to size or subject.

Austin returned. Daisy bounded in behind him and sat, her tail thumping the floor. Shaine stroked the dog's furry neck, slightly damp from her hurried trip in the rain.

Austin's idea was out of the question. She'd gotten this far, she'd just have to get him to change his mind.

"I'll carry your things upstairs," he offered.

"I can get them." She found her bags where she'd left them in the hallway. She glanced up at the loft, suddenly embarrassed. All along in her imaginings, Austin Allen had been a gray-haired old man. Whether he'd been married or widowed, the situation wouldn't have been as awkward as this.

He led the way up the log-banistered staircase set against the wall, and she followed. Reaching the loft, he flipped on muted track lighting above a massive oak headboard. The king-size bed occupied only a fourth of the room.

Shaine set her bags on the floor and moved to the open rail, peering at the room below. The pungent smell of the burning logs was strong up here.

The sound of rain drew her attention up to an enormous skylight. Water ran down the glass in silvery sheets.

With deft movements, Austin tugged a quilted hunter green comforter from the bed and stripped the sheets, then took a clean set from a huge oak armoire.

"You're giving me your bed," she said, and her face warmed.

He nodded and pointed for her to help with fitting the corners over the edges. "I have a sofa in my office. I sleep there half the time anyway."

Together they smoothed and tucked, changed the pillowcases and replaced the comforter. Finished, Shaine stood and met his eyes uncomfortably. He didn't look like a man whose mind would be easily changed. But she'd come this far. If he thought she could be diverted from her goal, he didn't understand the immediacy of the situation.

His gaze dropped to her sweatshirt and back to her face. "There's a half bath in there," he gestured.

"Okay."

He took clothing from the drawers inside the armoire and headed down the stairs.

"Thank you."

He nodded without turning back.

Shaine found the pair of flannel pajamas in her bag and undressed, feeling exposed in the open-aired loft. She pulled the pajamas on quickly and refolded the rest of her clothing, glancing around the room. Like everything else in the house, it screamed man. Only the bare essentials were visible, a ball cap and a jacket hanging on a peg near the bathroom door, a clock on a table beside the bed.

The long trip, her dealings with the man downstairs and her fight with the tent in the rain had caught up with her. She switched off the lights and crawled between the fresh sheets.

And stared at the rain running down the panes overhead.

On a clear night the skylight would provide a breathtaking view of the heavens. She glanced over to the wide vertical blinds that held the night out. Climbing out of the bed, she searched for a cord of some kind, her fingers finally brushing a doorbell-like button. She pressed it, and the blinds glided open until she could see the silver rain glistening on the trees and the mountain ridges above.

This house, this situation, this man was nothing like she'd anticipated. But then, what had she anticipated?

She needed his help. She'd set out with tunnel vision, and now here she was. Not exactly as she'd planned. Not anything like she'd hoped, but closer to her goal than she'd been the day before.

Hoped.

The word clung tenaciously to her mental vocabulary. Just as she clung tenaciously to its precept.

Sleepily, she studied the rain-laden heavens, wondering if there was an answer up there, if inspiration and insight and intuition came from the vast expanse of the universe and settled upon those open or willing or just gifted.

Exhausted, she climbed back into bed and snuggled into the downy covers. He had let her stay. He would work with her. She'd gratefully accept whatever shred of skill he would share with her. And—Shaine's eyes drifted shut—

she *hoped* she'd be able to change his mind about what he was willing to teach her.

Toby's welfare depended on it.

Chapter 4

Austin blew across the surface of his steaming coffee. He placed the mug beside one of the terminals, sat in his chair and logged on.

Last night he'd been unable to concentrate enough to get any work done, not after entering his bathroom and smelling the flowery fragrances of soap and shampoo and whatever all else the woman used to make the whole place smell like her.

There'd never been a guest in his home. Least of all a woman. Austin hadn't been very good company for a while. Twenty years maybe. He'd had enough of people to last him a lifetime. When he desired human company, which wasn't often, he drove to Gunnison to shop and eat.

Occasionally he took a trip and met with clients he normally only spoke with over the phone.

Once or twice a year he attended computer fairs where he checked out the latest developments and upgraded his equipment. And from time to time he met women who didn't require involvement or intimacy to have a mutually satisfying time.

And none of them knew him. Or knew of him. He'd made sure of that.

He slid a disk into the drive and pulled up a program he'd been working on for one of his clients. They'd been developing software for a major insurance company and thought it was finally perfected. Now his job was to make sure there were no glitches that could show up later down the line and cause an expensive recall or even open them to a lawsuit.

He was good at it. He'd found enough hidden errors and saved enough clients from potential disaster that he'd earned himself a name and the ability to demand high fees. And he didn't have to deal with people. Or their *possessions*. He clicked on an icon and sipped his coffee.

A couple of hours later, he got up to let Daisy out and nearly ran into his houseguest in the hallway.

"Oh, sorry," she murmured. She smelled like spring flowers, and he resented the fact that he'd noticed.

"That's okay. I didn't hear you get up." He'd been too engrossed in his work to hear her moving around. The sight of her in a slim pair of jeans and a little sweater thing that barely came to her waist gave him a restless feeling that didn't sit comfortably. The outfit accentuated her flat stomach and shapely hips, and gave him the urge to see if his hands could span that tiny waist.

"I didn't want to bother you. I didn't know if you were still sleeping or not." She tucked her hair behind her ear, and the sleeve of her white sweater slid back, exposing her pale wrist.

His insides knotted. She touched nerves he'd shielded for years. Austin looked away as if she'd revealed more than just the soft-looking skin of her arm. "I was working."

"Sorry."

Maybe that peculiar feeling in his stomach was because he needed food. *Right.* "Are you hungry?"

She shrugged.

"You must be by now. I've worked up an appetite."

"I don't want to be an imposition."

"Why don't we have leftover sandwiches?"

She slanted him a skeptical glance to see if he was serious. "For breakfast?"

"I'm not much of a cook. I eat what's easiest."

"Well, I'm a pretty fair cook."

"Knock yourself out." He let Daisy out and returned to show Shaine where everything was.

She dropped a knife, cast him a glance and washed the blade. Did his presence make her nervous? After several minutes, she relaxed and went about the chore efficiently.

Within no time she'd prepared pancakes with spiced apples cooked in the microwave. She set his plate before him and passed him the pitcher of hot syrup.

The smell of cinnamon reached his nostrils. "How'd you do that so fast?"

"I do it nearly every day. For sometimes as many as twelve people."

His fork paused above the steaming pancakes. He hadn't considered her family. Other people had families. Why did the thought disturb him? "Are you married?"

She shook her head and sat across from him.

"Kids?"

"No."

He poured them each a glass of orange juice. He hadn't cared one way or another, he was just making conversation.

"I'm co-owner of a bed and breakfast," she said. "I do most of the cooking."

"Where is this place? Omaha?"

Shaine nodded and watched him enjoy his breakfast. "Just far enough outside the city to be quaint."

She sipped her juice and tasted her pancakes.

"So Tom Stempson told you where to find me?" he asked.

Shaine laid down her fork. "He's been working with me for several months. My part's been rather halfhearted, I must confess. He wanted me to come back to the institute, but I wouldn't do it."

He didn't say anything.

"After the thing with the Deets boy, he told me about you. Said you'd had experiences like mine."

"Tom's never given me away," he said. "We only talk every few months, but he knows I don't want any part of this."

"I hope you're not angry with him."

"I value my privacy. He knows that."

She didn't know what to say. She'd invaded his solitude and, considering that, he'd treated her quite decently. She ate, wondering what had made him draw into himself and avoid people.

She had to change his mind about working with her, but she had to go about it delicately. He wanted to show her how to turn her dreams off. Her hope was that in the process, he'd change his mind—or that she'd learn what she needed, in spite of him.

"I don't want to be in your way," she began. "And I know you're a busy man. But how long do you think it will take to teach me?"

He finished his breakfast and pushed the plate back with a thumb. Placing both elbows on the table, he looked at her over his laced knuckles. "It's not something you can plan out, like a drive to Miami. There's no scale to work by, no directions or blueprint. We'll just have to see what happens."

He held her gaze.

"Okay," she said finally.

"I have a job to finish up today. Let me get the work finished, and then we'll get to it."

"I know I'm an imposition, but..."

"But?"

"But I want to learn whatever you'll teach me, as soon as I can. I need to make you understand how urgent it is for me to find my nephew."

"We'll work together this evening," he said.

"Okay."

"There's a television downstairs. There are weights...a treadmill..."

"I'll take care of my things, dry out the tent."

He nodded and headed for his office.

Meanwhile, Shaine finished assembling the tent so it could dry, then borrowed towels from his bathroom and dried her equipment.

By afternoon the sun grew blissfully warm. She pulled one of the wooden chairs into its heat and sat dozing, the melting rays soaking through her clothing and skin.

Later, she went in, acquainted herself with the downstairs and tested Austin's treadmill and weights. She quickly decided exercising was way too much work, flipped on the wide-screen TV and channel-surfed for an hour or so, until she figured she could go up and find something to fix for dinner.

Just as she headed up the stairs, his tennis shoes and muscular legs appeared, coming down. A sweatshirt with the neck and sleeves cut out revealed his broad chest, shoulders and well-defined biceps. Slowing down as he got closer, his face came into view.

"I—uh—was just going up to start some dinner."

"You don't have to do that."

"Do you mind? You do eat, don't you?"

"Yeah, I eat. I'll be down here for about an hour. After that I run and shower."

She moved to the right in the stairwell and turned sideways, allowing him to pass. From above, his shoulders appeared even wider. "I'll find something that takes a while to fix then."

He slid open a cabinet housing a stereo system, and vintage rock filled the room. Self-consciously she hurried up the stairs.

For someone who claimed to eat whatever was easy, his kitchen was well stocked. Humming along with the Rolling Stones, Frankie Valli, and The Drifters, she scrubbed potatoes and thawed steaks. Daisy kept her company. The music stopped. Daisy's nails scrambled on the kitchen floor, and she shot toward the front door. Shaine looked up in time to see Austin head outside.

Supper was nearly ready when he returned, his hair and shirt damp with sweat like they'd been the day before.

Austin paused awkwardly on his way to the shower. The appealing smells of food cooking had hit him as soon as he'd reached the porch. So foreign. So unexpected and out of his realm of experience. Like the woman standing in his kitchen. His stomach growled.

She looked up from behind the counter that divided the room, and smiled, an uncertain little lift of her lips that changed the focus of his appetite. Her mouth was a turn-on. He wondered if she knew that. Her mouth, that soft-looking pale skin, those legs. He frowned to himself. "I bagged up your tent and stuff and stored them in my garage."

"But—"

"But what?"

"But what about tonight?"

"You'll stay here."

She looked at him curiously, but she didn't argue. He'd never sleep if he had to worry about a helpless female exposed to the elements while he was tucked snugly in this house that had room for both of them.

She had salad plates on the table and wine poured when he returned from his shower and sat.

"I assume you like this dressing since it's all there was." She sprinkled a little on his lettuce. "I was surprised at how much food you had for someone who doesn't cook."

He studied her moving competently around his kitchen,

and didn't know how he felt about having her there. She disturbed him in more ways than one. "I didn't say I don't cook. I said I don't like to."

"What do you do in there all day?" she asked.

He took a bite of the salad, and answered after he swallowed. "I debug programs for software companies. Sometimes I beta test."

"What's that?"

"Play with programs before they get on the market."

"You do that from here?"

He nodded. "I get information over the modem, and they express-mail the disks to my box in Gunnison. I drive down a couple of times a week unless it's urgent."

"What about during the winter? The kid who drove me up says it gets nasty."

"I have a four-wheel drive. And a snowmobile."

"That sounds like fun."

He'd never really thought of it as fun, but he guessed he did enjoy riding it. He shrugged.

"How do you like your steak?" she asked, peering into the broiler oven.

Her jeans fit snugly over her curvy backside, the faded denim showing off the length and shapeliness of her legs and sparking his imagination. "Medium-rare."

"I knew you'd say that."

"Sure, you're psychic, right?"

The pleasure that had been evident on her face a moment before disappeared. "No. I'm nothing. At least that's what the tests show."

He picked up his fork and twirled it between his fingers. "I'm not used to this."

She sat across from him at the small pine table, her sleek hair tucked behind one ear, and folded her hands in her lap. "Did I do something wrong?"

He shook his head. There hadn't been a time since he was young that he'd entered his home and smelled supper cooking. He wasn't used to someone caring what he ate or how he preferred his steak. "I don't do this," he said, knowing his words were inadequate. "I don't make polite chitchat."

A blush rose in her cheeks. Her gaze dropped to the napkin beside her plate and remained there.

He didn't know how to act around her. He wasn't a people person. He resented having to call upon manners and polite conversation in his home. This was his sanctuary away from the entanglements of civilization, and he didn't want to deal with any encroachment, not even hers.

Getting up, she placed the steaks on their plates. The potato she set before him was still in its skin, but the fluffy insides had been mashed and dotted with chive.

She sat back down and, without a word, started eating.

Austin tasted the potato. It was delicious, as was the steak and salad. Best of all, he hadn't had to fix it himself. She'd tried to make herself useful. She *had* made herself useful. Somehow he understood she wasn't any happier with the situation than he was, but that she was just determined enough to secure his help that she'd overcome her reservations. He admired that.

He caught himself midthought. No. Stop right there. Any thoughts of acceptance would only lead to trouble. He'd cut himself off from people for a reason, and he'd do well to remember that. He knew better than to let horniness scramble his thoughts.

He ate, then got up to pour them each a cup of coffee. He'd opened up to someone once. And it had been the biggest mistake of his life. He wouldn't make it again. "The way to this man's heart is not through his stomach."

Her head shot up and she leveled that warm honey gaze on him. "I wasn't trying to bribe you."

"Good. See that you don't."

She picked up the broiler pan and placed it in the sink a little more noisily than necessary.

"Forget that. Come sit in here."

Hands resting on the edge of the sink, she straightened

her slender shoulders. Finally she turned and followed him into the other room, sinking onto a sofa.

Austin built a fire. The flames caught the sticks and eventually the split log. "Tell me what you did at the institute."

He could tell she was thinking over her attitude. She had to answer him to get anywhere with her situation. "I stayed a month. I took a lot of tests."

He sat on the hearth. "You said nothing specific brought on these dreams of yours."

"That's right."

"Can you remember your first dream about your nephew?"

Pain flickered across her face as plain as the firelight. "Yes."

"Describe it to me."

She did, with tears in her voice and in her eyes.

"Do you remember anything about the day or two before that first dream?"

"I remember everything."

"Tell me."

"I went to the cemetery that morning. On the way I stopped at the store and bought pink-tipped carnations. Maggie loved carnations. I left them at her grave. And a single blue one for Toby. There's a marker for him. There's nothing in the plot, though. But I didn't want Maggie alone there without him.... Somehow it seemed...I don't know...right. Maggie never liked being alone."

"What else?"

"There was a couple from Michigan at the inn that weekend. It was a Monday, and after lunch, I checked them out. Audrey took care of the room and the laundry, and I went through Maggie and Toby's closet and drawers. Toby's clothes and toys are still in my extra bedroom. I stored some of Maggie's things in the garage, the things I couldn't part with. And I took a trunk load to the Open Door Mission."

"They had been staying with you?"

"She moved in with me after the divorce. I helped her take care of Toby." Tears welled up then, and her chin trembled. She struggled to go on. "She made a lot of mistakes, but she was a good person. I loved her."

Austin had seen so many suffering people, it was a wonder he could still feel anything at all. But he did. He felt plenty. Her anguish. Her grief. Her confusion. *Damn her.* That's why he'd come here: to get away from feeling those things. She was exactly the person he'd avoided for the last twenty years.

To elude the dangerous wave of compassion that urged him to do something crazy like reach over and touch her and open up another whole set of complications, he turned and added another log. "Did the institute help you any?"

"They affirmed that I wasn't as crazy as the police thought when I kept nagging them about Toby still being alive. At first I couldn't separate the visions of Maggie and Toby in the car—under the water—"

She stopped. "Those were my fears, you see," she went on. "Maggie had always buckled Toby into his car seat, but when the search team brought the car up, he wasn't in it. Maggie's seat belt hadn't been fastened, either, leading the police to believe she'd attempted to free herself and Toby under water. They said maybe she got Toby out before she ran out of oxygen and was unable to get out herself. All the morbid possibilities of what could have become of his little body went around and around in my head until I thought I'd go crazy."

He said nothing, and kept his posture carefully guarded.

"Now I know differently," she went on. "The institute—Tom especially—helped me understand that my dreams were real." She waved a hand. "But I disappointed them all with my lack of abilities in any of their test areas."

Finally he turned back to her.

"I left after a month," she said. "I couldn't afford not to run my business, and we weren't getting anywhere. They wanted me to do more tests, but I knew it was pointless."

She raised her glistening gaze to his. "Did you take all those tests?"

The answer was out before he realized he was going to give it. "I spent years being tested and observed and recorded. Those researchers wait years for a find like me."

"And you were just a child?"

He nodded.

"How did you first know?" she asked. "That you had this...ability?"

Taking time to think about his reply, he left to refill their cups, and carried them out, sitting on the sofa across from her. She'd been honest with him. He didn't intend to get chummy, but she needed to know she wasn't the only one who had experienced these things.

"One day when I was about four or five," he told her, "my mother showed me my grandfather's war medals. I held one in the palm of my hand. I saw battles. I saw him in an army hospital. I saw his coffin covered with a flag, and I smelled roses. I described it all to my mother. She found a place in North Carolina to have me tested."

"What happened then?

"They drilled me with ESP cards, mind-mapping games, remote viewing exercises and every imaginable test." He ran a thumbnail along the crease of his jeans. "I had abilities in all those areas, but like I said before, my strength was in touching objects and getting pictures of the owner."

"That's incredible."

"It was pretty normal for me. I'd always done it in some way or another. Once I developed the ability, it was just my life. I didn't know anything else."

She leaned forward as if listening with her whole body. He'd never talked about this with anyone before, and he didn't know why he was telling her now, except that for some unexplainable reason he didn't want her to feel alone. He understood loneliness.

"I had a few dreams," he said, and her expressive eyes widened.

"Like mine?"

"Similar." A flush came to her cheeks and he knew she was relieved to hear him say these things. Her sincere reaction made him glad he'd told her. "Anyway, articles got published about the criminal cases. Once the ball was rolling, it gained more and more momentum until after a while all I did was find victims and tune in to killers. I couldn't go to school anymore because the kids and teachers knew about my talents and connections to the police."

"That must have been awful."

"My mom moved us around. But it was the same everywhere. We couldn't keep a low profile. My mom fancied herself an agent of sorts."

"What do you mean?"

"She'd get a call, book us a 'gig' and take money from people to find their loved ones."

"You had to live," she said.

"We could've lived like everyone else did. But she liked it that way. She took advantage of people who were hurting. I didn't realize until I was older, exactly what she was doing."

Though his voice and expression were carefully controlled, her expression said she'd seen through them to his pain.

"Sometimes," he said, more lightheartedly, "I'd pretend I wasn't picking up on anything, so I could have a rest from it. Sort of a vacation."

She studied the flames. "You were treated like a freak," she said softly.

He didn't know how he liked her easy assessment of his feelings. "I guess so."

"I know how that feels."

"You do?"

She turned her attention back, and an expression of discovery crossed her features. "I had dreams like these before...a long time ago."

He studied her in silence.

''When I was very small.'' She ran a hand through her hair in a nervous gesture. ''What had I done with those memories?''

''Saved them until you could deal with them, maybe,'' he replied.

She went on. ''Sometimes I didn't even have to be asleep to have one. One time I had an awake dream about my aunt Jackie being in a car accident. I cried and told my mother.

''A little while later, my mother answered the phone. She turned around and stared at me with this *look* on her face. I'll never forget it. I found out later that my aunt was in an accident. The next time something similar happened, my mother sent me to my room and told me never to speak of those dreams again. She said they used to hang women, burn them alive for having dreams like mine.''

''She was afraid of your sight, and made you think it was wrong,'' he said softly.

''More than wrong. She and my grandparents prayed and prayed over me. I didn't want them to think I was wicked, and I didn't want to be burned alive, so I let them think their prayers worked.''

''Maybe they did.''

''Maybe. I stopped having the dreams.''

''You learned to tune them out.''

''Is that what I did?''

He nodded. ''Until your sister and nephew died. Something there triggered them again.''

Shaine attempted to sip her coffee, but her hands shook, and hot coffee spilled over the side of the cup. That long-forgotten, well-hidden, slip of memory had come vividly into focus, and she wondered how she could have forgotten something so momentous. She blinked back moisture she didn't want him to see.

Austin took the mug from her and set it on the low table; then he took her hands, one at a time, and brushed her palms dry with his callused fingers.

She closed her eyelids against the gentleness in that

touch and held her breath so she wouldn't cry or groan or shame herself. He released her hands, and reached to take a strand of her hair and rub the tress between his fingers. She'd opened her eyes and was breathing again, but her heart forgot a couple of beats and then had to thump double-time to catch up.

He was so close, she could see the millions of tiny dark dots along his chin and jaw where he'd recently shaved. She wondered what it would feel like if she drew her hand along his jaw. Her palm burned with the temptation.

"First, Shaine, you have to learn to trust your instincts, your intuition." He released her hair.

She met his dark gaze, and without thinking about it, reached for his wrist. Her fingers wrapped around his warm flesh, the dusting of hair a pleasant sensation against her skin. "I trust the instinct that tells me Toby is alive."

Against his cream-colored sweater, his hair and skin were dark. His eyes closed for a brief moment, and when they opened again, they were grim. "All I can tell you is that in all the years I connected with victims, I rarely found anyone alive."

"But you did find some of them alive."

He was not a hard man by nature. Experience had driven him to protect himself. "The odds are not favorable," he warned. "Each time you open yourself to the possibilities, you take the almost inevitable chance of seeing and feeling things you don't want to experience. It's an unlucky crapshoot. And anticipating what you're about to open is almost the worst part of it."

His intensity would have convinced her if her reasons had been different. But this was Toby she was looking for.

He stared at her, giving Shaine an unexpected view into the pain-dimmed depths of his eyes, and for that instant, she shared his suffering. Thinking of his pain, her chest hurt.

Slowly his expression changed. That intense dark gaze

roved over her face, touched her lips, dropped to her breasts, warming her with its eloquence.

Her heart hammered against her ribs, and heat rose in her limbs. Beneath her fingers, his pulse quickened. His fierce expression didn't frighten her. Her gaze dropped to his mouth, and she saw his throat move as he swallowed. She barely knew him. But she understood him in some elemental way. And she wanted to kiss him. Oh, Lord, she wanted to kiss him.

Her entire body prepared for the experience. If he leaned forward and touched his lips to hers she would explode in a million pieces. And if he didn't…she would die.

His mouth came down over hers, his lips firm and warm and tasting of coffee, and the kiss seemed too beautiful and too fragile to bear. He tilted his head, aligning their mouths more perfectly, and her eager heart responded with a tumultuous pace. More than ever, the welling desire to cry rose up in her chest. Not from grief or empathy, but from the sheer joy of this man's touch.

He wasn't pushy. Or demanding. The ardent kiss was slow and easy, as though he wanted it to last. As if letting her know this was what making love with him would be like, too. It gave her time to imagine lying naked with him, to imagine his hands on her skin and his body pleasuring hers. He was a thorough kisser; he would be a thorough lover. His kiss slaked every hungering, thirsting ache she'd ever had, and she didn't want it to ever end.

But of course, it did.

As if by some sort of mutual amazement, they moved fractionally apart. His breath still touched her face. Reciprocal yearning configured his expression, and she prayed it wasn't just something she wanted to read.

"Is that what you meant by trusting instincts?" she half whispered.

The portal to the inner man she'd seen only a second ago disappeared, and his protective shell once again separated them. He moved back and released a pent-up breath.

"Didn't get anywhere with the food, so you'll try a new tactic, right?"

She blinked. "What?"

"Think coming on to me will win me over? Change my mind?" His mouth curved up in a cynical smile that pierced her to the quick. "I'll take you to bed. Bet on it. But I won't change my mind about what I'm going to teach you."

As if she'd intended for that to happen! As if she'd been the one to initiate it! Shaine picked up her cup and carried it toward the kitchen. "You're crude."

"No, I'm honest." The look on her face would have been the same if he had slapped her. Austin couldn't help watching her move around the divider. Was she a seductress or was he just a man too long without female company?

She ran water in the sink, and for some illogical reason he went after her.

She stopped scrubbing the pan and spun around, indignation burning in the depths of her gemstone eyes. "The thought of exchanging favors never crossed my mind, Mr. Allen. But if that's what it took to find my nephew, you can believe I'd do it. Sleeping with you would be a small price to pay for that little boy's welfare."

The anger dissipated from her body as though a force field of energy had been turned off. Suds dripped from her fingertips to the floor, and when she spoke again, her voice had lost its bravado. "If only it were that easy."

He didn't have the skills it took to relate to her, to anyone. His defensiveness was unbecoming, and he knew it. Immediately sorry, Austin started to move forward, but stopped himself before he invaded her space. Getting too close to her wasn't smart. "You're right. I am crude. I don't mingle with polite society much."

She shrugged as if it were of little consequence.

"I apologize."

"Might as well have it all out," she replied, dried her hands and opened the dishwasher door.

"Look, I haven't apologized to anyone in the last decade. You may as well acknowledge it because it might be another ten years."

"I accept your apology." She rinsed the plates and loaded them.

He put the wine away and took Daisy outdoors to give her the steak bones. The sooner this woman was gone, the better. She was beyond his experience. She wasn't a client or a one-night stand. He sensed the initial upheaval in his gut. She turned him on and had the ability to turn him inside out. She was trouble.

He wasn't going to let her open any old wounds or allow her to carve new ones. He'd desired a woman before. But not with this intensity nor with this chest-tightening longing that didn't really feel like a physical ache that could be appeased. And if he'd been hurt by that past desire, he could only fathom the devastation that would come from this hot and dangerous hunger.

Whatever happened and however he handled this time with her, he would either have to regret it or justify it forever.

Chapter 5

He loomed above her, his face hidden by deep shadows. His warm breath gusted against her chin, and the bare skin across her chest and shoulders tingled. He wanted her. As badly as she wanted him. In his arms she felt secure, desired, safe. His mouth came against hers, as eager and burning as she demanded. He urged her lips apart and his tongue invaded the recesses of her mouth, a welcome, rousing invasion.

Shaine crushed her body against his, sinuously pressing closer, as close as possible, yet not close enough. She wanted to envelop him, to possess him. She wanted to know passion with this man.

His voice, soft and low, spoke against her lips, uttering words that drove her out of her mind with need. He pressed a chain of kisses across her chin, down the column of her neck to her shoulder.

She writhed beneath him, her sensitized bare flesh eager for the touch of his hands. He didn't disappoint her. He whisked his thumb across her nipple, bringing the bud to *a peak, until she moaned, and then he took it between his lips. Heavenly.*

"Shaine," he whispered, his moist lips trailing from one breast to the other. "Shaine."

He touched and nibbled and suckled until she urged him fully against her.

He angled himself above, his chest hair rasping across her breasts, his manhood hot and hard and probing between her thighs. She'd never wanted anything as badly as she wanted this. Wanted him. Inside her. Now.

He kissed her throat, and she dug her nails into his hips, pulling him closer. Closer.

Her breath came out in a shudder.

From the other room a dog barked.

"No, no, don't stop," she cried, but her shadow lover had already left her.

A poignant emptiness ached deep inside her, and the unexpected night air chilled her heated flesh.

The dog barked again.

Heart pounding, Shaine leapt from the bed and raced to the railing, unable to see anything in the dark room below. Daisy's agitated barking continued. Assuring herself she did indeed have her cotton nightshirt on, Shaine groped her way down the stairs, clinging to the banister.

At the bottom, she ran solidly into a heated wall of flesh. "Oh!"

Hands gripped her shoulders to steady her just as she brought her fingers up and met the warm skin and springy hair of Austin's chest. She jerked her hand back like she'd touched fire. He released her.

"Daisy, no!" he commanded.

Immediately the dog quieted, and fur brushed against Shaine's bare legs. The air down here was cold and she hugged herself, rubbing her upper arms for warmth. "What's wrong with her?"

"She sets up a racket if she hears an animal outside," he said, his face hidden by the night shadows.

"A bear?"

"Sometimes. Sometimes a wolf or two. Could be only a raccoon." He moved to the window and peered out into the night.

"I'm glad you talked me out of sleeping in the tent." She skirted the furniture and joined him.

"It's getting too cold at night for someone as inexperienced as you to camp outside." Moonlight streaming through the window defined his handsome profile and the solid muscle of his shoulders.

The sight provoked the memory of clutching those bare shoulders in passion in her dream. "Not to mention the bears."

"They wouldn't bother you. Unless you had food."

"Yeah, well, I'll take my chances in here, thank you."

He turned to look at her, the angle of his jaw emphasizing the shadowy growth of his whiskers. She crossed her arms over her chest self-consciously, her body still tingling from the stimulating dream.

"Come here. I'll build up the fire so you can get warm." He moved away, and Shaine followed. He hunkered down to the chore, and she couldn't help but notice the masculine display of flesh above the pair of jogging pants he wore. The fire caught, and the golden light played across his muscled arms and shoulders.

He turned back, giving her a view of his matted chest. Her breath caught. She knew exactly what he'd feel like if she reached out and touched him—sleek flesh over sinewy muscle, the dark hair crisp and curling around her fingertips. At her side, her palm tingled with the disturbing knowledge.

A warmth pulsed at her feminine core, the arousing sensations shocking her. He hadn't touched her in that way, hadn't made a move except that innocent run-in at the bottom of the stairs. Why was her body responding in this inappropriate manner?

Guiltily she pulled her attention from his chest and sat beside the fire.

"Shaine." His voice held the rich seductive timber of her dream lover. A tingle ran up her spine and pebbled the flesh of her breasts.

She'd dreamed of him. Dreamed of making love with him.

She squeezed her knees together, not even needing to catalog the dream or the type. It had been a "knowing" dream.

Her skin burned hot. Her heart pounded. Her mind raced back over her recent dreams. The aproned woman. The boy. The dog. The diploma. If she walked into his office right now, she'd find a framed certificate on the wall.

Her knowing dreams always came true.

"Shaine?"

She jumped as if caught at something forbidden. She'd only had that dream because of the kiss they'd shared, she tried to tell herself. He'd made her feel guilty about that, and now she was feeling guilty about this.

"You warming up?"

She was warming up, all right. He had no idea. She nodded.

"I can stick that leftover hot chocolate in the microwave."

She shook her head and stood, grateful for something to occupy her mind and hands. "I'll do it."

She returned with two mugs and placed his on the stones without handing it to him. If he noticed her avoidance, he didn't let on.

He had pulled on a sweatshirt, and the sight eased her discomfort somewhat.

"Are you awake enough to work a little?" he asked.

She didn't think she'd sleep anytime soon. Not after that dream. She nodded.

"You sure?"

"Yes."

"I have a hard time getting back to sleep if I wake up during the night," he said.

"No problem." She settled on a sofa and pulled her feet up beneath her, trying to separate the reality of here and now from the equally convincing reality of her dream.

"You already know how to tell which dreams are precognitive," he said.

She nodded. She knew the difference. And she couldn't pawn off her last dream as anything other than what it was. The knowledge left her stunned—and a little ashamed. She barely knew him.

"Have you ever gone anywhere without a map?"

"Now that you've mentioned it, I guess so."

"There are things that you know in a part of your brain that has no language. You don't have to tell me how you know them. It doesn't matter. Just tell me the things you know. Don't let your emotions interfere."

She couldn't help a smile. "I know what you're asking."

"Go ahead," he urged, and reached over to switch on a table lamp. The warm light revealed his dark hair, attractively mussed. He sat across from her. Against her will, her attention dropped to his feet with their sprinkling of dark hair across the tops. "Elevators?" he prompted.

Shaine stifled her physical reaction to the man, and concentrated on his thought-provoking questions. "Sometimes I find myself standing in front of one before it ever dings," she replied. "Then it arrives and I get on, thinking that it was a coincidence."

He nodded.

Caught up in that revelation, she went on. "Once I went to the library for a book I needed for some research, and I didn't go to the catalogs first. I took the elevator to the right floor, got off and walked directly to the shelf. There was the book." She paused briefly. "Sometimes it's like I'm so preoccupied that I don't take time to think how I arrived somewhere or found something, and I don't give myself any time to think about it afterward."

"You've set up some self-preservation skills," he said. "You'll need to look at those and realize why you've done it. Then get rid of them."

"You're talking like you're teaching me how to use this so-called gift," she said warily.

"No. You have to understand it in order to not use it. How about parking places?"

She stared at him. "What do you mean?"

"Do you drive right up to a parking place close to a store?"

"No. Can you?"

"I could at one time."

"That's incredible."

"And your library book isn't?"

She shrugged.

"This is something you feel in kinesthetic form, a physical sensation somewhere in your body," he said.

"Yes." She understood his explanation clearly. "It's a feeling like when you drop something and you think it'll hit your toe, so you move your foot instinctively. That sensation between the dropping and the landing is what it's like."

He studied her with a new respect, she thought, though she couldn't figure out why. And when he spoke, the single word came out as though he were in awe. "Exactly."

"Is that how you felt the victims, too?" she asked.

He glanced down at his mug. "Sort of."

"Tell me. Tell me what you felt when you touched their things."

For a minute she thought he wouldn't answer, but then he spoke, his voice soft. "I'd get a warm feeling in my chest, and see a picture out of focus. Then I'd zero in on it, like turning a satellite dish or tuning in a radio station."

The mere thought of his incredible gift was beyond her reasoning. "Your talent is amazing," she said. "Did the doctors and scientists have any explanations after all that testing?"

He got up and used the poker to adjust the log. "Quantum physics and neuroscience have been trying to explain people like us away, to finds logical answers to this 'gift' of ours for years. Some think they can explain the ability or understand it with theories of electrons and upward causation and biophilosophy and mind and matter links. A lot of mumbo jumbo, but when they're all finished testing and theorizing, they don't really know why we can and others can't and what makes the difference."

"And what do you think?"

He studied her for a moment. "Just so you know, I wasn't the ideal subject, either."

"You weren't? But those researchers at the institute have spent their lives looking for people like you."

"Oh, I could do it all," he said. "I just didn't feel the need to explain it or qualify and analyze everything like they did."

He got up, moved to the bookcases Shaine had thought without order and promptly plucked out a worn leather-bound book. He opened it.

"The prophet Joel said, '....your sons and daughters will proclaim my message; your old men will have dreams and your young men will see visions.'" He looked up. "All through the Bible men had dreams. Remember the story about how Joseph interpreted dreams for the prisoners and for the king? There's nothing new about precognitive dreams." He closed the book, laid it on the table and returned to his seat.

Daisy padded over and laid her chin on his knees. He stroked her head. "Why do we need to analyze everything? Why not just accept it or reject it?"

Shaine wondered the same thing. But then her experiences at the institute had been unfruitful. "So, why do you think some people can do this and others can't?"

"I think all people are intuitive. Studies show over fifty percent of children depend on instincts. But by the time they're adults, only twenty-five percent rely on instincts.

The older people get, the more logical they get, and they talk themselves out of believing.''

"That's not your case."

"No."

"How did you talk yourself out of believing?"

"I didn't. I believe."

"Then why don't you use it?"

He studied her face for a moment, as though deliberating his words. Had she pushed too hard? "Did you want to stop what happened to that boy back home?" he asked. "Did it eat at you that there was nothing you could do?"

He'd spoken of this before. She didn't want to go there, but he was being candid with her, and she owed him the courtesy of returning his honesty. "I hated knowing and not being able to do anything about it," she said finally.

"There's some kind of scientific law in the universe," he said, stroking the dog's ears. "You can see these things and know them, and you want to reach out and change them. But you can't." His voice dropped off to a hoarse whisper that sent a shiver up her spine. "You can't."

"Maybe you can," she said.

He sat forward and leveled a stare at her. "If that were possible, don't you think I'd have done it?"

"You would have if you had known how," she agreed.

"Everything you see...*happens,*" he said.

Her thoughts jolted to the scene of her in his arms, their heated bare flesh straining together. Shaine's face and body flushed with heat, her throat filling with mute expectancy. He was right. Everything she saw in her dreams *happened*. And that's how she knew without a sliver of a doubt, that she would make love with Austin Allen—glorious, breathless, rapturous love.

She surveyed his dark hair, his golden skin and long-fingered hands, and embarrassment clawed its way to the surface of her mind, reminding her she barely knew him. She barely knew him, but she knew his touch inflamed her.

She knew the taste and urgency of his kiss and what his body felt like cradled between her thighs.

"Yes," she whispered. She didn't know whether to feel giddy or guilty to possess this disconcerting knowledge. "Everything I see happens."

And right now, she didn't know whether or not she would change it if she did have the ability.

Shaine awoke to the sensation of Daisy's tongue licking her hand. She opened her eyes and found herself lying on Austin's sofa, a soft blanket tucked around her. They'd talked into the early hours of morning, and she must have fallen asleep.

Wrapping the blanket around her shoulders, she let her nose lead her to the coffee in the kitchen. It tasted a trifle stronger than she'd have preferred, but she added a little milk and sipped it.

The whole time she showered and dressed, trying not to disturb Austin in case he was still sleeping, she went over the things they'd talked about the night before. He'd shown her things about herself—about her intuitive ability—that she'd never realized or *admitted* before.

How long would it take her to control it? To zero in on Toby and find him? How long did they have?

That afternoon and evening passed much as the one before, except that both were tired from the previous night and retired early.

Immediately, Shaine fell into exhausted slumber...and dreamed....

She entered his office and glanced at the unfamiliar surroundings: a soft-looking leather sofa and two chairs, a gigantic wraparound desk with two separate computers and accessories, a phone and a neat stack of reference books. An oak filing cabinet and an enormous aquarium stood on either sides of the uncovered double window.

The room was enormous and functional, yet possessed a prosperous air of comfort. Shaine stepped to the desk and studied the framed document on the wall behind it, trying to bring the words into focus.

The room grew too dark for her to see, and she groped her way to the door, where a sliver of light shone beneath it.

She reached for the knob and the door opened silently.

Toby sat on a floor that hadn't seen a vacuum for weeks—months maybe, his tiny fingers clumsily struggling over his shoelaces. A stale, sour smell assailed her senses.

"I'm a big boy," he said, the tiny voice precious and familiar. "Beebee's a big boy."

A loud slam sounded and struck alarm into his chest. She was coming.

The door opened and she loomed in the doorway, tall and unkempt and reeking of the stuff she drank all the time. "What're you doin'?" she drawled.

"I put my shoes on," he said, inching backward toward the bed.

"What the hell for? You're not goin' anywhere? Stupid little boys with stinky pants don't get to go anywhere."

He cringed, knowing what was coming.

"Stupid little stinky boys have to sit in the bathroom."

"No! I can't want to!" he cried.

"Don't you tell me no." She shook her finger under his nose. "Don't you ever tell me no."

He wouldn't look at her.

She jerked him upward by one arm, stripped his shorts off and sat him on the toilet. "And you stay there until I come and get you! If you get down I'll turn the lights off and leave you in here in the dark tonight."

"No!" he cried.

"Then mind what I say."

She turned and left the room.

Tears ran down Toby's cheeks and dripped onto his knees. He cried for several minutes, then stopped himself before she came and hit him. He stared down at the shoelaces dangling on the cracked and peeling linoleum floor.

Beside him, the faucet dripped in the rust-stained sink, the monotonous sound, his only company.

"Mama," he whispered.

A sob tore from Shaine's chest, a suffering so unbearable, she cried aloud with the pain.

"Toby!" she shrieked, jumping from the bed as if she had somewhere to go, desperate to reach the child and comfort him.

Orienting herself to her surroundings, she clutched her head in her hands and dropped to her knees, sobbing. "Oh, no, God, no," she cried over and over.

She became dimly aware of a light, and padding steps on the stairs. "Shaine?"

Her anguished cries had wakened Austin from a light sleep, and he'd hopped into his sweatpants and stumbled into the other room. From the loft above came heartbroken cries.

"Shaine?" he said, softly, kneeling down and reaching for her shoulder. Her slender frame shook with the force of her sobs. "What is it? What's wrong?"

"T-Toby," she said. "It's Toby."

"You had a dream?"

She nodded.

Awkwardly he tried to put his arm around her shoulders. He didn't have any experience at comforting hysterical women. "It's all right. It's all right," he soothed.

"No!" Her head shot up and her arm flung out, the backs of her fingers slapping across his bare shoulder. "It's not all right." She scrambled to her feet, her hair a wild disarray, her cheeks streaked with tears that shone silver in the light from below. "It's not all right," she clipped out, each word a shot. "Toby is not all right. He's scared and hurting. There's a woman who's mean to him. I've seen her. I've felt what he feels."

Austin stared up at her, not moving from his kneeling position.

"He's a little boy," she said in a tiny voice that broke.

"A little boy who misses his mommy and needs someone to take care of him. He called himself 'Beebee'," she said. "He couldn't pronounce his name when he was little. Even Maggie called him Beebee after a while."

"Shaine," he said, wondering if this was the right time to try to reason with her. "That doesn't prove that he's alive."

Her body stiffened with anger, drawing his attention to the soft curves beneath the short nightshirt she wore. Her legs, long and slender, were the kind of legs that gave a man erotic thoughts. He tried to draw his thoughts from her curvy body and exotic feminine scent to the subject at hand.

"Well, what does?" she asked, drawing his attention back to her words. "Last night you said yourself, the things in my dreams *happen*."

"Maybe this dream is something that already happened. In the past."

She shook her head vehemently. "No. He was never treated like that. Besides, I've told you, he's *older* in these dreams."

"That doesn't prove anything—"

"You have a big corner-shaped desk in your office."

He stared at her. "So?"

"It has two computers on it. There's a certificate of some type on the wall."

"And?"

"And I've never been in there. I've never set foot in that room."

"Come on, you could've gone in there any time while I was downstairs—or out running." Who was she trying to kid?

She took off down the stairs. "I've never been in there, I swear. There's a phone and a flat gray thing by your computer. You have a big oak filing cabinet."

He followed her through the main room and back into his office.

She stood in the middle of the room in the dark. "Turn the light on."

He flipped on the track lighting above his desk.

She glanced up at the certificate on the wall. "A degree?"

"Computer science. Pennsylvania State."

"I never knew what it said. I saw it in my dreams at home, too. I even saw Daisy. Back then I didn't know how those things were related to Toby. Now I do."

Austin sympathized with her. Really he did. But she was going to have to face the fact that her nephew was dead. She was trying so hard to persuade him otherwise. How could he convince her that the victims were rarely ever alive?

"Where's the fish tank?"

That stopped him cold. "What?"

She gestured to the empty space by the window. "Where's the fish tank? A great big one with a blue background and an oak cabinet."

Austin's mind reeled with the implication of what she'd just revealed. He stared at her. She returned his look, her eyes red from crying, her vulnerable mouth in a questioning line. An odd feeling crept in around the edges of his protective insulation. "How do you know about that?" he asked.

"I dreamed it."

He moved to sit in his form-molded office chair and let the information wash over him. He'd lived with his extra sense his entire life. He'd foreseen things about his own life, and in so many other people's lives that it ceased to amaze him. But he'd never before had anyone see things in his future. It was...weird.

"So where is it?" she asked.

He met her eyes. "It's in the garage."

"You took it down?"

He shook his head.

"What then?"

He stared at her, realizing the complexity and enormity of the sixth sense she had no idea how to control.

"What?"

"I haven't set it up yet. It's still in the cartons. And—" he pointed to the spot beside the window "—that's where it goes."

Expectant silence stretched between them. Finally she moved forward and leaned her knuckles on his desk, all her desperation and urgency written plainly on her features. She met his gaze and wouldn't let it go. A voice deep inside screamed for Austin to beware.

"You believe me now, don't you?" she asked.

Chapter 6

Did he believe her? Hell, yes. But was that even the right question? Deliberately, Austin rethought his initial reaction. So, she'd seen something he'd been planning. That wasn't all that surprising. It was possible to pick up on people's thoughts. Nothing was ever out of the question in his experience.

He'd convinced her to return to her bed an hour ago, but he'd been unable to force himself to follow suit. Idly, he'd been watching his Terminator screen saver blast cyberholes in the computer screen for the last twenty minutes. Okay. He'd finished with his last job. He'd devote every minute to working with Shaine now. The sooner he showed her how to block out the dreams, the sooner he'd have her gone and his life would be back to normal.

Normal. If living way up here away from everyone and everything and avoiding people was normal. But this was his life. It was how he lived with himself and the things that he'd seen and learned and been through. And he didn't know any other way.

Austin glanced over at the pillow and rumpled blanket on his too-short leather sofa, thought about the long-legged woman in his bed upstairs and shook his head. He'd already let his libido get ahead of his thinking where she was concerned. She was right: they didn't have much time. He needed to teach her and get rid of her before she gave him any more reasons why she should stay.

"So, what did the doctor say?" Shaine asked Audrey over the phone the next morning.

"He said I'm starting to dilate."

"Oh, God."

"Yeah, that's what I said. But he told me it could still be a couple of weeks."

"And I'm sticking you with all the work, Audrey. I feel terrible."

"He said to do what I normally do. Just not to overdo."

"And overdo is your norm. Did the Andersen woman work out?" she asked, mentioning the neighbor woman she'd hired to help Audrey with the work.

"She's a big help. She can't come until she gets her kids off for school, so I still have to do the early breakfasts, and then she leaves to go pick the kids up at three-thirty, but I have her all the rest of the day. Can we really afford her, hon?"

"Don't worry about that. Tell Nick to pay her out of my account. I'm the one who's not there to work."

"But what will you do? You can't afford that for long."

"I'll figure something out, Audrey. And I'll be there when you have the baby. I promise."

Shaine said goodbye and hung up. Hiring someone still didn't assuage the guilt she experienced over deserting Audrey at this crucial time, but what choice did she have? She knew beyond a shadow of a doubt that Toby needed her more than Audrey ever would. And in order to help him, she had to be here.

She rubbed the nagging pain in her ankle, remembering

the strange dream she'd had before waking this morning. The vision hadn't been of anyone she knew, and it had been an odd blend of sights and sounds. She'd had the impression of stumbling through the nearby woods searching for something. She'd eaten a filling breakfast, but her stomach felt oddly empty.

Shaking off the strange feeling, she wandered out to watch Austin splitting wood. He'd taken off his sweatshirt and, dressed in jeans, a snug T-shirt and supple-looking leather work gloves, he swung the sledgehammer, hitting the wedge and splitting the logs apart. A fine sheen of perspiration glistened on his skin. The muscles in his back and shoulders corded and flexed with each swing, and as he leaned into the action, she couldn't help but imagine the muscles in his buttocks and thighs doing the same.

She needed to think about something else.

A portable radio on the corner of the porch picked up an oldies station, and in amid bursts of static, the Beatles sang "Till There Was You."

"Aren't there gadgets that do that?" she asked.

He paused, catching his breath, and looked over at her. "Sure. Have one in the garage."

"Why don't you use it?"

"What? And waste the opportunity for all this exercise? I'm a computer geek, remember? I need the workout."

She lowered herself to the top step and stretched her legs out in front of her. "Somehow you're not what I imagine when I picture a computer geek."

His mild gaze raked the length of her legs before he met her eyes. "Really? And what do all the other computer geeks you know look like?"

"Well, I don't know any others."

"Then I'm flattered to be your first."

The rare smile at the corner of his lips wasn't entirely suggestive, but his words brought a tingle of embarrassment to her cheeks and added a strange warmth to the feeling already pooled in her abdomen. Sometime between her arrival and now, the atmosphere had changed.

She couldn't say it had been that kiss, because he'd been so quick to accuse her of trying to seduce him. But maybe it had been. Maybe as much as he wished that was how it had been, he knew that the kiss had been as spontaneous and as welcome on his part as it had on hers. Maybe he was just into deluding himself.

The same way he denied his gift.

But things had changed. It wasn't in anything they said…or necessarily did…but in the things that went unsaid and undone between them.

They were in that formative stage where each was wondering about the other. Wondering about past loves and past lovers. Wondering about intimate things that only another lover would know.

He bent to stack several chunks of wood before securing his grip on the wooden handle of the sledgehammer. He leaned into the task, his muscles bunching with each lift and swing. Lift and swing. Shaine watched with a mix of fascination and frustration.

The song ended and a news update crackled over the airwaves. "….students from WSC in Gunnison….reported missing since last night….sometime around six….last seen wearing…"

Shaine drew her legs up and straightened. The hazy dream image of the night before encompassed her thoughts, blocking out everything else. A young man in a red plaid flannel shirt, a dark green backpack on his shoulders, lay on a pile of dry leaves. His ankle throbbed inside his high-topped boots. The pain blotted out most of his thoughts, but he was afraid. She sensed fear and pain. And guilt.

She stood.

All those frightening forest sounds came to life. The young man shivered with the cold and rubbed his hands together, afraid to start a fire for fear of the wind coming up and fanning the blaze out of control. Bone-tired wea-

*riness stole his energy. Merciless pain throbbed in his ankle
until he wanted to cry aloud. But he didn't. He was keeping
up a brave front for someone.*

"Shaine?"

She heard Austin's voice and glanced over at him.

"What are you looking at?" He squinted into the woods.

"That guy."

"What guy?"

"That guy on the radio. He's out there."

"A deejay in the woods?"

"No, the student they said was missing."

Austin laid down the sledgehammer and pulled off his
gloves, wiping his sweaty palms on his thighs. He stepped
close to her.

"You've seen him?" he asked, realizing it wasn't a sight
she'd seen in the physical, natural realm.

She nodded.

"A dream?"

"A dream, yes. But then just now, when he was talking—" she waved toward the squawky radio "—I felt
him."

"Damn," he said under his breath. Some poor dead hiker
was lying out in the timber. He could just imagine animals
getting to the body. "Well, let's call a ranger."

"How long will that take?"

"I don't know."

She came down the steps toward him and circled his
wrist with her cool fingers. "Okay, let's call, but you know
these woods, don't you?"

"Yeah, but—"

"Then we'll just go get him."

"Just go get him! Shaine, we're in the middle of a forest,
in case you haven't noticed. A search like that has to be
done methodically."

She shook her head. Then she released his arm, took a
half step away and seemed to be listening. After a minute,
she pointed. "There. That direction. There's a clearing with

a natural windbreak. His ankle is sprained, or broken maybe, and he's dizzy and out of breath, like I was—no, worse than I was that first day.''

''I don't doubt your sense of direction. I don't doubt any of the details you just gave me.''

''Good—''

''Except your use of present tense.''

She frowned up at him.

''You've surely seen it all just as it happened. But by now the guy is dead. Or will be by the time someone gets to him.''

''No. He's not dead.''

''Shaine, he is.''

''Stay here then. I'll go.'' She ran into the house.

Austin followed and called up to the loft. ''You can't barge into the woods by yourself. Let's just call the rangers and let them handle it.''

She hurried back down, pulling on her denim jacket. ''Call the rangers. But I'm going.''

''I won't let you go alone.''

She turned and faced him. ''What are you going to do, sit on me?''

He glared at her, tempted.

''Come with me, then,'' she said.

''Fine.'' He snatched a hooded sweatshirt from its peg by the door, pulled it on and paused briefly to place the call.

He'd accompany her. Maybe she had to see once and for all. Maybe it would take something this awful to convince her that there was nothing she could do about her nephew. Stuffing a few items in a knapsack, he followed her out the door.

She pointed out the direction they needed to travel, and he asked for a description of the surrounding area. He led her down a sloping deer trail to the south of the cabin, often checking their direction against her internal compass. Daisy darted in and out of the brush, recurrently running off and returning later. They hadn't been out half an hour before Shaine stopped, both hands in the air before her.

"Here," she said. "Right here."

Austin inspected the ground and the surrounding area. Slipping between some willowy young trees, he discovered a spot where someone had camped. The nearby foliage was just as Shaine had described it, with the clearing and the windbreak. He dug up a patch of freshly disturbed earth and found two empty cans.

Someone had definitely been here. And not too long ago. But where was he now? There was no sign of blood or animal tracks that he could make out.

"This way." She moved off, in the opposite direction of his cabin, and sedulously he followed. She went as fast as the undergrowth would allow, finally breaking into an awkward run among the fallen and decayed limbs.

Daisy barked and led the way.

Austin saw the red flannel shirt on the ground ahead just after Shaine did. He reached out to stop her, but she hurried forward. To his utter amazement, a second person sat beside the one in the flannel shirt, a girl with a blond ponytail and an oversize sweatshirt. Tears streaked her dirty cheeks, and her eyes were opened wide.

"Tommy! Tommy!" she cried, shaking the shoulder beside her. "Someone's here! Look!"

The figure on the ground moaned and sat up, his youthful face distorted in a grimace of pain.

Shaine knelt beside the two young people. "Are you all right?"

"Thank God you found us," the girl said with a hoarse voice. "Tommy hurt his ankle and he can't walk. We've been lost since yesterday."

"How did you find us?" Tommy asked.

Shaine glanced back at Austin, an expectant look on her eloquent face. Austin tried to come to terms with the fact that she'd envisioned this, and that the young man sat on the forest floor, very much alive. His surprise stole every coherent thought.

"He's familiar with the woods," Shaine said, jabbing a thumb over her shoulder toward Austin. "He lives not too far away."

Her explanation hadn't told them anything, but they obviously didn't care.

"How are we going to get Tommy out of here?" the girl asked.

"We called the rangers," Shaine offered. "They probably have stretchers or something."

"That could take a while," the girl said, her face fallen.

Austin sized the college student up. "We'll make a travois and drag him back."

"Brilliant!" Shaine said with a smile that disappeared immediately. "How do we do that?"

He unzipped the bag he'd carried. "We cut down a couple of saplings and lash our jackets between."

Twenty minutes later, she watched him maneuver Tommy onto the makeshift conveyance. "How'd you learn to do that, anyway?"

"'MacGyver,'" he replied, and packed his survival gear back in the bag.

She giggled and took it from him, leaving him free to pull the travois.

The trip back up the trail took a lot longer than the one down, and even after pausing several times to rest, Austin had broken out in an honest-to-goodness sweat by the time they reached the log house.

Shaine and the girl they'd learned was named Tricia, helped Tommy into one of the wooden porch chairs.

Austin collapsed on the steps, and Shaine brought him a jug of water. "I think I'll skip my run today," he said, panting.

Shaine made sandwiches for Tommy and Tricia, and by the time the rangers came, the sun hung low in the sky.

* * *

Having caught his second wind, Austin watched the mud-encrusted Blazer leave, bent to pick up the split wood and carried it into the house. "Shaine?"

He didn't get a reply. He got the fire going, popped some popcorn and finally, checked the bathroom and the downstairs, looking for her. "Shaine?"

Concerned, he climbed the stairs to the loft. She lay on his king-size bed, still wearing her jeans, jacket and hiking boots.

"Hey." He touched her arm, but she didn't rouse. Unlacing her boots, he tugged them off, still not disturbing her. Sure that nothing would disturb her now, he rolled her from one side to the other, removing her jacket, then took the side of the comforter and tucked it around her.

On its own, his hand reached out and smoothed her hair away from her face. It was like touching silk. He ran his fingers through the strands, wondering at his impulsive inclination to touch her.

He'd thought he was safe up here away from people. Away from the hurts of victims, away from the warped appetites of criminals, away from feelings. Away. Period.

But this woman had shown him he'd only been deluding himself. He couldn't live the rest of his life without feeling something.

And right now he was feeling pretty confused. What had happened today was a one-in-a-million chance. He didn't have much to measure it to, and he'd had some wild experiences. Rarely had he tuned in to anyone he could actually help. Oh, the victim's families were often grateful to have a body to bury and to set their minds at ease. And the police and the FBI knew he had done them a service.

But reaching a victim in time to prevent a tragedy wasn't the norm.

Shaine had done just that. She'd been lucky.

Hadn't she?

Or could she do it again?

With every fiber of his being, he'd discouraged her belief

that her nephew was alive. He knew the pain and disappointment and guilt that accompanied being too late, and he didn't want that for her.

But what if…?

What if there was an iota of a possibility that the child really was alive? He thought back over all the information she'd given him and her reasons for her belief. If there was a chance, even the *smallest* chance in the world, didn't he owe that to her?

Austin combed his fingers through her hair one last time, lingered over the soft skin of her cheek and tenderly drew a line across her parted lips.

He thought it over carefully, making very sure he wasn't doing this because he had a case of the hots for her. He was doing this because she deserved her chance.

And so did her nephew. If he was still alive.

"Okay, sexy lady," he said aloud. "We're going to do it your way."

He adjusted the coverlet one last time and left her to her sleep.

"What you have to learn," he said, with a startling new intensity behind his eyes, "is how your own intuitive sense works."

Still fighting the groggy effects of the day before, Shaine concentrated on absorbing his words. Her morning cup of coffee had chugged life through her veins, and she'd stepped out on the porch for some fresh air. That's where Austin had found her. "Okay," she said. "I learn how my intuitive sense works."

He leaned a hip against the porch rail and nodded, raising his own cup to his lips.

"And you're going to tell me how to do this?" she asked.

"Give the sense your own definition," he explained. "Not a label someone else calls it. Not even a label I call it. Give it a name and a color and credibility and whatever else it takes to know it. You have to acknowledge that you have this capability."

"I have the ability," she said with some assurance in her voice. "And Tom taught me to give my dreams names. That's how he taught me to differentiate between them."

"Good. So you understand what I'm saying."

"I think so."

"Now, you use your strongest experiences as points of reference."

"What do you mean?"

"Take the experiences that are vivid for you. Things you knew without a shadow of a doubt."

"Like my aunt Jackie's accident?"

"And the Deets boy. Every detail about those incidents will help you in the next."

It hit her then that he was giving her practical, completely understandable information on how to use her own skill. Excitement built within her chest, and her heart pounded erratically. "Austin?"

The warmth of his flint-colored gaze touched her every bit as directly as the heat from the morning sun. She'd never felt quite so alive.

"What?" he replied.

She tried to form words around the pressure in her chest. "Wh-what are you doing?"

He leaned forward, his intriguing dark eyes suffused with a challenge...and something more.... "I'm going to give you what you're asking for. So you'd better *hope* it's what you really want."

Joy sprang up inside her, but warily she forced herself to double-check his meaning. "You're going to teach me how?"

As if she were seeing too much, he cast his gaze toward the fall-dressed mountainside for several seconds. When he looked back at her, she read his uncertainty. "Yesterday shook up my conviction about your nephew."

"Oh, Austin." She allowed the expectant thrill of his

decision to wash over her. He believed her! He believed she could find Toby! Impulsively she stepped closer, wanting to touch him, needing to share her feelings and oh, so grateful to him for caring enough to change his mind.

"Whoa!" he said, as his coffee sloshed over the side of the cup and dotted the porch floor. One arm went around her, and quickly he set the cup down and used the other to steady her against him.

"Thank you," she said, and placed her hands on his cheeks.

Against her breast his heart thundered. Around her, his arms were solid and reassuring. For the first time ever, she didn't feel all alone. This man understood her. He cared enough to help her. He wasn't afraid of her, nor did he want to examine her head to satisfy his curiosity.

His hand opened in the middle of her back, but it didn't pull her toward him. Heat radiated through her sweater and raced along her spine.

She stared into his dark eyes and wanted to kiss him. She wanted to feel that pulse-drugging excitement once again. His cheeks were warm and smooth beneath her palms. She raised her face until her lips were only inches from his.

"Don't do this just because I'm helping you," he said, his voice a low warning.

She had to think a moment. Had to clear her head and recognize what he was saying to her. Don't kiss him? Don't throw herself into his arms? Don't what?

"I'm doing this because I want to," she said, and moved her hands to his hard shoulders.

The way he sat on the rail had her pressed into the V of his jean-clad thighs where hard muscle encased her hips. His hand moved up her back, still not demanding, still not pressing her toward him. When he reached her hair, he twined his fingers through the tresses and found the sensitive skin of her neck.

The caress transmitted a betraying shiver through Shaine's body.

His eyes darkened. His lips beckoned. Shaine leaned into the kiss, meeting his mouth, wrapping one arm around the back of his neck to retain the delicious connection.

His lips were warm and pliant and starved for the taste of hers. Not gentle. Not patient. Not at all like the last time. Passion swept through her with the onslaught of his hungry quest for more. He had an array of kisses, and she wanted to sample them all.

He slid his hand through her hair to cradle the back of her head, and the kiss became daring, fiery, ardent. Shaine cupped his jaw, ran her thumb over the warm supple skin of his cheek.

He framed her face with his hard-palmed hands and unsatisfactorily kissed both corners of her mouth, nipped her chin, touched his tongue to the tender skin below her jaw. Shaine's shallow breath fluttered through her lips.

"You'd better decide," he said against her throat.

Shaine opened her eyes, but saw nothing. "Decide what?"

"What kind of a relationship you want, here." He nipped her ear, and a soft sound of pleasure escaped her.

The air cooled her damp fevered lips. She ran her tongue over them. "What do you mean?"

"I told you I'd take you to bed. I will. We both want it." He held her head still and looked into her eyes. "But I won't get involved. If you need a commitment, I'm not your man. If you want to share some good times and go your separate way afterward, that's how it'll be. But I won't mislead you."

She eased back, slightly embarrassed, more than slightly uncertain, and he allowed her the freedom, his hands sliding to her waist. "We kissed," she said with a shaky laugh. "That's not a lifetime commitment."

"Okay. I want it straight between us. No misunderstandings."

"No misunderstandings," she agreed, the delicious glow he ignited within her a restless flame she would live with now. She couldn't afford any complications interfering with her search for Toby. It was easy to see she could fall for Austin in a heartbeat, and he had no intention of reciprocating. She'd be wise to place her arousing feelings for him out of the way and concentrate on the matter at hand.

After *this*, however, that would be no easy task.

She'd never before known the desire or tender feelings she'd experienced in his arms. He made her feel alive and beautiful, he made her want to give, but need to take, all at once. And Shaine knew, just as she knew many things without positive proof, that this feverous, frightening passion Austin had made known wouldn't be easy to forget or ignore.

Self-consciously, she pulled away from his easy embrace and faced the mountainside, folding her arms and holding her elbows. "Well, what next?" she asked finally. "How are you going to teach me?"

He tossed his cold coffee over the porch rail and stood. "For the next few days we'll go over these things we've talked about. How to use your experience with the Deets boy and the others as a guideline to direct your perception. I'll ask you too many questions and make you crazy, forcing you to remember all the little details."

"Whatever it takes," she said, turning back to him.

"In a few days I'll be getting mail in Gunnison. We'll have to go down for it."

"Okay. A job?"

"No."

"May I ask what?"

"A package from a friend of mine."

He still hadn't told her anything, but she waited. If he wanted to, he would.

"He's with the FBI."

Shaine searched his rugged features, her interest piqued.

"I asked for files so you'd have something to practice on."

Her heart leapt into her chest. "What kind of files?"

"Missing persons."

"And he's just sending you this stuff? Aren't they confidential?"

"Families and detectives only seek my kind of help as a last resort, so by the time this stuff gets to my friend, it's a desperate measure." He ran a hand over his face. "This was what I did for years and years, Shaine. I've worked with the FBI on hundreds of cases. They're eager to have a fresh lead or a new clue."

She stared at him nervously. "What will we do with these files?"

He contemplated her once again. "Sit down a minute."

"Why?"

"Just sit down. Am I the teacher? Sit down."

She backed onto the chair and he crouched in front of her. Daisy joined them then, laying her snout on Shaine's knee. Shaine petted her distractedly.

"I think you have the same ability I do,' he said gently. "We're going to test it."

"What do you mean? What ability?"

"To touch things and get impressions."

"That's impossible, why would you think that?"

He shooed Daisy away and took her hand. "You told me you started having the dreams of Toby after you'd packed away his and Maggie's things."

She thought a minute, remembering the details she'd shared with him. "That's not exactly what I told you."

"No, you told me about signing out guests at the inn, and visiting the cemetery, but in there was the part about packing their things."

She acquiesced. "Okay."

"You held something of Toby's, didn't you?"

She recalled crying all the while she packed the clothing and toys, deciding what to give away, what to keep. Unconsciously her fingers tightened on his. "Yes," she whispered.

"And after that you dreamed of him."

She'd been staring unseeingly at the sky, but she focused on him, on his words.

"From childhood you'd trained yourself not to have the visions. As a defense, you learned to shut them out. But whatever you held of Toby's triggered your perception, and your subconscious released it in the form of dreams."

Stunned, Shaine clutched his hand until her knuckles turned white. A sudden grasping fear clawed her insides. "What does this mean?" she asked. "What will we do with those files?"

"You'll touch their things," he said. "We'll see if you can get impressions from them."

Her heart had a frantic workout against her breast. Alarm spread through her body until her hands shook. Lord help her, this was what she'd wanted. This was why she'd left Audrey alone with the inn, why she'd made an idiot of herself coming up here and why she'd hammered at Austin tenaciously for the last week.

This was what she'd wanted.

And heaven help her, he was giving it to her.

Chapter 7

The ride to Gunnison was a pleasant one. Shaine had always loved fall, and autumn in the Rockies was a breathtaking sight. Deer bounded across the road, and Austin drove his Jeep Cherokee slowly. Once, several porcupine lumbered across, and he waited patiently while they moved aside.

The past couple of days had been revealing, in more ways than one. Not only had he shown her insight into her own ability, but he'd unwittingly revealed his own caring, vulnerable nature, the side of him she'd suspected was there all along.

Austin had a sixties CD blasting from the rear speakers, and tapped his fingers on the steering wheel to Dion singing ''The Wanderer.'' As she'd overheard from time to time since her arrival, he sang a few lines here and there in a surprisingly good voice.

She smiled and leaned back in the comfortable seat. The play of sun through the leaves of the gold and yellow trees dappled the windshield and dash and glinted highlights off Austin's dark hair.

He plucked a pair of sunglasses from the console and slid them on, glancing over. Instantly he pulled them back off and held them out. "Want 'em?"

She shook her head and he slipped them back on.

"Why this music?" she asked.

"What?" He leaned forward and turned the volume down.

"Why do you listen to oldies and nothing else?"

"I have other stuff."

"But you don't listen to it."

"It's the *only* kind of music," he said with a grin.

"Maybe you're trying to recapture the years you didn't get to be a kid."

"Maybe you're making a pretty lame attempt at psychoanalysis."

"Hey, I'm free."

The Kinks belted out "You Really Got Me" just then and Austin turned the volume back up. "Maybe you should just let yourself enjoy it, and not wonder why," he said over the song.

She applied herself to just that.

Gunnison streets weren't busy that morning as he drove to the post office. He came out with two boxes and loaded them into the back of the Cherokee. Shaine surveyed the packages and followed him with her gaze as he strode to his door.

Austin slid into the seat and recognized the apprehension on her face. She'd been trying her best to cover her uneasiness over what they were going to do, but he knew the fear she hid.

"How about some lunch before we get groceries?" he asked, hoping to give her a change of scenery and lighten her mood.

She agreed with a nod.

"You've been cooking and eating meals I like," he said, thinking out loud. "What do you like?"

"I haven't had a pizza for ages," she suggested.

"Pizza it is." He parked in front of place called Bob & Tony's and led her inside. "Smells good."

They slid into a booth, sat across from one another and agreed on toppings. Austin placed the order and they helped themselves to salad.

"Have you eaten here before?" she asked.

"A couple of times. Not in the last five or six years. It's a college hangout on the weekends."

"I had a dream last night," she said.

So had he. An erotic dream about her. The remembrance half aroused him, and he deliberately brought his thoughts under control. "Really? Which kind?"

"Knowing," she replied, and pushed her salad plate away.

"Toby?"

She nodded, and then he understood the shadows beneath her eyes. "Tell me."

"He was at a chrome table with a yellow top. I could see the whole kitchen as plain as I can see the restaurant here. There was some kind of macaroni on his plate. Some peas. He didn't like the taste, but he was hungry, so he ate some. The woman was there and she sat across from him, smoking. Staring at him.

"'Where's Dave?' Toby asked. The woman got this hateful look on her face, and her voice was full of venom. 'Dave left. He left us because you were a *bad boy*.'"

Shaine's voice quavered on the words. Tears filled her luminous eyes. "How can she treat him like that?"

Austin reached over and covered her hand with his. "I never understood the rotten people I envisioned. Even being in their heads I didn't understand."

"He's just a little boy, practically a baby still," she said, straining for composure. She locked her fingers as though to keep them under control, and leaned forward. "How did she get him?"

Austin shook his head. He'd had to change his whole way of thinking for her benefit. He had to go under the assumption that this child was alive. And if he believed that as strongly as she did, he'd wonder, too, how the child had gotten from the scene of the accident to this place where he was now. He gave the question his full consideration.

"If someone discovered him, along the riverbank somewhere, they'd have called an ambulance, called the police, notified someone."

"You would think," she replied.

"Even if no one found him and he wandered off by himself, a lost child is turned over to authorities."

"Unless someone unscrupulous found him," she said.

He considered that possibility. "So if this woman—or her husband or boyfriend or whoever—came across him, what are they still doing with him?"

"Mistreating him."

"Yes, but why? A person doesn't hang on to a strange kid they don't want to take care of."

"Maybe there's something in it for them," she suggested.

"Ransom? They wouldn't have known who he belonged to."

"Unless they saw the accident on the news or in the papers. Toby's photo was in all the papers."

"Okay," he said. "They could know who he was, but then they would have made an attempt at ransom."

"Nothing like that happened," she told him.

The waitress brought their pizza and Austin placed a slice on a plate for her. They ate in silence until another thought came to him. "What about his father?"

"Whose father?"

"Toby's."

She wiped her lips with a napkin and sat back against

the vinyl booth. Finally she said, "My sister didn't have successful relationships with men. Or boys for that matter. All through junior high and high school she went with one jerk after another."

She hadn't answered his question, but Austin waited for her to say it the way she wanted to.

"She just couldn't stand to be without a boyfriend. Not even for a day. For some reason she needed those jerks to make her feel good about herself, I guess. But they never did." She glanced down at her plate and back up. "Make her feel good about herself, I mean.

"The time she and Toby lived with me was the first time she'd looked out for herself and what was best for her. She was finally pulling her life together."

The waitress refilled their glasses, and Austin thanked her.

"I don't know who Toby's father was," she said, finally. "She married this guy named Perry just after Toby was born, but Perry wasn't the father. She told me it wasn't important, because the father hadn't known she was pregnant, and he wouldn't have cared."

A fatherless child. The correlation between Toby and himself gave Austin pause.

"What's wrong?" she asked.

"That's too bad," he said. "About Toby's father."

"Maggie was doing just fine without a guy messing up her life for a change," she said.

"A boy needs a father."

Her gaze penetrated his attempt at nonchalance. "Did you have one?"

He admitted, "Sure, I *had* one, he just happened to be married to someone else besides my mother, so he didn't recognize me as his."

"Even a father who acknowledges his kids as his, doesn't necessarily make a good dad," she returned.

"You speaking from experience?"

"My dad let my mom raise Maggie and me. He went to

work, paid the bills and hung out with his cronies on weekends. After my mom died, he moved into a trailer and took up with someone new. We didn't see each other much. He died a couple of years ago.''

Austin turned the subject back to Maggie. ''Do you believe Toby's father wouldn't have cared?''

She gave a disgusted sniff. ''Oh, yeah. I met the guys she went with. I picked up the pieces after those relationships went bad. She was above those jerks, she could just never see it.''

''So there's no way that Toby's father could have planned this to get his son.''

She gave him a puzzled frown. ''Planned what?''

''Planned to do away with her to get the kid.''

Her topaz eyes widened. ''No! They were selfish jerks, but none of them cared enough to be a murderer. You're suggesting that someone deliberately killed Maggie. That's impossible. Besides I'm sure that whoever Toby's father was, he never knew it.''

''Okay.'' He pushed the dishes aside and spread his hand over hers on the table. ''We needed to consider all the possibilities. The police aren't going to be any help. You know that.''

Her gaze dropped to his hand on hers, before fluttering back to his face. ''I know. They consider the case closed, and they think I'm crazy.''

''Shaine.''

She cocked her head in reply.

''When we get more to go on, I'll contact my FBI friend. He couldn't do anything officially, but he may be able to help.''

She turned her hand beneath his and squeezed his fingers. ''Do you think so?''

''I don't know. It all depends on what you come up with in the next few days.''

Apprehension flitted across her features. He wouldn't let himself back out because of what she might have to go through next. This was what she'd wanted from the beginning. But he knew.

He knew.

She had no idea what she was letting herself in for.

Shaine put away the groceries while Austin worked out and went for his run. They were still full from their meal in town, so they'd planned to have fruit and cheese later in the evening.

After his shower, Austin tended the fire and brought a couple of files and envelopes from his office.

With a nervous trembling in her limbs, Shaine surveyed his approach. He placed the items on the low table and sat beside her on the sofa. "Ready?"

Apprehension crushed her resolve. "Are you sure this is necessary? Couldn't you just tell me how? Talk about it some more?"

He read through a folder. "We've talked for days, Shaine."

"I know, but—"

"Look. This is what you came here for. Why you badgered me into hearing you out. You convinced me to see it your way. I could be doing a dozen other things far less unpleasant, but this is what you asked of me."

Shame clenched into a fist in her stomach. He was right. He'd warned her a hundred times. He'd tried to talk her out of it, convince her otherwise, but she'd insisted on him teaching her.

Besides, there was no other way to help Toby.

She swallowed her squeamish cowardice and sat up straight. "You're right. I'm ready."

Austin went into the kitchen for a minute and returned with a pair of tongs. He looked into a bulky manila envelope, used the tongs to remove an object and held it toward her.

Shaine stared at the small pink ballet slipper with an alarming mixture of dread and anticipation. Her hands were glued to the knees of her jeans. She couldn't have reached for the satin slipper if she'd wanted to.

"I didn't have to touch anything to see the Deets boy," she rationalized. "Or Tommy in the woods. I just dreamed about them and knew where they were."

"That's right," he said. "You don't have to touch things to get random readings. But we're not looking for a chance vision. We're zeroing in. This will help you do that. You'll see more clearly and more specifically."

He didn't share her hesitation. He grabbed her right hand, turned it over and placed the object in her palm. Dropping the tongs on the table, he took her other hand and closed it over the slipper, holding both her hands between his.

"It's like going to sleep," he said. "If you try too hard, or concentrate on doing it or not doing it, you'll lay awake all night. Just let it happen."

For a second Shaine thought she might faint. For another second she thought she had. But then she realized the sense of vertigo wasn't physical.

"It's there, Shaine," Austin said softly near her face. "The picture is there. You feel it. You sense it. Let yourself move toward it. Remember everything we've talked about. Remember the exercises. Use your reference points. Nobody is going to care that you can see it. I want you to see it. You want to see it. Don't fight it. Let go."

Colors exploded inside her head. Soft colors. Gentle colors. Aqua. Fluffy yellow. *Pink.*

And in the midst of that half-defined palette of pastels, she saw what he wanted her to see.

Chapter 8

Oh, but she was a beautiful girl. Her gilt-framed photograph sat on a glossy piano in a sunny plant-filled room. In the picture she wore a pink leotard and white tights. The laces of her satin slippers twined up her calves. A ribbon-festooned garland of white net wreathed her head, and hidden beneath the headpiece, her hair was dark and smooth, fashioned into two braids.

A man sat at the piano, his hands moving over the keys, music resonating from the instrument and filling the room. Mozart, but Shaine couldn't identify the piece by name.

"There's more," she whispered, instinctively understanding another realm of this vision waited just out of reach. Frustration and panic warred for prominence, and she clenched her hands into fists.

"Relax," he said, his voice soothing her apprehension. "Turn with it, Shaine. Let it take you along. Don't adhere to the boundaries of your natural mind. Go outside them. You're making all the rules. There's no wrong or right."

In her mind she searched until the image came into focus.

"It's a headstone. There are…pink azaleas planted at the foot."

"Someone's seeing this, Shaine. Who is it? Whose eyes are you seeing through?"

Deep despair welled up inside her—anguish and suffering and…anger. Anger over her loss. Anger that the life of her child had been snuffed out. Anguish sat like an anvil on her chest. "Her mother," she whispered, finding it difficult to breathe.

"Don't stop there. What else do you see? What does the marker say?"

Shaine reached out and touched the cold granite stone, her fingers outlining the rough-texture of the words and the drawing above. "Ballet slippers, with the laces dangling down."

"Where are they?"

"They're carved in the stone. And numbers."

"Read them."

"Seven-seven-eighty-five to three-six-ninety-six."

"What else?"

"A dog. A small long-haired white dog with a rhinestone collar."

"Where's the dog?"

"I don't know. In the car. Waiting in the car."

"Where's the car?"

"Up on the road. It's long and silver."

"What kind?"

"I don't know. I don't know cars. A Cadillac maybe."

"Can you see the license plates?"

"Seven dash C three one twenty-nine."

"What state?"

"I can't read it from here."

"Describe it."

"It's white with blue numbers. There's a thin red border. There's something red in the middle."

"What is it?"

"It's—it's the Statue of Liberty. My chest hurts."

"It's okay. That's enough." He pried open her fingers, letting the ballet slipper fall to the floor, and took her hands in his. "Shaine?"

The vision swam out of focus and the warmth of his hands on her ice-cold skin brought her back to the log house and the sofa where she sat. She turned astonished eyes on him. "What was that? What did I see?"

He released her hands and opened the folder. "Tamara Sue Jenkins. Birth date July 7, 1985. Abducted March 5, 1996, estimated date of death one day later. Father, a conductor for the New York Symphony." He looked up. "And I'd bet money they drive a long silver car, have a little white dog and that New York license plates are white with a red Statue of Liberty."

Feeling as though she'd just awakened from a drug-induced state, Shaine grappled with the heavy sense of misery that had accompanied the vision. Something horrible had lurked just out of reach. Shaine hadn't seen it, but she knew of its existence. She felt it in her being. "What happened to her?"

He scanned the computer printout. "Abducted outside a dance school, missing for three months, until the FBI called in a psychic who located the body with this." He used the tongs to pick up the shiny pink slipper and place it back in the envelope.

Watching him, she couldn't help wondering why he used those tongs to avoid touching the slipper if he'd done as good of a job of shutting out his telekinesis as he claimed. However, a crushing sense of sorrow weighed on her heart and diminished the thought. "Do they have the person who did it?"

"Nope."

"I wasn't any help then."

"That's not why we did this. We did this to see what you could do."

"And?"

"And I'm amazed at the accuracy of what you learned.

I've seen cases where the detectives would have given anything for a license plate number or even a state to start in. Your vision is incredibly detailed and accurate.''

"But worthless."

"In this case perhaps. But this child was already found."

Shaine stared hard at the envelope, thinking of how careful he'd been not to touch the girl's slipper. "If you held it...would you see the person who killed her?"

His jaw tensed, and he raised his chin just a notch. "Maybe." A minute passed and he met her eyes. "Probably."

But he'd worked determinedly to put a lock on that ability. It wasn't her place to judge him on that. She hadn't experienced half the trauma he had.

"Note the way you did that now, Shaine. Do you remember how you got there?"

"Kind of."

"Do you remember how you felt? Physically?"

She nodded. "My chest hurt. My hands were cold."

"Those are reference points. Physical ones, but you have mental ones, too. Recognize them now and store them for next time."

Exhaustion swept over her like a tidal wave. He must have seen it in her face or the way she let her boneless body sag back against the sofa cushions. "Need to sleep?"

She nodded. "How did you know? Did this happen to you afterward, too?"

"No." He brought the blanket from the arm of the other sofa and draped it over her. "I recognized the pattern from your dreams. I was quite the opposite as a matter of fact."

"How's that?"

"After I'd done a session, I'd be wired for ten or twelve hours. I couldn't have slept if I'd wanted to."

"Funny," she murmured.

"Yeah." Austin tucked the blanket around her and watched her eyes drift shut. Her gift was extraordinary. At the institute he'd met others with differing abilities, but he'd only known one or two who could actually find a location like Shaine had. He was grateful her first "hands-on" experience hadn't been a grisly one. He wished he could guarantee she wouldn't have to go though anything worse. But he couldn't.

Sooner or later, she'd learn why he'd had to divorce himself from all this. Sooner or later, she'd come face-to-face with something she wished she'd never seen.

And he was leading her right toward that day.

Toby awoke instantly. Beneath him the sheets were warm and wet. He hadn't meant to do it.

He climbed from the bed and clumsily peeled down the resistant pajamas. From a pile of unfolded laundry by the door, he found a clean pair of underwear and pulled them on backward.

His damp skin sent a shiver through his body, and he wished he could get back into the bed to keep warm.

Dimly, in the back of his mind, he remembered a soft nubby blanket and a faded terry cloth bear. Memories of comfort. Memories of another place. Memories before her.

He tugged a scratchy blanket from the back of a straight chair, got his small pillow and curled up on the floor.

It was scarier down here. He could see the dark places under the bed, and the black shadows in the corners of the room. If he cried she'd come hit him.

When she'd see the bed, she'd hit him, too. His little body trembled with the thought and he cried anyway.

Once there had been the mama who held him when he cried, who hugged him and let him sleep with her. He couldn't remember her much anymore, but sometimes he remembered how she made him feel.

The door flew back against the wall.

His body stiffened and he blinked against the harsh light in the hall.

"What's the matter now? Don't you have any sense? It's the middle of the night. What's that smell?"

His cries froze in his throat and his heart beat so fast, it hurt.

She smelled worse than his bed. She came toward his place on the floor, and he shrunk back, coming up against the metal leg of the bed.

"You did it again, did you?"

He saw her foot coming, but he couldn't squeeze under the bed in time to prevent it from catching him in the leg. He howled with pain and fear.

"Come out from under there! Come out now! If I have to get down there and drag you out, I'll close you in the bathroom for the night! In the dark!"

She would anyway. She would anyway.

Was there anyplace he could hide? Was there anyplace she couldn't find him?

Her hands hit the floor and her indistinguishable face appeared. The bad smell of her breath reached him.

"Okay, stinky boy," she drawled. "So that's how it's going to be, huh?"

She reached for him, and he shrieked in terror. "No!"

"No!" Shaine screamed the word and lunged up on her knees in the bed. The tangible horror of the dream cloaked her in overwhelming distress. She bent forward, pressing her face to the sheets and sobbed, "Oh, baby, honey, oh, Toby!"

Austin's footsteps pounded up the stairs. "Shaine?"

In helpless frustration, she beat the mattress with a fist and screamed a curse.

Austin took her by the shoulders and pulled her up to face him. With one hand, he raked her hair back so he could look at her. Dimly she realized he'd turned on a light below, and in its muted glow, his features were full of concern. With his thumb, he brushed tears from her cheek.

"I can't take any more," she said in a hoarse and pleading voice. "I can't take any more of these dreams."

He pulled her against his chest. She resisted at first, and then gave in to his genuine warmth and caring. With gentle fingers, he stroked the tangles from her hair. Her head rested against the steady beat of his heart. The warmth of his skin penetrated his T-shirt.

He maneuvered them so that his back rested against the headboard, and she lay partially in his lap. His hands continued their comforting caress of her hair, moving to her shoulders, and magically stroking her bare arm until the tension left her body.

It felt good to have his hands on her skin, in her hair. His rock-ribbed body gave her warmth and comfort and a sense of security she'd long been without.

The cotton beneath her cheek was damp from her tears, and the sensation reminded her of Toby's wet sheets. Another sob escaped her, and she related the dream to Austin.

"You're right," he said after several minutes.

"What?" she asked, wiping tears from her lashes.

"These dreams aren't getting us anywhere. You can't see enough from Toby's viewpoint to detect where he is. All the dreams do is torture you."

"And what can we do about that?"

"We're working on it. As soon as you've honed your skill, we'll have you hold something of Toby's. Maybe that will show you how he got where he is."

"Do you think so?" She raised up enough to look at his face.

"I don't know," he replied, as honest as ever, and equally as unwilling to give her false hope. "There's no given in any of this."

She placed her head against his chest again.

"Until then," he said.

"What?"

"I'll sleep up here, too. When you start having a dream I'll wake you."

Sleep up here? Shaine pushed herself to a sitting position and sized up his serious expression.

"I'll sleep on the floor. There's plenty of room."

There was at that, she couldn't deny.

"I've already seen you in your jammies," he said with a teasing note in his voice.

The thought of having him stay close was comforting. And if he could help her stop the dreams, she'd be grateful. At last she nodded. "Okay."

"If you're all right, I'll go get a couple of things."

"I'm all right."

The light below went out. Minutes later, he returned with a sleeping bag and pillow. In the generous moonlight coming through the skylight, he spread the bag out in the expanse between the bed and the railing and settled in. Shaine lay down and watched him fold a pillow beneath his head.

She couldn't remember anyone ever being as concerned about her as he'd been. Perhaps, in the beginning, he'd only resisted her pleas for help in order to protect her. He didn't seem like a selfish man. Not at all. In fact, she'd never known anyone as caring. Her mother had loved her, in her own way, but she and Shaine's grandparents had held her at arm's length, always a little afraid of her. Her father'd been more concerned with his bowling average than his family.

Maggie had loved her, but her sister had been too involved with the unfolding drama of the string of men in her life to give Shaine much of her time or energy. There had been a couple of men she'd dated, but a connection had never developed. Perhaps the bond she felt with Austin was simply because of the miraculous way he'd opened her mind to her gift. Or because he truly understood her the way no one ever had before.

Maybe he didn't feel the same connection she did.

She liked Tom Stempson a lot. And she didn't believe he meant her any harm. But she was a subject to him. Someone to study and learn from.

Austin, on the other hand, didn't need anything from her, so he had no ulterior motive beneath his concern. Shaine noted the direction her thoughts were taking and, recalling the kisses they'd shared, warned herself not to get caught up in needing him for anything other than to help her find Toby.

Her sister had been a prime example of a woman being unable to function without a man in her life. Shaine had told her time and again that she needed to look out for herself, that she didn't need a man to make her complete.

Now here was Shaine. Thinking that Austin Allen made her feel complete for the first time in her life. How could she be falling into that same pit?

Forewarned is forearmed, she thought, and thanked her internal alarm system. She wasn't going to read any more into this "connection" between them than was there. She needed his help. He empathized and was willing to work with her. They were alone in the mountains and physically attracted to one another. That was normal.

Shaine rolled to her back, so she wouldn't be tempted to watch him all night, and studied the starlit sky through the panes above. This isolated log house with its flickering fires and panoramic view of the heavens and mountains was a lovers' paradise. And Austin, whom she'd originally imagined to be an aging recluse, was one of the sexiest men she'd ever run across. The combination could mean trouble for her.

She'd better remember that.

He woke her twice during the night, and she marveled at how he could detect her dreams.

"I'm a light sleeper," he explained over coffee and toast the next morning. "That's why I like it up here away from people and traffic."

"There are other reasons you moved here, too," she said as a question.

He looked into his steaming mug. "I've lived fairly secluded my entire life," he said. "Growing up, I spent most of my time at the institute. I was accepted there. Revered almost. And even though they pried and prodded, I was more comfortable with them than with outsiders.

"My mother and I spent a lot of time traveling, staying in motels, assisting detectives. The researchers back at the institute were like my family, and though I was glad to get back each time, the constant expectations wore me down."

Shaine imagined the life he spoke of, remembered him saying how difficult school was, too. It was a wonder he'd turned out the compassionate man he had.

"I didn't even have to tap into the money my mom had socked away. Tom found me all kinds of endowments and scholarships, and I wanted to study computers. I loved the learning part of college, but I hated the idea of all those people in the dorms, so I lived off campus."

"What about after college?" she asked.

"I worked for a company in Chicago for a while, another in Minneapolis, always keeping a low profile, but always being sought out. I decided then that I would never be happy in a city, so I built this place and have worked on my own ever since."

Shaine studied his tanned features. "When did you stop—touching things?"

He contemplated her question and leaned back in his chair. "Do you have any idea of the number of things a person touches unthinkingly?"

She shook her head.

"I had to learn that early," he said. "I had to shape the ability in such a way that I could deliberately not read objects I touched. Block the perceptions out. I had to use it for crime detection, but I didn't want to see things from the objects I had to touch everyday. It's a curse to know things about people that you don't want to know—that you should never have to know. And worse is knowing *about* people...the way they think. So I gave it an on-off switch in my head. By the time I was twenty I'd turned it off permanently."

She thought of him using the tongs on the ballet slipper, but didn't mention it. "And you're happy here?"

"Yeah."

She believed him. He seemed content in his home and with his work. But didn't he get lonely? "Don't you miss people?"

"I never knew a person I wouldn't rather get away from than stick around," he replied with a shrug.

"What about companionship?"

He raised his dark brows. "Have you forgotten Daisy? She's never caused me a moment's grief—well at least not after she stopped chewing my shoes to shreds. And she doesn't have an errant thought in her canine head." Grinning, he placed his dishes in the sink.

"That's not what I meant."

He dried his hands. "I know. Are you ready to work?"

Her heart faltered, but she firmed her resolve. "I'm ready."

"Shall we sit in there?" He indicated the living room with a nod, and she agreed, leading the way.

After disappearing into his office, he returned with another file folder and envelope, the sight of which prompted nervousness.

"Relax, Shaine."

She took a deep breath and blew it out slowly, settling comfortably on the cushions and drying her hands on her denim thighs.

"I read through the file this morning," he said, and picked up the tongs still lying on the table.

From the envelope, he produced a black watch. Shaine's hand trembled a little as she reached for it. She held it in her palm and placed her other hand over the top. The glass face felt warm against her skin.

Closing her eyes, she blanked out everything except the warmth of the watch and the shine of silver that flashed in her mind's eye.

"Where are you?" Austin asked.

She shook her head.

"What do you see?"

"I—I don't see anything. I know there's a boy. I know

he's dead. The number seven came to me." This was unlike the day before, unlike the distinct pictures and scenes she'd seen.

"Use your reference points."

"This isn't the same as last time. I'm not getting anything to draw me in."

"Give it a little time."

She did. Seven came to her again. "There's a divorce," she said after a minute. "That's all. I just don't have anything."

"Here."

She opened her eyes to see he held the open envelope out for her. She dropped the watch in. "That's okay," he said. "You did get something."

"What?"

He opened the folder. "Eleven-year-old boy. Stabbed seven times."

"Do they have a killer?"

"No."

Disappointed, she leaned back against the cushions.

"That's perfectly okay," he said. "You can't get a perfect connection every time."

"Did you ever not get anything?"

"Once in a while. Want to try another one?"

"Yes."

He brought another file and handed her the envelope this time. She glanced in and tipped it to slide the locket into her hand. The instant the piece of gold jewelry hit her palm, a jolt like electricity shot through her.

She gasped and closed her ice-cold fingers around the necklace for fear she'd drop it.

Shaine didn't know if her eyes were open or closed. It didn't matter. She'd found someone.

Chapter 9

She saw the motel room as clearly as she'd seen Austin walk toward her with the files. A faded orange print spread draped the double bed. The stale smell of cigarettes hung in the air.

A hot plate, a cooler and a coffeemaker testified that this wasn't a one-or two-night stay.

"She's in a motel room. She's been there for some time. A couple of months maybe. There's a folded apron on the little table, the kind they give employees at fast-food restaurants."

"What color?"

"Dark green. The bathroom light is on. It—it smells like..."

"Like what?"

"Hair dye. She just dyed her hair."

"What color?"

"I don't know."

"Are you her?"

"Yeah. But I can't see me—her. Her feet hurt. She stands a lot at her job."

"Is she afraid?"

"No."

"What else? What else is in the room?"

"He's not there right now, but a guy's staying there with her. His shoes are by the door. The TV's on."

"What's on?"

"She's flicking channels, a soap opera, a game show, 'Barney...'"

"Who?"

"'Barney.' I'll tell you later."

"What else?"

"A movie. I've seen it before.... It's...oh, it's one of those bandit movies with Burt Reynolds. There's the news. WMBB, channel 13."

"Perfect, baby," he said. "What's on the news? Did they say the date?"

"No. She flicked passed it." Shaine stayed with the vision until nothing more unfolded.

She let it go and turned to Austin. He'd unthinkingly called her "baby." The endearment made her wish it hadn't been a slip.

"She wasn't afraid?" he asked. "There was no one with her?"

"No."

He rubbed his neck. "Maybe if we try it again later. Or tomorrow."

"Why, what did you want me to see?"

"What happened to her. Who killed her. What else?"

"No one killed her. She's not dead."

"How can you say that? How can you sound so sure?"

"I don't know. I knew that boy was dead, didn't I? And I knew the girl yesterday was dead. This woman is not dead. She's in that motel room."

In agitation, he jumped up and stood in front of the fireplace, a frown gracing his otherwise handsome features.

Shaine slipped the locket back into the envelope.

After a long, pensive silence, Austin disappeared into his office and returned, jabbing numbers into his portable phone. "Ken, Allen here. You know the number. Call me."

He sat across from her.

"Who'd you call?"

"My detective friend."

"What for?"

He pointed the rubbery antenna to the folder on the table. "Look at that."

She hesitated.

He urged her with a flick of his hand. "Go ahead. There aren't any crime scene photos or anything."

She picked up the folder, opened it and glanced through the file. "Gloria McCullough, thirty-eight, reported missing July 4, suspected foul play. She had told police on June 12 that she thought she was being stalked."

"There's no body yet. Maybe they'll find it somewhere around that motel."

The phone rang. He clicked it on. "Allen here. Yeah. The McCullough case. Check on a motel where WMBB, channel 13, is aired."

"Orange flowered bedspreads," Shaine interjected.

Austin repeated her description to the man on the phone. "And she was working at a fast-food place where the employees wear dark green aprons.... No, that's it.... Do that. Yeah."

He hung up. "He'll get back to me."

Shaine gave the room a restless once-over without really seeing anything. "How long do you think it will take?"

He shrugged. "Might be later today. Might not."

Dreading the wait, she got up and moved to the window. "There's a moose out there."

With a skeptical expression, he joined her. "That's an elk."

"Oh." He didn't touch her, but his body radiated warmth. He had a musky outdoorsy smell all his own. She wished she could turn and fold herself against him. From experience she knew how comforting his arms were and how arousing his kisses could be. From her dream she knew he would set her on fire and do everything within his power to see that she enjoyed him dousing the flames.

If she closed her eyes, she could feel his flesh against hers. See the passion in his eyes as he took her breasts in his hands. Taste ecstasy on his lips and his skin.

"Don't see a lot of elk near your inn?"

His words contrasted with her thoughts. Regretfully opening her eyes, she shook her head and watched the animal strut through the foliage at the edge of the clearing.

"Tell me about it."

His voice so close behind her was a distraction. "The inn?"

"Yeah. You've done enough work for one day. Aren't you tired?"

"A little. Not exhausted like after the other visions."

"Hmm. Well, we can't just sit and wait for Ken to call."

The elk disappeared behind Austin's log garage. "Aren't you going to run?"

"No. I'll wait with you," he said near her ear.

A shudder passed through her body, and she prayed he hadn't detected it. She was almost ashamed at how easily he affected her. She certainly didn't want to succumb to her desires for a man she'd barely met. That was something Maggie would have done. "I have a thought."

"What's that?"

"We could set up your aquarium." She turned, surprised to find him looking at her rather than out the window, and hoped he'd be willing to go along with the idea. She didn't want to think about the call they waited for, neither did she want him to see how he affected her.

"Not a bad idea. I just haven't taken the time to do it."

Austin carried the packing crates in and they spent the remainder of the day assembling the base and tank.

"The inn used to be Audrey's grandmother's home," she

said, picking up the conversation they'd started earlier. "She's in a nursing home now, and when her family put all her things and the house up for auction, Audrey wanted it. I was working with her at a collection agency at the time, and we decided we'd rather have our own business, so we went out on a limb and financed the place together."

Listening, Austin used a screwdriver to tighten the screws holding the cabinet doors.

"Audrey's husband used his connections to have a lot of the work done, and the rest we did ourselves—all the stripping and sanding and painting and staining."

"Sounds like a lot of work."

"It was. Only a few of the pieces of furniture are original. Audrey's family sold it all off and divided the money. We couldn't afford to buy any of it then, what with getting the house itself, so it's taken us about five years to replace furnishings."

"They're all antiques?"

"Mostly. We even scoured farms and ranches and found old claw-foot bathtubs that were being used to water livestock. Each room needed its own bath, you know."

"Big job."

"It's rewarding. We run an authentic Victorian bed and breakfast, and we're working for ourselves."

He stood, a look of admiration in his eyes, but he turned his attention to their handiwork. "Shall we fill it?"

"Why not? Won't be much fun to look at without water."

"Won't be much fun to look at it without fish, either," he replied.

"Where are we gonna get fish?"

He shrugged. "I'll check an on-line directory and find someone who will ship me some."

"You mean—" she glanced toward his desk "—like order them on your computer?"

He nodded.

"No way," she drawled.

"As long as there's a place on-line."

"I saw that Sandra Bullock movie," she said, following him. "She ordered pizza and plane tickets, and she had people chasing her all over for top secret information."

"My job isn't quite that exciting," he said, slipping into his chair and pulling up a new screen.

Shaine stood behind him and watched, fascinated by his rapid keystrokes and his assurance as he maneuvered on the Internet. "Here's something interesting," he said.

She'd taken to studying his broad shoulders, his dark, finger-combed hair and his profile. She had an overwhelming desire to reach out and lay her hand against the skin of his neck or his tanned cheek. Putting the aquarium together had only been a delay. His nearness still drove her crazy.

The early evening had grown fairly dark, and he hadn't bothered to turn on a lamp. The ghostly light from his computer screen flickered across his intent features.

In Shaine's mind, another image superimposed itself over this one. The same handsome profile, a similar flickering light, but an expression of torment and indecision.

The man at the window.

The man in her dreams.

She hadn't had the dream since coming here. *Of course* that man was Austin! Why hadn't she realized that before? What was going to happen to cause him such anguish? Who was going to do that to him?

Her.

No. She didn't want to think that. That wasn't why she'd come. She'd never considered the possibility that his helping her could hurt him so much. Was knowing ahead of time that hurt was coming enough to keep it from happening? She couldn't quit now. Wouldn't. She was too close to finding a way to get to Toby.

Strong. Solid. Assured. Those were the only ways she'd seen this man until now. But now she knew, understood somehow, that a profound vulnerability lurked just beneath the brawny surface.

She didn't want to be responsible for the pain she believed would be his once her dream came to pass. She knew no way to stop it, however. Not without packing her things and heading back to Omaha.

And that was out of the question.

She did what she'd resisted, and placed the backs of her fingers against his neck, just below his ear.

His hands paused on the keyboard.

She turned her hand and stroked his skin, tested the thick texture of his hair.

He typed a couple of words.

She stepped behind him and kneaded the muscles of his neck and shoulders, loving the warmth and strength beneath the soft sweater.

Her own boldness surprised her.

He made a deep-souled sound, not quite a groan.

She locked her fingers in his hair, and he dropped all pretense of trying to find what he was looking for and rested his head back against her midriff.

After stroking his temples, she ran her hands down his stubbled cheeks and brown throat and across his chest.

He swiveled the chair so she was at his side, and with a gentle tug, pulled her down. Shaine fell into his lap, heedless of the chair arms cutting into her back and legs, and searched his dark eyes. The same fire burning in her breast, gave his expression a sultry ardency.

He'd told her he'd take her to bed. He'd warned her he wouldn't commit himself. Was that enough for her? Was this passion something that could be quenched by a few nights together? She didn't think so.

Nor was it something she'd be able to pretend she'd never felt and go on without learning what could have been.

"What are you doing, Shaine?" he asked, his voice a husky rasp.

"I don't know."

He tucked her hair behind her ear and cupped her cheek,

his thumb stroking the crest of her cheekbone. "Well, you're distracting me."

"You were distracting me," she countered.

"I wasn't doing anything."

"You don't have to."

His brows rose.

She blushed, but with his knuckles, he prevented her from ducking her chin to hide.

Austin's gaze took in her lovely long-lashed eyes, the sweeping bow of her tempting lips, and didn't miss the fluttering pulse that beat at the base of her throat. He moved his thumb to that susceptible point. His hand looked dark against her lovely pale skin.

She didn't weigh much, but her rounded bottom in his lap created a pressure of another kind. He felt himself stiffen, almost embarrassed at his immediate response.

He drew her toward him until he could kiss her throat. She smelled wonderful. He opened his lips on her soft flesh. She tasted wonderful. A tremor ran through her body, and she released a sweet sigh. Against his chest, she clutched his sweater in a fist.

Her reactions were genuine. Marvelously eloquent. His touches affected her in a wholly gratifying manner. Lord, she was beautiful and sexy and passionate, and she *wanted him.* Her silky hair, her wide eyes, her slender body and those incredibly long legs had turned him on from the first time he'd seen her. The thought of her undressed, willing and wanting, filled him with a fierce sense of possessiveness that gave him pause.

With her hands on his shoulders, she pulled back and smiled, a sweet uncertain smile that he knew he didn't deserve. He'd acted like a jerk since the moment she'd arrived. He'd behaved purely out of self-preservation, but she'd had no way of knowing that. And still she had that expectant look in her eyes whenever they were close. Each time he held her, comforted her, she responded to his touches the same way a stick of dynamite responds to a match.

The same way she did now as he slid one hand underneath her sweater and flattened his palm against her back. If excitement vibrated through her at that, how would she respond to more intimate caresses? He would love to find out.

He took her lips with his then, exultantly, riotously, graphically, showing her the enthusiasm was mutual.

She kissed him back, running her hands over his shoulders, his neck, his jaw. He touched his tongue to her lips, and she met it with her own. He groaned and ran his other hand beneath her sweater, inching it upward.

Shaine helped him, tugging the garment over her head and dropping it heedlessly. Her white lacy bra seductively pushed her breasts upward. She turned her upper body to face him more squarely. He framed her ribs and kissed the pale exposed skin above the fabric.

Delicious tingles spread through her body at his intoxicating attention. He made her feel so good. So good about herself. So good about them together.

She wanted to feel his skin beneath her palms. She slid her fingers inside the neck of his sweater, and he didn't need any more prompting. He leaned forward so that she had to grip the arm of the chair to keep from falling.

Beneath the sweater he wore a form-fitting cotton undershirt. It disappeared as quickly.

Oh, my, his skin was warm. Warm and supple, and a sensual delight beneath her greedy hands. She leaned down to kiss him again, indulging her craving to know more, taste more of this man who set her senses aflame. She traced his collarbone, the defined muscles of his shoulders and upper arms, seeking, discovering, acquainting. She couldn't seem to know enough of him.

He kissed her harder, deep and determined, and pulled away momentarily, and they both caught their breath. "You could drive a man mad," he breathed against her lips.

In the minimal light from the computer screen, his dark eyes were filled with glinting desire, his hair mussed. She used the opportunity to touch his lips and feel the heat and moisture.

"You know what you're doing to me," he said.

She gazed into his eyes. "I know I've never felt this way with anyone before. I'm afraid to miss anything."

"I won't let you miss anything." Bracing an arm across her back, he moved upward out of the chair, and she clung to his neck to keep from falling. He didn't get far, lowering her to the floor and stretching out, his weight partially on her.

He kissed her, and this time she could reach the broad expanse of his back. Their kisses grew demanding, unsatisfying. Austin wedged his knee between hers, and their bodies strained against one another.

He engulfed her breast with one hand, kneaded her flesh through the flimsy material, lowering his head and plucking moist kisses as far as he could reach.

His caresses made her wild with need. Shaine thought she might explode if he continued the unmerciful arousal of her body and senses. He nuzzled her stomach above her jeans, ran a hand over her hip and thigh and brought it up to cup her through the denim.

Stars burst behind her eyelids. Her breath abandoned her in a rapturous gasp. She curled her nails against his scalp.

"Look at me."

She did. She could barely make out his face in the near dark.

"This is getting serious," he said. "Do you want to go on?"

She'd never wanted anything as much as she wanted him to take her all the way. He'd been clear about his feelings from the beginning. She could expect no more than this from him.

Knowing that, did she want to go on?

Chapter 10

Shaine wished she could see his face better, see the hard curve of his biceps and the flat plane of his stomach. He was so beautiful. So special. And if this was all she could expect, then she wouldn't ask for more.

This impetuous, yet totally absorbing and erotic delirium he'd created was more than she'd ever expected to experience. Having this much of him was better than having nothing or no one at all. She'd been lonely for so long. She'd never known anyone who'd made her feel so good about herself.

"Yes," she said. "I want it very much."

He brought his hand to her cheek. "You are so beautiful," he whispered.

The words amazed her more than anything that had happened so far. Feeling beautiful beneath his hands, she smiled.

"Tell me how to please you," he said.

"Turn a light on."

She thought his brows rose in surprise. He ran his hand

down her bare arm and drew her fingers to his mouth. "Shall we go upstairs?" he asked, kissing them.

She nodded.

Standing, he pulled her to her feet. He turned on a lamp as they passed through the living room, and rested his hand on her hip as she climbed the stairs ahead of him. She reached the bed and sat to remove her boots and socks.

Austin did the same, and then they stood, facing one another.

There was just enough light to see him, tall and broad and breathtakingly handsome. She would remember this always.

He reached for her waist and she helped him remove her jeans. She stepped out of the denim, and heard his intake of breath.

"You have the longest, sexiest legs," he said, his voice gruff with excitement.

"You like long legs?"

"I do now." Austin reached behind her and unfastened her bra, dropping it to the side.

Lord, she was beautiful. Long, silky legs that went on forever, perfect mauve-tipped breasts and a waist that dipped in and flared out over rounded hips. She looked as good as he'd imagined all along. He slid her white briefs down her legs, and she kicked them away. He gazed at her, desire and tenderness warring inside him.

He was the one uncertain of how to go on. He'd never made love to a woman that he actually knew anything about, a woman he knew had feelings and a history, and that he'd come to care for more than he should have. He knew he could please her physically.

That's not what gave him hesitation. He found himself wanting to fulfill her emotionally, as well, and that was an entirely new concept. It was also a mistake.

He'd told her from the beginning that he'd take her to bed without a second thought. Now here they were; she'd understood the rules, so why was he having any doubt at all?

He should have been tumbling her on that bed and wrapping those gorgeous legs around his waist, oblivious to anything else.

But he wasn't. He was wondering how many other guys had known her passionate nature and taken pleasure in her body, and he was hating himself for it. He had no right to wonder. None.

"Austin?" Her voice held a quiver and her nipples tightened.

"Get into bed before you freeze." She obeyed. Conscious of his responsibility, he went to his travel kit first, then slipped out of his jeans and joined her.

He kissed her and she clutched his shoulders.

He nuzzled her neck and she sighed.

He lowered his mouth to a tightly beaded nipple and she gasped.

She was the most responsive woman he'd ever known. She gave herself over to her senses without inhibition, her earthy gratification evident in the way she touched his hair, his skin, pressed her nose to his chest and inhaled.

He couldn't wait any longer to have her. He rolled her to her back. She breathed a sound of surprise and pleasure into his ear when he entered her. She met him kiss for kiss, thrust for thrust, breathlessly sharing the steady climb to ecstasy.

He loved the feel of her hands in his hair, almost more intimate than her silken thighs around his hips, because he'd never before known a nurturing caress.

With breathless words and eager motions, she told him what pleased her and begged him not to stop.

He couldn't have stopped if his life was threatened. He joined her in rapturous fulfillment and sprawled beside her.

"Don't leave yet," she said softly.

"I won't. I didn't want to crush you."

"I don't mind."

He eased back over her damp body, twined a leg with hers and rested his head on her pillow.

He didn't think he'd ever want to move again. Slowly his heart resumed a natural cadence.

Shaine gloried in Austin's weight and heat, feeling safe, secure, desirable—all the things she'd needed to feel for a long time, all the feelings that had made her forget what she was really doing here.

Finally Austin moved to her side, taking her with him, and she cuddled against his chest, replete.

The phone rang. The covers tugged away as Austin reached for the receiver. "Allen here."

Shaine blinked, trying to orient herself. The shrill ring still echoed in the room, and she realized that it had been the first phone call she'd heard here.

Austin ran a hand over his eyes, exposing his underarm. Shaine stroked the sleep-warm skin with one finger, drawing his gaze.

"Mmm-hmm," he said to the person on the line. "What's this guy going to do now?... No... You'll call? Thanks." He hung up and lay back down.

Holding the sheet to her chest, Shaine leaned up on an elbow. "Well?"

"The McCullough woman's working at a hamburger joint in Panama City, Florida. They followed her to the Starlight Motel. Later, a man joined her. Detectives went to the door and confronted her. She left her husband and took off with this guy last July. They traveled around some, but have been holed up there for over a month." He lay on his back and stared at the skylight. "You were right."

She absorbed his words, as well as the unspoken distress beneath them. "That's good, isn't it? That I found her?"

He faced her. "It's good. You solved a missing-persons case."

"Why do I have the feeling you're not entirely comfortable with this?"

"There's nothing 'comfortable' about the whole process. It's hell, and you'll have to see that sooner or later."

She knew that. He'd made it clear from the start. She lay back down. He hadn't really answered her question. Her finding the McCullough woman wasn't sitting right with him.

Shaine studied the heavens above the skylight.

"It's not always like that," he said finally. "Try not to count on it."

"Didn't you ever find anyone alive?" She waited.

"I can count them on one hand. We see so differently, you and I." Thoughtfully he said, "I just can't quite put my finger on something important we're not understanding."

"This proves that I can do it, though, doesn't it?" she asked.

"Oh, you can do it," he replied.

"What now?"

He sighed and rolled toward her. "You have to touch something of Toby's."

Her stomach clenched. He was right. This was what all their work together boiled down to. "His things are in my extra bedroom."

"I know you're upset about leaving Audrey there alone for so long. Would you like me to go to Omaha with you?"

She raised herself up again, laying a hand on his warm shoulder. "Would you do that? You wouldn't mind?"

"You want my help, don't you?"

"Yes."

"And getting back to the inn would solve one of your problems. I can wait a while to take more work."

"Oh, thank you, Austin." She leaned into a kiss, and his arm came up and pulled her against him.

"I do like the way you show your appreciation," he said with a seductive growl.

His playful words nagged her briefly. She did appreciate him. She did need him. But she wasn't willing to analyze her reasons just then. She gave herself over to this man whose lovemaking was the stuff dreams were made of.

And Shaine saw stars again that night.

He actually did make the plane reservations from his computer. Shaine called Audrey and they packed. Austin knew someone in Gunnison who cared for Daisy when he traveled. With a grin, Shaine watched him tell the dog goodbye.

They caught a commuter flight to Denver, and a late flight out of Denver to Omaha. It was after midnight when Nick Pruitt met them at the baggage claim.

Shaine introduced him to Austin.

"Sorry to keep you up so late," Austin apologized.

"No problem. Shaine and Audrey have met me at the airport plenty of times."

Shaine sat between the two men in Nick's pickup, seeing the familiar sights of her hometown without much feeling. Her thoughts centered on the task looming before her.

What did her friends think of her bringing a total stranger home? She decided it was only fair to tell Audrey exactly what was going on.

Golden light spilled from the lace-curtained windows of her Victorian Inn, and finally Shaine felt a sense of coming home. Audrey was waiting for them in the kitchen.

"Shaine!" She gave her a welcoming hug, her belly huge between them.

"Oh, my gosh, Audrey, look at you!"

"I know. If this kid doesn't come soon, I'll be the main attraction in the pachyderm complex at the zoo."

Shaine laughed. "It's not that bad. This is Austin Allen."

Austin moved forward and Audrey shook his hand. "I got a room ready. The Sophia room, if that's okay," she said, looking to Shaine.

Shaine glanced at Austin, and knew he wouldn't object. They hadn't thought to discuss arrangements, but he wouldn't want to embarrass her. She couldn't picture him in the lace-curtained room with its antique furnishings, and no twentieth-century embellishments. Besides, she wanted him near for as long possible.

"Thanks, Audrey, but he'll stay with me."

She had to give Audrey credit for hiding her reaction. "Whatever you want, hon. I made tea."

Shaine reached into the cupboard for cups. "Tea sounds great. And I want to tell you what's going on."

They settled at the round oak table, and Shaine poured. "Austin is helping me." Her friend already knew some of the situation and about the dreams of Toby. Beginning with the incident about Jimmy Deets, Shaine explained what had happened and why she'd been in Colorado.

Audrey accepted the information without batting a lash. "You've always had a second sense," she said calmly, and turned to Austin. "A customer lost a wallet once, and she suggested he look under his car seat. There it was."

Shaine looked at her in surprise. "I hadn't attributed that to anything other than a lucky guess."

"Well, you make a lot of lucky guesses," Audrey said with a tired smile.

"Come on," Nick urged his wife. "Off to bed with you." The Pruitts said their good-nights and headed for their small house across the street.

Shaine rinsed the cups and turned out the lights. Together, she and Austin got their bags from the back porch and Shaine led the way around back and unlocked the door to her downstairs apartment.

She flipped on the lights and showed him the bedroom and bathroom. "It's pretty small," she apologized.

"We'll just be all the closer then, won't we?" He slipped his arms around her, and she leaned into his embrace gratefully.

Thinking how much he disliked being around people, and how hemmed in he would feel here, she appreciated his sacrifice all the more. "Thank you for coming with me."

He stroked her hair. "We're going to see this thing through together," he promised.

He'd awakened her to an incredible talent that had lain dormant within her all this time; incredible but frightening when so much was at stake. And he hadn't let her come back here to face it alone. She had so much to be grateful to him for.

As soon as tomorrow she might know where Toby was.

Having nothing to eat in her apartment, Shaine took Austin upstairs for breakfast. She shooed Audrey into a chair and took over the preparation. There were only two rooms occupied, so when Marge Andersen arrived, Shaine left her to clean and do laundry, then led Austin to the small bedroom Maggie and her son had shared for those few precious months.

He moved the stacks of poorly labeled boxes she'd packed Toby's things in. Finally she opened a carton, and beneath a blanket, found toys and clothing. Overwhelming sadness gripped her, along with a fresh attack of nerves. Her stomach knotted. "Here," she whispered.

Austin glanced inside. Their eyes met, his filled with a deep understanding concern. He picked up the box.

In the living room, Shaine seated herself on the edge of her sofa. The surroundings were all different. Austin's secluded log home had seemed the perfect atmosphere for a task like this. Would being here make any difference? Was she deliberately placing stumbling blocks in her own path? Yes. She tried not to think of all that was at stake.

"You're as white as a sheet," he said, dropping to his knees in front of her. "Relax."

He rubbed her hands between his, and gave her a supportive smile. Her gaze moved from his hands to his lips, and thoughts of the previous night together brought a new warmth to her heart. Her bed was small, but he'd said they hadn't used half of his anyway. He'd awakened her twice when she'd begun to dream.

She'd never spent the night in a man's arms until Austin. She'd never known pleasure like she'd known at his hands and lips and body. She'd never felt these tender, yet fierce feelings of need.

He kissed her—an indulgent kiss that bolstered her confidence.

Without touching anything himself, Austin turned the box on its side, so that the contents tipped, a few things falling to the floor.

Shaine looked them over, remembering packing them, remembering Toby playing with them. A worn terry-cloth bear caught her attention. "He slept with that," she said, gesturing. "That's Bear."

"Go ahead."

Shaine picked up the bear and brought it to her lap, placing both hands on it.

Her chest grew warm.

"Go with it," Austin said softly. "Use your reference points."

She did. Her hands got colder. Her chest got warmer, the heat dipping into her stomach. The picture swam into focus.

Toby. He was sitting at a small table with some other children. They had crayons and papers in front of them. The other children were coloring, but Toby only watched.

Finally a woman knelt beside him and spoke softly. Shaine couldn't see her face, but she wore camel-colored slacks and a beige sweater. She hugged him, and he wrapped his little arms around her neck. Still she talked, her voice gentle and assuring.

One of the other children handed Toby a purple crayon. He released his hold on the woman and accepted the crayon. Soon he had drawn a circle with eyes.

Shaine explained the scene to Austin.

"What's in the room?" he asked.

"Brightly painted shelves with toys. Noah's ark is painted on the wall."

"Any signs? Any other people?"

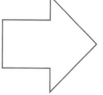

NO COST! NO OBLIGATION TO BUY!
NO PURCHASE NECESSARY!

PLAY "LUCKY 7"
AND GET FIVE FREE GIFTS!

HOW TO PLAY:

1. With a coin, carefully scratch off the silver box at the right. Then check the claim chart to see what we have for you—FREE BOOKS and a gift—ALL YOURS! ALL FREE!

2. Send back this card and you'll receive brand-new Silhouette Intimate Moments® novels. These books have a cover price of $3.99 each, but they are yours to keep absolutely free.

3. There's no catch. You're under no obligation to buy anything. We charge nothing—ZERO—for your first shipment. And you don't have to make any minimum number of purchases—not even one!

4. The fact is thousands of readers enjoy receiving books by mail from the Silhouette Reader Service™ months before they're available in stores. They like the convenience of home delivery and they love our discount prices!

5. We hope that after receiving your free books you'll want to remain a subscriber. But the choice is yours—to continue or cancel, anytime at all! So why not take us up on our invitation, with no risk of any kind. You'll be glad you did!

NOT ACTUAL SIZE

You'll love this exquisite necklace, set with an elegant simulated pearl pendant! It's the perfect accessory to dress up any outfit, casual or formal — and is yours ABSOLUTELY FREE when you accept our NO-RISK offer!

PLAY "LUCKY 7"

**Just scratch off the silver box with a coin.
Then check below to see the gifts you get.**

YES! I have scratched off the silver box. Please send me all the gifts for which I qualify. I understand I am under no obligation to purchase any books, as explained on the back and on the opposite page.

245 CIS CA99
(U-SIL-IM-09/97)

NAME

ADDRESS   APT.

CITY   STATE   ZIP

 **WORTH FOUR FREE BOOKS PLUS A FREE SIMULATED PEARL HEART PENDANT**

 **WORTH THREE FREE BOOKS**

 **WORTH TWO FREE BOOKS**

 **WORTH ONE FREE BOOK**

DETACH AND MAIL CARD TODAY

THE SILHOUETTE READER SERVICE™ - HERE'S HOW IT WORKS:

Accepting free books places you under no obligation to buy anything. You may keep the books and gift and return the shipping statement marked "cancel". If you do not cancel, about a month later we'll send you 6 additional novels, and bill you just $3.34 each plus 25¢ delivery per book and applicable sales tax, if any.* That's the complete price—and compared to cover prices of $3.99 each—quite a bargain! You may cancel at any time, but if you choose to continue, every month we'll send you 6 more books, which you may either purchase at the discount price...or return to us and cancel your subscription.

*Terms and prices subject to change without notice. Sales tax applicable in N.Y.

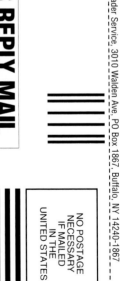

If offer card is missing, write to: Silhouette Reader Service, 3010 Walden Ave., PO Box 1867, Buffalo, NY 14240-1867

BUSINESS REPLY MAIL
FIRST-CLASS MAIL   PERMIT NO. 717   BUFFALO, NY

POSTAGE WILL BE PAID BY ADDRESSEE

SILHOUETTE READER SERVICE
3010 WALDEN AVE
PO BOX 1867
BUFFALO NY 14240-9952

NO POSTAGE
NECESSARY
IF MAILED
IN THE
UNITED STATES

She shook her head. "The edges are fuzzy."

"Stay with it. Something will come."

She stayed with the vision until it dissipated like fog on a sunny morning. "That's all."

With disappointment, she looked at the bear in her hands.

"That's okay," he said. "You saw something different."

"But not helpful."

"Not painful, either," he reminded her.

"Thank God."

"Try something else. You have so many to chose from. Something will be the catalyst."

Shaine placed the bear aside and selected a plastic car. After five full minutes with nothing, she tried a small figure of the type kids get at the drive-thru.

This time, physical responses cued her to something new. Toby lay on a bed in a room she'd never seen before. A room with toys on shelves and a rocking horse in an alcove. Bear was snuggled beneath his chin.

"I've never seen this place before," she said.

"You wouldn't have seen it if it's where he's at right now, Shaine. Describe it."

She did, giving him as many details as she could.

They went through the entire carton with similar results. Throwing the objects back in and closing the lid to hide them, she curled up in the corner of the sofa, disappointment knifing through her chest, exhaustion creeping into her bones. "I didn't get a thing! Not a thing!"

Austin paced the small room. Finally he flipped on her television and watched the news.

"Mind if I run?" he asked later.

She shook her head.

"You need to sleep," he said.

"I want to check on things upstairs first. There's not much to do in the evening, but I want to make sure Audrey is resting." She went to a drawer in the kitchen and took out a key. "Don't forget this."

"I would have. You had to remind me to lock my own house when we left it."

"I don't expect the moose have much experience at hocking software."

"Elk," he corrected, and kissed her nose on his way to change.

She checked on Audrey before returning and falling into wearied slumber.

She awoke early, discovering the other side of the bed empty. She found Austin seated on one of the stone benches beside the herb garden she'd started last year. He held a coffee mug and studied the plants.

"Hey," she said.

He slid over to make room for her. She pulled her robe around her more tightly and sat beside him.

"Couldn't sleep?"

"I slept."

She buried her hands in the pockets of her robe, grateful the mornings here weren't as cold as in the mountains.

"I've been thinking," he said.

She turned her face to him.

"If Toby's not dead, maybe it's Maggie's things you need to hold."

"What good would that do?" she asked.

"I'm not sure. It's just a hunch I have."

She trusted his hunches. She remembered the horrible feelings of loss and anger she'd experienced through the little girl's ballet shoe, and wondered what would come of touching something belonging to the sister she loved so dearly.

"It's up to you," he said.

Of course it was. It had all been up to her. And if this was the only way to get a handle on this whole crazy situation, then she'd do it. She'd do whatever it took. Undoubtedly Austin knew that, too. "After breakfast and a few chores?" she asked.

He nodded. "Mind if I do a little yard work?"

"Gee, I'll have to think that one over. Hmm. No, go right ahead. Tools are in the shed there. Key's on my ring."

She took his empty mug and headed for the inn, her mind leaping ahead. Perhaps touching something of Maggie's rather than of Toby's was what had initiated her dreams.

Maybe there was something among her sister's possessions that held the answers she insisted on having.

At the same time she dreaded it, she hoped like crazy it was so. She didn't know how many more disappointments she could handle. Nor did she know how long Austin would hang around to assist her. He'd get bored and restless here soon, and she had no right to expect him to stay.

She needed results. Now.

Chapter 11

Austin raked leaves and banked them around the rose bushes that lined the stone walkway through the ornamental garden. He paused to watch squirrels gathering food for winter, his thoughts on Shaine's growing frustration and her inability to read anything concrete in the boy's possessions.

She should have been able to see something. Her accuracy with the FBI's files had proven that. Maybe she was too close to the case. Maybe...

He didn't know what was holding her back, but he still had the nagging feeling that there was something obvious he should have recognized by now.

At least she'd been able to sleep last night, and that had been a blessing. Obvious in the smudged-looking skin beneath her eyes and the slight trembling in her hands, this ordeal was wearing her down. Today's session had to go better. For both their sakes.

Since he was already dirty, he decided to run and then grab a shower. He'd dressed and was tying his shoes, when the intercom in the kitchen crackled. "You there? Meet me at the garage."

Meeting Shaine as she unlocked the side door, he helped her sort through boxes until she decided on one. He carried it to her apartment.

This time she knelt on the floor beside the box and reached in without hesitation. Perhaps she'd spent the morning doing as much self-talk as he had.

She pulled out a photograph of the boy he knew from her expression was Toby. Straight blond bangs and a dimpled smile characterized the tiny boy. Austin watched her for a reaction, but the only one was a natural one: sorrow filled her eyes, and she laid the picture on the floor. A small jewelry chest came next, and opening it revealed more mementos than jewelry. Shaine fingered ticket stubs, a silver charm and a small plastic hospital ID bracelet.

"What is it?" he asked.

"It was on Toby's ankle when she bought him home from the hospital."

He studied her closely for a connection to any of the items, but she displayed no signs of sensing anything.

Finally she held a watch and placed her other hand over the top. Minutes passed. Her breathing remained steady, her eyes open and serious.

"Find somewhere inside to start," he advised gently. "A guiding point."

"There isn't one."

He placed his fingers over hers, finding her hands warm, not cold the way she described while she channeled in.

"I remember things," she said, opening her eyes and going through the contents of the chest. "These things all have memories and feelings attached, but nothing more. There's no—" she made a fist, searching for the word "—connection. It's like I'm trying to tune in to a station and the radio's not plugged in."

"Try something else," he suggested, losing hope fast.

She did. She went through the entire box, holding one

thing after another, until in frustration, she dumped it all back in and hit the lid with her fist. "It's no use! I can't do it!"

He placed the carton by the door and stood at the window, staring sightlessly at the already leaf-strewn side yard. Doggedly, he went back over all the dreams she'd described: the woman with the apron; the Deets child; Toby; Daisy. And the visions: the hiker in the woods; Tamara Sue Jenkins' mother at the cemetery; the McCullough woman at the Florida motel.

She'd known the Jenkins girl was dead, but she'd seen only her parents and her headstone. She'd known the boy who'd been stabbed was dead, but she'd seen nothing. She could see nothing of her sister, but had nightly dreams of Toby.

What was the difference? What was the connection?

A nagging idea occurred to him. His first reaction was to dismiss it, but nothing was too bizarre in matters of this nature. How could he test his theory?

"Shaine?"

She looked up, her eyes dark with misery.

"Where's Audrey?"

"At her house across the street."

"The little white one with the porch?"

"That's it. Why?"

"I'll be right back."

He shot out the door and sprinted across the lawn. With a curious expression, Audrey came to the door when Austin knocked, and opened the screen.

"Give me something for a few minutes," he asked. "Something close to you. Something with a lot of meaning and emotion in it."

"Are you guys still testing Shaine's vision?"

He nodded. "This is important, Audrey."

"Okay." She thought a minute, and then waddled back into the house and returned with a ring between her thumb and forefinger. "I haven't been able to wear this for a couple of weeks."

He looked at the wedding band in his palm.

"Lose it and you're dead meat."

"I won't lose it," he promised.

Shaine hadn't moved from her place on the floor, her elbow draped on the sofa.

"Here," he said, kneeling beside her. "Hold this."

"What is it?" She looked at the ring curiously.

"It's a ring, obviously. Now just take it in your hand and focus."

She released a sigh, but did as he instructed, opening her palm and closing her fingers over the band. Her lips moved.

"Relax," he told her. "Feel the impression of the gold in your palm. Let it show you."

Seconds passed.

"I'm warm," she breathed.

"Good. Go with it."

She squinted a little. "The sun's so bright."

"Where? Where are you?"

"There are blinds at the window, but I don't want to get up to close them. There, the nurse did it for me. That's better."

"Where are you?"

Behind her closed lids, her eyes moved. She frowned in concentration. "A hospital room." A smile came to her lips.

"What's in the room?"

"The usual stuff. A shelf with flowers and cards. A balloon bouquet. A little plastic crib." She sucked in a breath. "Oh, he's beautiful."

"Who?"

"The baby. He has the sweetest little face, and his mouth is pouty. His hair…oh, his hair is the softest stuff I've ever touched. It's dark with a curl by his ear."

"What else, Shaine? Look around."

"He's wrapped in a faded blanket that smells hospital clean. There's a blue card above his head."

"Read it."

"'Pruitt. Six pounds, five ounces, Dr. James.'"

He watched her face as she enjoyed the tranquil scene, not disturbing her again. Finally she opened her eyes and blinked to focus on him.

He smiled at her.

"I saw Audrey's baby."

"You sure did. Did she know it's a boy?"

She nodded. "They told her that months ago."

"And you knew her doctor's name?"

"I'm sure I've heard her mention it." She examined the ring in her hand. "But now I know what he'll look like and how much he'll weigh."

Austin couldn't suppress a chuckle. He took the ring from her and slipped it on his little finger.

"I have the feeling you planned this for a reason. Austin, what does this prove?"

"You've only been seeing the future," he said.

"What?"

"All the dreams you've had, all the visions, they all took place in the future. You saw the Deets boy as he'd be the next day, and your navigating instinct led you to the body. You saw his mother before she was on television. You saw Daisy before you got to Colorado."

"I saw Tommy hurt in the woods," she went on for him. "But what about the Jenkins girl and the McCullough woman?"

"You didn't see the girl because she was dead. She's in the past, but you saw her parents as they are today or tomorrow. You saw the McCullough woman as she'd be the next day or so, just as the detectives found her. She'd been a redhead, by the way, but she had brown hair when they talked to her."

"That explains the hair dye. Then Toby..." she said, a furrow across her brow. "What does this say about Toby?"

"That you're seeing him in the future."

She grabbed his wrist. "Oh my God!"

"What?"

She jumped to her feet and raked her hair back. "Some of those things, some of those awful things may not have happened yet!"

He read the mixture of relief and dread on her face. If everything she'd seen was in the future, then it was entirely possible that the things she'd seen happen to Toby hadn't come about yet.

On the other hand, if she couldn't see into the past to learn what had become of the boy, they had no immediate way of preventing those things from happening.

He could probably teach her to access that aspect of her vision, but it would take too long.

The only way to do get the information they needed quickly enough would be through someone who could readily experience the past.

Someone...like him.

Chapter 12

He didn't sleep that night. The sounds of traffic disturbed him. He needed to find a gym for a good workout. Shaine's tiny apartment and the neighbors crushed in on him.

Even Shaine kept him awake, with a recurring dream that he wouldn't allow her to experience.

All of those things were the cause of his unease.

Not the fact that he alone held the key to releasing Shaine from her torture and possibly finding the child he now agreed was probably alive.

It had been twenty years since he'd deliberately held an item and searched for its owner. He had sworn to himself that nothing could ever make him do it again. He had worked and strove and built a new life, a life that had nothing to do with taking on the burdensome cares of the world.

From time to time in the past, a tenacious relative or detective had sought him out. And he'd been able to convince them that nothing—not money or guilt tactics or threats—could make him break his vow.

Why then, when she hadn't even asked, had the crazy thought of actively joining Shaine's efforts skimmed across his mind?

He was tired, that was it, and antsy to get back to his mountain retreat. He was eager to get this thing over with and get his life back to normal.

Lying facing him, she sighed and kicked the covers off, the light from the streetlamp fingering through the blinds and revealing long shapely legs. Desire radiated through his once-sated body.

He touched her hair, straight and silky, her shoulder, smooth and lustrous, her hip, warm and bare. Sleeping with her was the most significant commitment he'd ever made to a woman. It was also one of the poorest choices he'd ever made concerning his own welfare. Sleeping together was more personal, more intimate than the act of lovemaking. Sleeping together meant knowing another person's personal traits, their bathroom habits, their idiosyncrasies. Sleeping together meant waking up together.

And all that meant more involvement than he'd ever planned on. It meant caring. And he didn't want to care.

She stirred beneath his hand, and he flattened his palm on her rounded bottom and brushed the velvety skin, thinking how perfect she was, how she seemed made just for him and his pleasure.

"Was I dreaming?" she asked sleepily.

"No."

She snuggled closer. "Good. That means you feel this nice for real."

He smiled against her hair. Her marvelous hands moved over his torso, stroked his chest, pulled his hand to her breast.

He kissed her, and she slid one leg over his hip.

He urged her astride him, and joined their bodies. Shaine inhaled sharply, followed his gentle urgings, and led them both to sublime exhaustion.

She lay in the crook of his arm, her head on the pad of

his shoulder and savored the steady beat of his heart beneath her palm. *He was thinking of leaving.*

The alarming knowledge wounded her, though she'd known all along theirs was a fated relationship. He'd always been honest. But she'd been hungry for his attention, his affection.

For him their relationship was physical.

For her it was so much more.

She'd go on after it was over. Even living on the outskirts of the city with people in and out of the inn every day, she was pretty much a loner. She wasn't her sister. She could get along fine with her own company. She had friends. She had the inn. A man was nice, but she didn't have to have one to make her a whole person.

But after Austin, going on alone would be different. Because with him, she'd known more joy than she'd believed could be hers. In him she'd found someone who really knew her, and liked her for herself, in spite of her differences. For the first time she'd been herself without hesitation or reservation.

And although she told herself she could be a complete person without him, she wondered who she was kidding.

Shaine helped Audrey with the morning jobs and did the week's shopping. They still had a week and a half left before the baby came, and after having left her for so long, she wanted to help all she could.

Dumping flour into a canister, she paused, the white cloud settling on the front of her sweatshirt, and digested what she'd just thought. A week and a half. She knew the exact day Audrey's baby would arrive. How?

She called up the vision of the baby in the hospital, the flower-strewn room, the blue name card on the bassinet. *There.* The date had been there.

She grinned to herself, and continued putting the food away. This insight could have its advantages, she thought wryly. Should she tell Audrey what she knew?

Footsteps sounded overhead, and she stopped. Their guests had checked out, and more weren't expected until the following day. Nick had another day job, but maybe Marge Andersen was doing some heavy cleaning.

Shaine climbed the stairs and peeked into the room she'd heard the sounds coming from. A clunk and a few grunts led her hesitantly to the bathroom doorway.

Fully clothed, Austin stood in the antique bathtub wrestling with the shower head and a wrench.

"What do computer geeks know about plumbing?" she asked.

He turned to where she leaned against the doorjamb. "I live a long way from maintenance men, remember? Besides, you can learn a lot of useful stuff on the web."

She crossed her arms over her chest and watched.

He finished and placed the tools in a metal box. "So, some old cow used to drink out of this tub, eh?"

"And before that," she countered, "when it was an original fixture, some old cow probably took a bath in it."

He laughed out loud, a rusty sound she hadn't heard before, and she was glad she was the one who'd drawn it from him. "Think we'd fit?" he asked, with a lift of one arched brow.

"I don't know. Want to sneak up and try tonight?"

He stepped out and looked at the tub. "If we got wedged in, someone would have to grease us to get us out."

"Why don't we just grease up before we get in?"

He turned and looked at her then, a look of teasing humor, but something more. Something almost sad. Almost pensive. She thought of her dream, the one of him in the window, and the torment she'd sensed. Never spoken between them was the fact that Austin had the ability to do what she didn't seem able to. He was the one who glimpsed the past.

But she would never ask him. She remembered his anguish in the dream, and remembered, too, that she'd known she had the ability to take it from him.

Perhaps this was how it could be prevented. By not asking. If she'd seen Austin in the future, then she could prevent him from suffering that anguish. And she would.

She wanted to kiss him hard and keep him with her forever. She wanted him to go before it hurt more than this.

She wanted him to let her love him.

But of course, he wouldn't. And she couldn't.

She turned and hurried back to her groceries.

He found a gym in the phone book and borrowed Shaine's car to go and work out. When he returned, she was sitting on the floor, looking through a photo album. "You're late," she said, glancing up.

"All those babes in their thongs distract me." He dropped a bag near the door. "Can I do a couple loads of wash?"

"Sure. Did you eat?"

He shook his head.

"I'll slice some of that roast and make you a couple of sandwiches."

He caught her wrist before she could head for the kitchen. "No. Sit down."

She frowned at his curt order, but his intense expression convinced her to listen to whatever he had to say. She dropped onto the sofa and waited.

He sat on the chair across from her, elbows draped on his widespread knees.

He's leaving.

His dark gaze touched her face and softened.

She'd known it last night. *Don't prolong it. Just say it and go.*

"You know, don't you," he began, "that there's only one thing left to do?"

She nodded. *Say goodbye.*

"The ironic thing is, you've never asked it of me." He gave a little snort. "If you'd have begged or cajoled I'd have said no. But you didn't ask."

Asked him not to leave? She wouldn't do that. That wouldn't be fair. Confused now, she asked, "Asked what?"

"What we both know I have to do."

"You're leaving."

He blinked, brows climbing his forehead. "No, no, I'm not leaving."

She closed her eyes. Seconds later, his warmth touched her knees and his hands took hers.

She opened her eyes to see him kneeling before her. "I'm not going anywhere. Is that what you thought?"

She nodded.

"No." He hooked his hand behind her head and pulled her forward to kiss her. "I want to see this through with you. I want to help you find Toby."

She'd tried to swallow her fear that she wasn't going to find her nephew. Who would keep the dreams at bay when Austin was gone?

"I want to find him for you."

"I know you do. You've done all you could to help me, and I—"

"No, I haven't."

She stared at him.

"There's more I can do, and we both know it."

Shaine's heart took off like she'd been given a shot of adrenaline. He meant he'd do it! He meant he'd get impressions from Toby's things for her! "But you turned that off years ago," she said in disbelief. "You said you'd never do it again."

"And I wouldn't," he replied. "Not for anyone but you."

His willingness was too good to be true. Guilt surged inside, forcing her to be certain she wasn't taking advantage of him. "That time I told you I'd sleep with you to help Toby—"

He covered her lips with his fingers. "Don't *even* say it. That's not what this is about."

"But we—"

"No. What we have together is not about bargaining or ploys. Did you want to make love with me?"

"Yes."

"And I wanted to make love with you. And I want to do this. That's all there is to it."

This was a monumental decision. Shaine didn't take his offer lightly. Neither did she intend to argue with him any longer, for fear he'd change his mind. "Thank you."

"Thank me later."

"My gratitude doesn't hang on what we find or don't find. I'm thanking you now because you were willing to do this for me."

He sat back on his heels and took a deep breath.

"When?" she asked. "Tonight? Tomorrow?"

"Might as well do it now. Where's your key ring?"

She pointed to the divider between that room and the small kitchen.

He plucked the keys off the counter. "Sit tight."

Nerves clenched Shaine's stomach into a knot. She chewed her lip and waited for his return.

Minutes later, he appeared with both cartons they'd gone through previously. Shaine moved to sit on the floor beside him.

"What's first?" she asked.

"Go for the gusto." Boldly he reached into a carton and pulled out the worn bear. Shaine watched him make himself comfortable and take slow, deep breaths. He was relaxing, just as he'd taught her.

He held the bear between both palms, and she waited, her breath caught in her throat.

It had been so long. Could he still do it? Did he have the simple on-off switch he'd told her he had? What if he'd forgotten? Let the gift lay dormant too long?

It was taking too long, way too long. She bit her lip to keep from asking questions and distracting him.

The color beneath his tan deepened ever so slightly. She

wouldn't have noticed if she hadn't been observing him so closely. *Say something! Say anything!*

Did he need her to talk him through it like he had her? Oh, she should have asked!

Minutes ticked by, and she wanted to scream.

Finally, calmly, he opened his eyes and set the stuffed toy down.

"Well?" she expelled in a gust of anticipation.

"He got it for his first birthday. There was a purple animal on the cake—"

"Barney!" she said excitedly.

"Whatever. Toby was happy and content. You were there."

She nodded. "What else. Did you see Maggie?"

"I felt her more than saw her—sort of a warm, comforting presence. Sometimes it's difficult to read from a baby's perspective," he said.

"Well, other things then. His cars." She dug into the carton, found a plastic container filled with die-cast cars, opened it and held it toward him.

He took several cars and repeated his relaxation and concentration exercises, relating images of people and activities, but nothing that aided their search.

"Don't look disappointed," he said, and cuffed her chin gently. "I didn't really expect to get anything from his things."

"You didn't?"

"Nah. I was just warming up."

She cast him a fierce look.

He grinned.

Her gaze drifted to the box of Maggie's things.

Austin pulled it toward him. Gingerly he opened the flaps and looked in. "What shall I use?"

"The watch," she replied without hesitation.

"Was she wearing it?"

Shaine nodded.

He took the watch and folded his long fingers over it. His eyes closed. His breathing was almost imperceptible.

Austin forced himself not to fight the searing spark that shot up his arm into his heart. His entire chest warmed, the sensation flooding to his abdomen. With steady control, he directed the energy toward unlocking the vision that grew stronger and clearer. It had been so long, so long since he'd been down this corridor, but maneuvering it was effortless.

A sensory onslaught threatened to overwhelm him, and he had to remember to back off to the edge and absorb the sights and sounds and colors and emotions at his own pace.

There were so many images, so many emotions and abstract entities to sort through, it took him a while to find the ones he wanted.

"She loves her son so much," he said. He'd felt these emotions before, experienced them through relatives of missing persons. "Her regrets are destructive. I can identify her fear and rejection. They almost crush her, but she's a fighter. She doesn't want to be cheated or deprived. She wants to be a good mother."

"She was a good mother," Shaine said softly.

Austin guided the energy away from the intense impressions, so he could isolate the incident he searched for without the overwhelming emotional distraction.

"A Sentra," he said, catching a glimpse. "A red one."

Shaine gasped. "That's her car! The one that went into the river!"

He pedaled backward, sensing he'd gone too far past.

"I'm standing on a road. She walks toward me. I'm with a woman. Maggie gives us directions and points back the way we came. She's nervous because the kid's in the car, and she inches toward the Sentra."

Austin barely sensed Maggie's confusion and her protective instincts as she moved closer to her car, and toward the woman. He wasn't tuned in to Maggie; he was picking up on the man who was a dark threat to her.

"She's off guard now, there's fear in her eyes. It takes

no effort at all to grab her around the waist and press the gun to her head.

"'Get the kid!'" Austin related.

"The woman yanks open the car door and grabs the boy. The mother's fighting now, using all her strength, and she manages to break away for a moment. The woman has the kid out of the car, and he still hasn't shut up.

"She's surprisingly strong now, but a knock on the head with the gun fixes her.

"Have to be careful of fingerprints. Get the gloves on. I drag her to the driver door and force her in. She slumps over to the side, but I jerk her back up. I have to lean across her to start the engine. I crank the steering wheel to the right and pull the gearshift lever down.

"The car rolls toward the embankment, and I slam the door shut, then run behind and push so it'll pick up speed.

"There's got to be enough momentum to get the car off the road and down into the water. She isn't dead, and if she doesn't drown, she'll be able to identify me. This kid is worth a bundle.

"The woman is waiting by the car on the road. It's a white Corsica. New Mexico license plates." Austin rattled off the numbers and letters.

"'Piece of cake,'" he went on in the man's viewpoint. "The Sentra's slowly sinking into the water. I get back in the white car. 'Shut the kid up! It'll take twelve or more hours to reach the contact and get the money, and I'm not going to listen to that crap the whole time.'"

Shaine's soft crying shifted Austin's attention from the vivid scene in his vision to her misery.

She stared at him in shock, huge tears rolling down her colorless cheeks.

"I should have done that by myself," he said gruffly, his mind's eye still elsewhere. "I shouldn't have put you through it."

"I had to know." She shook her head. "It's what I've needed to know all along. That man *killed* her!"

Helpless anger arced through her like a bolt of lightning. She'd been killed! Her sister had been murdered!

The high color that had been evident on Austin's face moments ago instantly drained, leaving his tanned cheeks startlingly pale.

"What is it?" she asked, leaning forward.

His expression blanched, and she reached for him.

He gulped for air like he couldn't breathe. Was he having a heart attack? What was happening to him?

"Austin!" She bracketed his face, but his eyes were glassed over with pain and horror. "Austin!" Caught up in a terror all his own, he couldn't hear her.

His entire body tensed. Shaine placed her hand over his pounding heart, her own pulse racing with fear.

"Austin, answer me!" She ran her hands over his shoulders, down his arms—and discovered his clenched fist.

The *watch.*

It took all her strength to pry his fingers open and wrench Maggie's watch from his grasp. She dropped it and brought his hand to her face.

Slowly his breathing calmed. His body relaxed. And finally, at least a minute later, he focused his gaze on her. Unimaginable suffering dwelled in the depths of his burden-dark eyes.

"You were there," she said in a hoarse whisper. "With Maggie. Weren't you?"

His eyes didn't change. Only his lips moved when he said, "Yes."

Shaine dropped her head forward, her hair hiding her face. He'd gone through that for her. He'd experienced the pain and horror again.

But Maggie—her heart broke all over again with the knowledge—Maggie had experienced it. And died. The loss and the unacceptable thoughts of her sister's pain and terror pierced Shaine anew. How did the people left behind live with this? How did they cope and go on with their lives?

"We have something to go on now," he said.

She raised her head and threaded her hair back. The glimmer of hope that she'd clung to glowed bravely. "Yes," she whispered. "Thanks to you."

The intercom in the kitchen crackled. "Shaine?" Nick's voice, sounding concerned, came through. "Can you come up here right away? Audrey's going to have the baby!"

Her eyes met Austin's. "Let's go."

Chapter 13

"Audrey, you can't have this baby tonight! You're not going to have it until next Thursday."

"Nick, run home and get my bag." Audrey turned back and looked at Shaine like she'd predicted an ice storm in July. "What are you talking about?"

"I saw the baby, and I saw his birth date. It's not time yet."

"Yeah, well, tell that to him," she said, rubbing her distended belly. I'm having this baby, and I'm not waiting until you think it's the right time."

"Okay." Shaine gave her a quick hug. "I'll take care of everything here."

"I know you will."

Nick returned and the Pruitts drove off.

Six hours later, Nick brought her home, tired, cranky and still very much pregnant. "False alarm," Audrey told her over the phone. "And if you say 'I told you so,' I won't talk to you for a month."

"I wasn't going to say that."

"Nick says the guys at work have a baby pool going. He wants to know how much the baby will weigh."

Shaine told her and Audrey relayed the message.

"And, Shaine?"

"Yes?"

"Is he all right? I mean, he's healthy and all?"

"He's perfectly healthy, hon. And he's beautiful. Now get some rest. I'll do everything in the morning. You stay home."

"I will. Until I can't stand sitting around any longer."

Shaine hung up and snuggled against Austin. She'd barely fallen asleep when Audrey's call had come. She'd lain awake thinking of Austin's vision that day, hurting for her sister, worrying about Toby and blaming herself because Austin was the one with the bad dreams that night.

He'd been mumbling, turning from his side to his back again and again.

He'd left a message for his FBI friend. She had to believe that soon they'd have something on the people who killed Maggie and took Toby.

"You awake?" she asked, knowing he'd heard the phone ring.

"Mmm-hmm."

"What proof will we have on these people?" she asked. "How will your friend prove they had anything to do with Maggie's death?"

"Usually, by the time I'm called on a case, he doesn't have much to work with. Anything I come up with is a gold mine to the department." Austin turned to face her, and his voice grew stronger. "One thing leads to another. We have the plates to go on. The description of the car and the kidnappers. I might get something else."

"How?"

"The channel's open, Shaine. I'm not going to close it now."

"You mean you could just see something? Or dream something?"

"I could."

"You've done that before?"

"Yes."

She thought a minute. "Did you hear yourself?"

"What?"

"You're hoping."

He was silent so long, she thought he'd fallen asleep. When he spoke, his voice held a note she'd never heard before. "The only thing I'm hoping right now is that you're not too hurt when all is said and done. I've learned to *expect* the worst. You haven't even begun to *comprehend* it yet."

"Ken's lined up a meeting with the composite expert at OPD," Austin told her late the next morning.

"Who's that?"

"The person who puts together likenesses of criminals and missing persons."

"An artist?"

"Not really. It's all done by computer now, and I guess she's one of the best."

Shaine drove and parked on the street near the police station downtown. They checked in and waited. Within five minutes an attractive young black woman greeted them and led them through several doors and to an elevator.

As Ken had promised, Treasy Browne was good, and Austin had obviously done this before. He helped with features and expressions, and before long they had computer composites of the man and the woman he'd seen. Treasy faxed the pictures to Ken's office and made copies for Austin and Shaine.

"How could you describe him so well, when you were seeing through his viewpoint?" she asked on the way back to the inn.

"I don't know. It must be because I got there through Maggie. And Maggie knew what he looked like. There are never any rules to follow. One time to the next can be different. You just take what you get and work with it.''

The delay wore on their nerves. Neither of them slept well. Austin found things to do, even painting the back fence, cleaning the garage and waxing Shaine's car and Nick's pickup.

Finally, two days after Austin had had the vision, Ken called with news. "The kidnapper's car was licensed to a woman named Lorenz in New Mexico," he informed Austin. "It was reported stolen three days before Maggie's death, and it turned up forty miles away from the Lorenz woman's home one day after."

"What do you figure from that?"

"He was probably driving from Arizona or New Mexico and stole the car, leaving his somewhere nearby. They got to Nebraska, watched Maggie for the opportune time, nabbed the kid, then returned to their own car."

"Where did the stolen car turn up?"

"A convenience store in Silver City."

"Evidence?"

"The police have a file and a couple of items in evidence."

"Can you arrange something?"

"You going to come?"

"As soon as I can."

"I'll meet you there. It's been a while."

"I'll probably have a woman with me."

"Interesting... Call when you get there. They'll page me."

"Gotcha." Austin hung up, found Shaine and relayed the news.

"I'm coming," she said.

He knew she wouldn't be shaken from the idea. "Are you comfortable leaving Audrey?"

"She has another week. This will take us a couple of days. I'll see that Marge Andersen fixes the breakfasts until

I get back. The guests will just have to eat after her kids go to school.''

"When shall we leave?''

"First flight out,'' he said.

"You'll have to phone for reservations.''

"I'll manage.''

"I'll pack.''

Their flight arrived in Las Cruces shortly after seven that evening, where they ate and caught a commuter flight to Silver City. Standing in front of the car rental booth, their luggage at their feet, Austin reached over her shoulder and selected a color folder from a rack. "A Spanish-style bed and breakfast.''

"Where?''

He opened it and studied the miniature map. "A few miles from here. Want to check it out?''

"Let's call and see if they have an opening,'' she suggested. "We can find something to eat on the way.''

The inn did indeed have an opening, and the short drive was worth the few extras minutes it took Austin to locate it. The inn was beautiful, the young couple who owned it gracious, and by ten, Shaine and Austin had settled in their room.

Austin turned the bathroom light out, glanced around and got into bed. "Is there a TV hidden somewhere?''

"Guests come here to get *away* from the twentieth century,'' she said, smiling. She picked up a journal from the nightstand and flipped through the pages. "At least there's something riveting to read. Notes from the guests who've stayed in this room.'' She glanced through the pages.

The place made Austin uncomfortable, but he'd known she would enjoy it.

"Look,'' she said, holding it toward him. "A lot of them are couples celebrating anniversaries or taking a weekend holiday away from their families. Isn't that romantic?''

He took the book. A disquieting tremor ran up his arm and he pushed the journal right back at her.

She gave him a questioning glance. "What's wrong?"

He shook his head.

"Tell me."

"I don't like holding it."

"Really?" She looked at the book like he'd given her a whole new perspective, then gave him a wide-eyed stare. "Are there impressions stored in it?"

"Hundreds."

"But you've got the switch turned off, right?" He didn't say anything, and she went on. "That switch isn't a hundred percent effective, is it? That's why you're careful not to touch things."

"It works most of the time. But every so often something slips past the barrier."

She returned the book to its place and appeared thoughtful. "I truly understand why you needed to make a place for yourself away from all this. I enjoy my antiques, and I like to imagine who owned them, but if I really knew their histories, I'd probably feel differently."

Her words meant more than she knew. He'd often considered himself strange, and hadn't shared anything personal with anyone since the girl he'd foolishly trusted in college. It was hell going through life not trusting anyone. Not being able to share the real him. Never getting close enough to form any kind of attachment.

He'd thought he was resigned to that life. And he had been. Until Shaine.

She snuggled down beneath the covers, and he turned to study her features. She appeared thoughtful. He could lose himself in her eloquent eyes. He ran a finger across the alabaster skin of her cheek.

"What are we *really* doing here?" she asked a little later.

"What do you mean?"

"I mean it's been a year since those people took Toby and left the car near here. No one will remember anything."

"Probably not, but there's still the evidence."

"What kind of evidence?"

"I don't know. I guess we'll find that out tomorrow."

"I should check with Audrey."

"There's no phone."

She arched a brow. "We'll make our calls in the morning. There's a phone at the desk downstairs."

"Your rooms are nicer," he said.

Her eyes widened. "Mine don't have phones or TVs, either."

"It's just the thought that went into planning them. They're more…welcoming."

"Well…thanks."

"A racket, when you think about it."

"What's that?" Her eyes were closed now.

"You guys don't have to pay for cable or phones and lines, but you charge more than the nicer motels."

"Atmosphere is worth something."

He had to get out of bed to turn off the fake gas lamp on the wall. "Right."

"Well, it is. These rooms and all this furniture have a history."

"Tell me about it."

"They make you uncomfortable?"

"Sometimes."

"Can you fall asleep dreaming of the people who lived here, raised families…?"

"Knocked off a chunk in this bed every Saturday night," he finished.

"Austin," she reprimanded with a laugh in her tone.

He pulled the covers away a little and kissed her neck. "I've never made love in a crowd before."

Laughing, she threw the covers completely back and embraced him.

Austin called Ken in the morning, and after a quick breakfast in the inn's dining room, he and Shaine set out to meet him at a roadside café a short distance from the convenience store where the white Corsica had shown up.

Once there, Austin led Shaine to a booth. "Shaine, this is Ken McKade. Ken, Shaine Richards."

"Miss Richards." He was a little older than Austin, not as filled out, with dark hair graying at the temples. He wore a pair of brown slacks with a neutral shirt and tie.

"Call me Shaine," she said.

"All that exercise is paying off, Allen," he said, with a wry grin. "You still look like you did years ago."

Austin shrugged. He ordered coffee and brought the conversation to the point. "Shaine is the one who saw her nephew alive."

"Saw him?" Ken asked. "How?"

"She saw him in a dream."

"Oh." Obviously used to Austin's extrasensory skills, he accepted that information and turned to her. "Where was he?"

"I don't know. I couldn't get a handle on the location." She explained her dreams and the visions she'd experienced while holding Toby's toys. "Austin's the one who held them and got the couple with the Corsica."

"Could have knocked me over with a feather," Ken said with a shake of his head, "hearing you'd taken it up again."

"I haven't," Austin clarified. "Just this one case. Just to help Shaine find her nephew."

"Okay. Well, you know I'm not a skeptic. That's why I dropped a couple of other cases going nowhere to back you up when you called. If you're seeing it, it's coming down."

"Thanks, Ken."

"We'll walk the perimeter of the store first. You can go inside. It's been a long time, though. Thousands of people have come and gone." He stirred sugar into the coffee the waitress had placed in front of him. "But you never know."

Shaine sipped her coffee and listened, fascinated by the respect between the two men.

"Then we'll go to this Lorenz woman's place and see

the car. By then I should have the paperwork through to check out the evidence.''

The plan sounded solid, and Austin showed no signs of uncertainty. Finished with the discussion, the three of them parted and met again in the convenience store parking lot.

Shaine hung back as Austin and the agent walked around the lot and the building. While the two men went inside, she glanced around. Cars and distracted customers came and went. A year ago, the kidnappers had stopped here with Toby. He'd been a tiny boy in a strange car and a strange city without his mama. What kind of people stole a baby? And what had the kidnappers done with him? Sold him? The idea was sick.

The men returned. Ken reached into his navy blue sedan and found a slip of paper for Austin. ''The address in case I lose you.''

Austin and Shaine got into their rental and pulled out into traffic.

The woman was expecting them. She offered coffee and chocolate chip bars in her comfortable living room.

''That's all I know,'' she said, after relating her version of the missing car and its return.

''Did you notice anything unusual about the car when you got it back?'' Ken asked.

''It stunk to high heaven,'' she said with an irritated grimace. ''I had to have it professionally cleaned to get the disgusting smell of cigarette smoke out.''

''Anything else?''

''Well—'' She pursed her lips thoughtfully, and wrinkles radiated from her narrow lips. ''It seems like I do recall the police asking me if a couple of things found in the car belonged to me. Yes, that's right, they did. Maybe a toy of some kind—I don't remember—and a shoe they had bagged in plastic. I don't have any children riding in my car, so I told them they weren't mine.''

She picked up her cup and saucer. ''Imagine someone

with children stealing a car to go joyriding,'' she scoffed. "What kind of an example are parents setting these days?''

Shaine's attention had been riveted to the objects found in the car. "Did you know about that evidence?'' she asked Ken as they headed toward the garage.

He shook his head. "I knew they had prints because the car was broken into. A window was out and the steering column busted in order to hot-wire it, so the crime lab did a routine investigation.''

Expectation welled in Shaine's chest. Something belonging to Toby! The police had something she could identify as his! That would make the case official, wouldn't it? They would believe her now!

Spontaneously she took Austin's hand and squeezed it. He returned the touch, searching her face with questioning eyes. "You okay?''

She nodded.

Mrs. Lorenz let them into her garage. Austin walked around the white car.

"Mind if we sit inside?'' Ken asked her.

She looked puzzled, and somewhat put out, but she unlocked the doors.

Ken gestured for Austin to sit in the driver's seat. He got into the back, and Shaine seated herself on the passenger side.

Austin placed his hands on the steering wheel and closed his eyes. A nervous tremor ran through Shaine's stomach. How could he act so calm when she knew he detested this? She decided to follow his example, determinedly relaxed, and placed her hands on the fabric seat on either side of her legs.

The clock on the dash ticked in the ensuing silence.

She must've been sitting like that a good five minutes when she heard Mrs. Lorenz's shoes on the garage floor. Shaine opened her eyes and glanced over at Austin, surprised to find him looking at her.

"Anything?'' he asked.

She shook her head in disappointment. "You?"

"Nothing I could pick up on. A few blurry images. I think they were hers," he said, meaning the Lorenz woman waiting impatiently.

Shaine took her turn thanking the woman for her time. Austin and Ken talked, and they separated, getting into their vehicles.

Ken pulled onto the street and drove on ahead of them. Austin gave Shaine a glance and pulled her to him. "We're getting a little closer all the time," he said.

"I want this to be it," she said, her fist clenched against his chest.

"We have a lot more to go on than we did a week ago."

"And we have Ken," she agreed.

"He's a believer," Austin said.

"So am I," Shaine said. "So am I."

The detective Ken had contacted led the three of them to a lower-level office that had seen its heyday in the seventies. They seated themselves on duct-taped blue vinyl-cushioned chairs and waited for Detective Parker to check out the evidence and return.

Ken paged through the file and explained the routine fingerprinting.

Parker returned with a plastic tub containing three manila envelopes. He opened the first and slid a pink baby bottle out onto the blotter on his scarred wooden desk. "Look familiar?"

Ken and Austin looked to Shaine for a reply. She shook her head.

The next envelope held a small white shoe with yellowed laces and a pink and blue flower embroidered on the top. Ken made a note in his pocket spiral. He raised a brow at Austin and Shaine.

Shaine had never seen the shoe before. "It's a girl's shoe, and besides, it's too small."

The final envelope held a miniature spoon with rubber protecting the bowl.

Again Shaine shook her head, this time with confusion and discouragement weighting her thoughts. "Are you sure you have the right things? We're looking for the items left in a white Corsica on—what was the date?"

Ken filled the date in for her.

The detective slid the file toward himself and pulled out several blown-up photographs. "Here are the photos from the scene. You can see the shoe just under the edge of the passenger seat." He thumbed through the papers. "The spoon was found behind the rear seat, the bottle in the trunk behind a box of old magazines that the Lorenz woman was planning to take to a thrift store.

"That's not Toby's shoe," Shaine supplied. "He was too old for a bottle, and there was no spoon in Maggie's car when he was taken. This stuff belongs to another child."

Horrified at the implication, she leaned her forehead into her hand and gripped her temples against the headache she could sense building.

"Can we have about thirty minutes?" Ken asked.

She looked up to see the detective glance from Ken to Austin. "The evidence stays right here."

"We're not going anywhere," Ken replied.

With a slightly offended attitude, Parker silently swaggered from the room.

"What's this about?" Shaine asked almost resentfully. "None of this stuff is Toby's."

"But it's from the car," Ken said logically.

"And it hasn't been touched or otherwise contaminated in all this time," Austin filled in, getting up and moving to sit in the chair Parker had vacated.

Shaine took her hand from her forehead and stared at him. If this meant what she thought it meant, they'd gotten

themselves into something bigger than they'd anticipated.
"What are you going to do?" she asked.

Austin looked her in the eye. "I'm going to find out what
these things have to do with Toby."

Chapter 14

Austin used one of the empty envelopes to pull the small white shoe toward him. He studied it for a few seconds, preparing himself, relaxing.

Ken, who'd seen the procedure many times, settled into a chair to wait.

Austin tuned out Shaine's tense energy and picked up the shoe. A familiar, yet still surprising current ran up his arm. The leather was soft and pliant, the soft gray sole unscuffed. He covered it with his other palm and turned his perspective inward.

A dynamic force of energy swirled and stretched and bent itself into colors and sounds and smells that he absorbed, sorting the senses and forms into manageable snips.

"Her name is Amy."

It was even harder to pick up on intelligible information than it had been from Toby's perspective, but he had her, and now all he had to do was traverse the collective and developing images until he found something he could lock in to.

It took a while to sift through and find what he wanted, but no one said anything to disturb him.

"Someone watched her for weeks," he said finally. "Her mother's young. Very young. The same man is here. I can sense him, but he's not alone. He didn't do this by himself, and he didn't choose this baby."

Rossi. The name came to him like a divine gift. "Rossi staked out the mother and baby as easy prey. Then he…" The picture shifted and took a new shape, and Austin knew the man who'd taken the baby was only part of a bigger scheme. The one who took the most risks. The one who believed he deserved the most money.

"I have the baby," he said, inside the kidnapper's head now. "It's so stinkin' easy to get these kids." Austin detailed directions to a remote location with the word *Greasewood* in it. It was off Highway 191, which ran north and south from Interstate 10. "There's a house. Some outbuildings. It's hot and dry. I leave the kid here and pick up my money at a post office box."

"See if you can get something more on the baby," Ken said, his words a gentle direction.

Austin refocused and found a guide point to search from. He scanned each new page that opened to him, backing away from the cloudy unfocused pictures he recognized as the baby's, and concentrating on the man's.

"Here she is. She's practically waiting for me. The roommate's gone. The teenybopper mom is on the phone in the other room. Don't these stupid little bitches have more sense than to get knocked up while they're still wearing training bras?

"The baby was asleep, and she didn't wake up. I didn't have to use the chloroform."

Shaine's indrawn breath registered dimly.

"I put her in the car," he said. "The white Corsica. Doris is in the driver's seat. The back seat is empty except for the baby. The house. I look back at the house. It needs paint. It's white with most of the blue trim chipped off. There's an intersection just ahead. It's…oh."

"What?" Ken asked.

"There's a highway sign. It's Kansas."

"Hot damn!" Ken said, slapping a palm on the desk.

Austin's focus changed then, shifted, dipped and turned, and a consuming sense of shock and alarm spread through him. "Amy!" The young girl was frantic. "Amy!" She screamed the name again and again. She blamed herself. Her mother had told her she wouldn't be able to take care of her baby and work and go to school. Her mother would be glad. Maybe she'd planned it!

No one could help her. The police had nothing. The FBI had nothing. She had nothing. No mother. No husband. No Amy.

Grief, like a gaping pulsing wound, blotted out all other sensations, and Austin couldn't fill his lungs with air.

The shoe was tugged from his fingers. Ken set it on the desktop. Austin concentrated on breathing evenly and remembering the pain wasn't his.

But it was. It was.

He knew just how deeply the girl grieved for her baby, how scared and alone and desperate she was. For that abysmal time it had all been his, and feelings as deep as those were not easily forgotten.

Ignoring whatever Ken might think, Shaine pulled her chair beside Austin's and took his hand. He met her eyes, and the depth of emotion in his took her breath away.

"This is the only chance we'll have to hold these things," he said to her. "Take the shoe."

The sound of a train roared in Shaine's head. Why did he want her to do this? What if she saw something awful? What if the future was worse than the past?

She remembered her dream of Austin, the image of pain and suffering on his face. The pain had all belonged to others. He'd made it his. *For her.*

His hand in hers was strong and warm. Imbuing courage. And hope.

Shaine released him and faced the desk where the tiny white shoe lay. Swiftly, so she wouldn't have time to anticipate, she swooped forward and took it. The laces dangled between her fingers. She shut her eyes, maneuvering the reference points Austin had taught her to use.

It was surprisingly easy. As soon as her chest warmed and her fingers grew cold, she knew she was there—and she flowed with it. The heat plunged to her abdomen.

A toddling girl with a pink dress and floppy bow in her fine hair wobbled across a large room filled with a dozen other children. It appeared as some kind of day-care facility. Children banged toys and whooped. Occasionally one cried.

"Amanda, they call her," Shaine was able to tell them.

"See her mother," Austin said hopefully. "Can you find her?"

Shaine tried. She waited patiently for another avenue to open. Nothing came. Finally she shook her head and returned the shoe to the desk. "We know she's okay," she said without much excitement in her tone.

She glanced over at Austin, and did a double-take at the look of awe his face. "You saw her," he said, his voice low.

She nodded.

"We *both* saw her."

Comprehension at his incredulity sunk in. He'd rarely envisioned a live victim. This was almost miraculous for him. Shaine couldn't help thinking of the stories she'd seen on CNN after the Oklahoma City bombing. Even the search-and-rescue dogs had to find a live body once in a while or they became depressed and quit looking. It was a silly analogy, but an obviously true one. If the need for hope and encouragement affected dogs that way, Shaine could imagine how such a thing would effect a human being.

Especially a compassionate man like Austin.

"We have about ten minutes before Parker comes back. You want to do these?" Ken pointed to the bottle and spoon.

"Yes." Austin held the objects for impressions, coming up with the same as he had before. Shaine didn't get much more, either.

The detective returned, and they ended the session. The afternoon had grown hot beneath the dry sun.

"You gave me a lot to work with," Ken said, loosening his tie as they walked back to their cars. "The name Doris isn't much to go on, but I'll bet I have the young mother and the locale where the baby was taken from by tonight. The other place, the one with Greasewood in it? Do you think that's the drop-off point?"

"I think so," Austin replied. "It was the man and woman's destination. Once they got the kid there, they were home-free, and the money was theirs."

"Will you guys be staying or heading back?"

Shaine looked up at Austin.

"You'll need to rest," he said, then glanced back at McKade. "We'll stay another night, and head back tomorrow. I'll call your pager and leave the number where we'll be tonight."

"Gotcha." Ken walked off.

"We'll get a place with a phone and a TV," Austin said as they got into the rental.

"You can rent space in an airplane hangar, and I'll sleep," she replied, leaning her head back against the seat. "Of course you'll be wide-awake."

"That's why we need the TV."

"I'm sorry I didn't get more," she said, regretting being unable to help.

"You did fine." He merged the car into traffic and switched on the air-conditioning. "We wouldn't have gotten this far if not for your dreams."

And he wouldn't have had to see and feel the things he

had if not for her sake. She closed her eyes against the thought.

He woke her what seemed like seconds later, but when she glanced around, they were in front of a hotel.

"Where are we?"

"Las Cruces. I felt like driving off some energy, and you seemed comfortable. We can catch a flight from here in the morning." He checked them in and carried their luggage.

They stepped into an elevator. "Nice place," she commented.

The door slid open. The faint smell of chlorine met her nostrils. "Don't tell me. There's a pool and a hot tub and exercise equipment."

He led her down a hallway. "Okay."

"Okay, what?"

"Okay, I won't tell you."

He set their bags down and inserted the plastic card in the lock.

"Hungry?" he asked.

She shook her head.

"Maybe you should eat before you fall back asleep."

"How do you know I'll fall back asleep?"

He adjusted the thermostat on the wall. "Because you only slept about an hour and a half. You've got at least another six and a half to go to catch up."

"I feel like I need a shower."

"Go ahead."

She brushed her hair and teeth, peeled off her clothes and stepped beneath a tingling spray.

"Shaine?" Austin called a minute later.

"Yeah?"

"I'm going to head down to the gym."

"Okay."

She rinsed her hair.

"This smell drove me crazy the first couple of times you used my shower," he said, his voice closer than before, surprising her. "I imagined you standing naked in my bathroom."

Shaine wanted to invite him to join her, but she didn't want to seem too bold or embarrass herself. "Austin?" she called softly, seeing if he was still there.

"Yeah."

"Want to see the real thing?"

"Yeah."

Unable to suppress a smile, she pulled the shower curtain away from the end of the tub so the spray didn't flood the bathroom.

He'd dressed in his shorts and a form-fitting T-shirt. His gaze slid over her body and perceptibly darkened. "You are beautiful, Shaine."

Her shy smile almost excited him as much as the sight of water dripping from her nipples and sluicing down her thighs. She was by far the most beautiful woman he'd ever seen. And the only one he'd ever want from now on. As long as he lived, there would never be anyone to compare to her. Spending these past days and nights with her had shown him that.

"You're making it difficult to leave," he said dryly.

"Maybe there'll be babes in thongs," she said.

His gaze slid down her lithe body. "Maybe."

"Maybe you'd get a better workout here." She bit her lip.

He laughed out loud. God, she was fun. And a little uncertain of him. Of them.

He stripped off his clothes and shoes and stepped into the warm spray beside her. Her palms came up to his chest and his body responded immediately. Her lovely tawny eyes widened. A rivulet trickled down her neck and he bent his head to lap it up.

Her hot wet skin made him crazy. He stroked her flesh from her jaw, down her collarbone and breasts, to her flat stomach and down her legs, coming back up to cup her buttocks and pull her flush against him.

The water made their bodies squeaky-slick. Austin enjoyed her smooth satin texture against his hair-roughened skin, framed her jaw and kissed her long and lustily.

She wrapped her arms around his back and her breathing came in uneven bursts against his cheek. She pulled him closer like she couldn't get enough of him. The feeling was mutual. He wanted her, body and soul.

He brought a hand between their bodies to touch her, and she gasped against his mouth. Instinctively she raised one leg aside his hip to give him access, and he leaned her back against the tiled wall.

She exhaled in shaky pants against his jaw, an incoherent word escaping here and there.

"Raise your other leg," he coaxed.

She obeyed, grasping him around the neck and helping him ease inside her. "Oh, Austin…"

Her nipples pebbled tightly with her excitement. He held her hips securely with one arm and rubbed the other palm across the hard peaks.

Fierce pleasure shone on her flushed face, and he felt the surging tension in her limbs.

Austin didn't know how much longer he could hold back. She felt so good, and her vivacious energy spun him to the edge. "Tell me when," he groaned.

Eyes closed, limbs taut, her body tensed and she dug her nails into his shoulder. "Now."

The most liberating word in the English language.

Austin cupped the fleshy globes of her bottom and rapturously surged into her straining body. She cried out and clung to him, and he rode the wild crest of pleasure in her wake.

Water pounded his shoulders.

Minutes passed.

Their breathing calmed.

"Good thing we didn't try this at my place," he said finally.

She stirred against his neck. "Why?"

"Hot water would have run out long ago and we'd have frozen to death."

"I don't think so."

He eased her thighs from his waist. "You don't?"

She shook her head with a grin. "We generated enough heat to not notice."

"Trust me. We'd have noticed." He turned and rinsed quickly, then stepped from the shower and grabbed towels.

When she shut off the water and stepped out, he enfolded her in a towel and his embrace. Blotting her hair, he kissed her temple and hugged her close.

"I've never known anything like this," she said, her cheek against his chest. "Like what we have together."

"Neither have I," he admitted.

"Have you ever been in love, Austin?"

The question caught him off guard. He stroked her hair. "Once."

"What happened?"

"I was young. Twenty maybe. Horny. She was doing a thesis on extrasensory phenomenon. She found out a little more about me than she was comfortable with. After a while she was afraid of me. I confronted her with it. She got defensive, called me a freak, and that was that."

"I'm sorry."

"It was a long time ago."

"It hurt you."

"I got over it."

"Did you?"

"Yeah."

She pulled back and looked up at him. "Then why did you run away?"

"I didn't run away from her. Or from that one experience. I ran away from all of it. The researchers. The institute. Tom. The cases."

She flattened her palms on his chest. "The victims and their families."

"Especially them."

"I understand."

"I know you do." And he did. For the first time in his life, someone shared and understood the nightmares this ability brought with it.

But as with Tom and even Ken, he was providing something for her that she still couldn't do herself. She'd needed him. And he'd been just lonely enough to become entangled, regardless of what would happen.

Her whole objective had been to find her nephew. He didn't believe she'd used him or bribed him in any way. What they'd shared and her responses were too genuine to be anything other than mutual attraction.

But whether she found Toby or not, she had a life to go back to. A life filled with people and objects and things he wasn't willing to deal with day after day. Just these few days in crowds and motel rooms had been enough for him. He was ready to go home.

This was why he'd protected himself for so long.

But Shaine Richards, with her hopeful search, her quirky smile and her seductively long legs, had broken through years of self-protection and unlocked that place of need deep inside.

He would never be the same.

But he would know that he was capable of something he'd never before allowed himself to discover.

He could love.

Chapter 15

His hair had grown a shade darker, but he still flashed the same dimpled grin. Toby. She'd know him anywhere, no matter how old he was. He sat on the wooden edge of a sandbox, a baby playing in the sand at his feet.

The other child's hair was dark, his hands and legs chubby like Toby's had been once. The tiny boy poured sand on Toby's tennis shoe with a plastic shovel and laughed aloud when Toby pretended to get mad.

A horn sounded and both boys looked up.

"Daddy!" the small one squealed, and Toby had to help him over the side of the sandbox so he didn't fall on his face in his excitement.

He stayed where he was, watching the child greet his father, turning to intently observe the bird's nest on the limb of the towering tree above.

"I brought something for you," the man said, and Toby looked down, discovering the man's long shadow on the grass.

"You did?"

"Want to see?"

He nodded and turned.

He took the heavy ball of tissue paper and unwrapped a sliced geode. Thousands of purple crystals shimmered in the midday sun that filtered down through the leaves. He raised an uncertain blue gaze. "Cool."

More than anything he wanted to hug the man who already held the other little boy against his chest. He longed to feel that same security, be a part of what they shared. "Thanks," he managed.

"You're welcome. Coming in?"

"Sure." He stood, and the man's hand rested on his shoulder.

Without having to say more, they turned toward the house.

When they reached a wide porch, the man set the boy down and he tottered noisily across the wooden boards toward the door. The man turned back to Toby and, without a spoken word, folded him against his chest.

It felt good. It felt warm and secure and right, and not at all babyish like he'd been afraid.

"I'm gonna put this with my other one," he said, pulling back and clutching the precious rock in both hands.

"Okay."

"C'mon, Daddy!" the toddler sang out. "C'mon Toby!"

"We're coming," the man replied, and reached his hand down. "C'mon, son."

Shaine rolled to her back, and opened her eyes to blink into the velvety darkness of the unfamiliar room.

"A dream?" Austin asked from beside her.

As usual, his alertness surprised her. "How did you know?"

"I can tell. It wasn't bad, was it?"

"No. It was strange. But it wasn't bad."

"Was it... What kind was it?"

"Knowing."

"What happened?"

"Toby was older. Four maybe. And a baby boy was with him."

"A playmate?"

"Smaller. Like a brother. He felt like a brother."

Which they both knew was impossible since Maggie was dead and no one knew who Toby's father was. An adoptive brother? One wherever he would be living in the future?

"He was happy. Content. And loved."

"That's good."

"I just…"

"What?"

"I couldn't see who he was with. I want it to be me, but—I'm still afraid I might not find him."

His hand located hers resting on top of the sheet.

"I'd be able to live with that now that I've seen he's happy," she said into the darkness. "You gave me that peace."

"Not me."

"Yes. You taught me how to use my vision, and because of that I worked past those first awful dreams into the future, and I would be all right with this much."

"Where's your hope?"

A long minute passed. A siren screamed in the distance. "I don't know."

"We're going to find him, Shaine."

"You believe that?"

"I want to believe that."

She pulled his fingertips to her lips. "Even if we didn't find him, I'd always be grateful I took off for the mountains looking for an old recluse."

She knew he smiled.

"Glad I found him, too."

His stubbled chin touched her bare shoulder.

Austin breathed in her sleep-warmed skin, detected the soft flowery fragrance of her freshly washed hair and pressed his lips to the satin smooth skin of her shoulder.

The next few days would be the pivotal point in this search. And in this relationship.

He fell asleep with her alluring scent pervading his senses, and he awoke to the shrill ring of the phone.

"Allen," he said gruffly.

"Austin."

Ken's voice brought him alert instantly. "What did you get?"

"Amy Cutter. Reported missing from Thomas County, Kansas, the day before Maggie's death and Toby's disappearance. The mother was eighteen, living with a girlfriend. The baby came up missing when she checked on her after an afternoon nap. She had to be sedated for several days and is still in counseling."

Austin didn't need to be told of the mother's distress. He'd experienced it firsthand. Ken was, however, confirming his sighting.

"We have a case," Ken stated.

"Kidnapping."

"Thomas County is in the upper left corner of the state, a hop, skip and a jump out of the way from Silver City to Omaha. A well-laid plan."

"Incredible," Austin said, lying back and rubbing his eyes.

"And I have a good hunch that if we can track down Amy Cutter, we'll find Toby Richards."

"It's that place in Arizona, Ken. That's where they fence the kids. Did you check it out?"

"I have two men there right now."

"Good. Let me know. I'll be back in Omaha today."

"I'll call you there."

Austin hung up and noted the sun streaming through the crack in the drapes. Shaine still slept soundly. He'd get up, grab a run and a shower before she woke.

Watching her sleep, he considered his options. How long could they go on like this? The closer they grew to one another, the harder it would be to part when the time came. And that time sped imminently closer.

The wisest thing he could do would be to back off now. Chalk up the great sex and this insane need for her to a fleeting loss of good sense and move on.

Was he wise enough? Was he strong enough?

He had to be. She had established a great life for herself. She'd worked hard to get the inn operating, and she loved it. The Pruitts were wonderful friends.

This last week only reinforced how impossible it was for him to live anywhere but in the mountains. He'd been a solitary man for as long as he could remember. Up on his mountain, away from the people who made up this society was the only way he could survive. He'd been inside too many sickos' heads, seen too much through their eyes and their senses to want any part of living among them.

Though his intuition occurred in a part of his brain that had no language, and he couldn't explain it, he'd learned to trust it. He knew he wouldn't be able to live the way she did.

His adoring gaze took in the sweep of her long lashes against her creamy-skinned cheek, and he thought of the color of her eyes when they were lit from within with passion. He studied the perfect symmetry of her bow-shaped lips, knowing how soft and utterly kissable they were. The scent of her hair stabbed him with insatiable desire.

He reached as if to touch her face, stroke her hair, but drew his hand back.

There was no way he could expect such a vibrant young woman to cut herself off from humanity. Besides, he hadn't been fooling about believing they would find Toby. When she had her nephew with her, Austin's importance would fade. Even if it didn't, the boy would need to go to school, and the Colorado mountain roads were treacherous in winter.

One or both of them would regret letting things go this far. He was to blame. He'd known the impossibility of it all, but as soon as he'd touched her and stopped letting his head do the thinking, he'd lost his grip.

Maybe it wasn't too late. Maybe she was still operating out of gratitude and physical attraction; those were both normal motivations. Maybe it wasn't too late to prevent her from being hurt when their liaison ended. It was entirely possible that he was the only one who'd leapt off the deep end and fallen in love.

Perhaps Shaine Richards's feelings could still be spared. He could only hope.

Austin explained Ken's findings on the way to the airport.

"So they're actually looking for this Cutter child?" she asked as they checked their bags and waited for their flight.

"Yes. She was reported missing the day before Maggie's death. Toby was assumed dead, and there was no evidence of foul play. But this kid disappeared out of her crib."

"How fortunate for her."

She knew her sarcasm was ugly, but the whole thing was so unfair. No one had ever even looked for Toby.

They boarded and found their seats. The flight attendant brought them juice and flirted with Austin.

"Amy's going to lead us to Toby," he said sometime later.

"You're right. This is our only chance now."

"Not the only one. Just the best one." He opened a trade magazine, but seemed to grow tired. He hadn't slept much at all. He probably couldn't wait to get home to his quiet haven and his view of the heavens.

"Why don't you lean back and close your eyes?" she suggested.

He did. And before long, his breathing grew deep and even. Shaine had never watched him sleep before. He was such a light sleeper, and she just the opposite. She was careful not to wake him, and he slept the rest of the flight.

"We'll be landing soon." The attendant stopped beside him and laid her hand on his.

Austin's eyes opened.

The attendant's eyes widened and her hand jerked away like she'd been pricked with a needle.

They stared at one another until the flustered young woman straightened and hurried away without another word or a backward glance.

He rolled his head and his dark eyes met Shaine's.

"What just happened?" she asked.

"My perceptions are a little unguarded when I'm asleep. I'm not always able to make sure the switch is off."

"You saw something?"

"Yeah."

"What about her? Why did she look so funny?"

"I'm not sure. It's kind of an electrical impulse, like when one of us touches an object. But I don't know if people's minds are able to sort through the impulses and recognize what's happened or not. They must know something, because the experience gives them the willies."

Another painful reason why Austin Allen had closed himself off from the world. Another reason why she disliked herself for bringing him away from his place of safety and opening him up to the very things he'd determinedly left behind.

Another reason she'd never be able to repay him.

They refastened their seat belts and prepared for landing. The attendant who'd touched Austin stayed at the back of the cabin until they disembarked.

Shaine realized he was used to the avoidance. He accepted it without obvious concern. But that didn't mean he liked it. He simply knew it was something he couldn't change and had dealt with it in the best way he could.

Now that she knew, now that she'd seen firsthand the emotional trauma and the physical toll his ability wreaked, Shaine understood him. She knew a person couldn't endure the experiences he had without eventually cracking under the strain. Self-preservation had driven him to Colorado.

His home was a lot like him. It was rustic on the outside, but high tech on the inside. To all appearances, Austin was a closed-off man with little ability to have feelings for others. In reality, feeling too much had brought him considerable suffering.

Austin hailed a cab so they wouldn't have to call the Pruitts, and they said little on the drive home. Reaching the inn at last, Shaine unlocked her door and dropped her purse on the counter.

Austin placed their bags on the floor.

"Are you hungry?" she asked.

He shook his head.

She kicked her shoes off. "It feels so good to get home." She met his eyes. He said nothing.

He was ready to leave. This time there was no mistake.

The thing she'd wanted for so long, finding Toby, would be the thing that released him to go home and end their time together. She still wanted Toby. There was no question about that. But she'd discovered something else she wanted in the process.

"They think they've found a place in Arizona," Shaine told Audrey the next afternoon. "A farm of some sort where the children are taken and hidden until they're delivered to the people who've paid for them."

"That's terrifying." Instinctively Audrey brought a protective hand to her round stomach.

"So, how are you feeling?"

"Gross. But I don't want to talk about me. Marge has been just great. She had some ideas about finishing off that back porch and making an eating area for nice weather." Audrey detailed the plan.

"That's a good idea."

They went over the grocery supply, making a list for

Marge, then Shaine closeted herself in the small office behind the dining room.

She caught up on paperwork, not realizing how late it got, until finally, she turned out all the lights and went downstairs.

Austin was watching a football game, his legs, in a pair of sweat shorts, stretched from the sofa to her coffee table. She didn't remember him coming to bed the night before, and when she'd awakened he'd been gone. "You okay?"

"Yeah."

She sat facing him on the sofa. "I know you're getting antsy to go home."

"It won't be long now," he replied without looking at her.

Inevitable. They both knew it. They'd never made any plans together, never spoken of a future beyond finding Toby. Shaine didn't know how to have a casual affair.

She studied his profile. She didn't know how to share what she'd shared with him, how to form an emotional and physical bond and then just sever it. He was obviously used to the process. He didn't make attachments. The thought angered her, but she tamped it down. She'd better learn fast.

"Ken called."

She focused her attention on his words. "What did he say?"

"They've confirmed the place I saw. It's east of Tucson, between a couple of mountain ranges, isolated. A couple in their forties going by the name of Holbrook keeps the kids until money is transferred and then they deliver them."

"That's awful."

"Altogether, they figure there are about eight people involved in the operation."

"What are they going to do?"

"They need another day or so. There are a couple of kids there right now, and they plan to follow the Holbrooks and catch them in the act of transferring."

"Selling," Shaine corrected.

"Yeah."

"Then what?"

Austin turned and looked at her. "Well, caught red-handed, they'll have to start talking unless they want to go down alone."

Everything about her seemed weary. He hated the toll this ordeal was taking on her.

"This is so unbelievable," she said. "It's like something you see on 'America's Most Wanted.' If I didn't know what they'd done to Maggie and Toby, I wouldn't believe it. I feel like I've been having one big long nightmare for the past year."

Austin aimed the remote at the screen and flicked off the game. "Come here."

She leaned forward until her head touched his chest, and he smoothed her silky hair, holding her head against his chest, wishing he could impart comfort and strength through that simple touch.

He wished he'd been able to do more. He despised the familiar helplessness that swamped him when situations were out of his control. "I know something that'll cheer you up," he said.

She lifted her head. "What's that?"

He picked up the remote he'd found in an electronics store that day.

"Where'd that come from?"

"I bought it." He aimed it at her stereo. The first chords of Little Eva's "The Loco-motion" filled the room. She didn't have a disk player, but he'd found a couple of tapes to liven the place up.

She grinned. "There are customers two floors above us who paid to spend the night in the 1800s."

He turned the volume down. "They could have spent the same money and had this great toy. Look, it works on the TV, the stereo. I'll bet I could get it to turn on the coffee-maker."

She laughed out loud. "You're right. It cheered me up."

Relieved to see her mood lighten, he sat up straight. "Want to go out? A movie maybe?"

Shaine glanced at Austin's expression, knowing he'd suggested it only for her. "We should stay near the phone."

"No problem." He stood, picked up something from the counter that divided the rooms, flipped it open and showed it to her.

"A phone?"

"Yep."

She grinned. "Okay."

He headed for the bedroom. "I'll change clothes. It's getting almost as cold here as it was in the mountains."

In the background, the softly playing music ended. Things had changed between them. Shaine couldn't put her finger on the exact time or place it had happened, but it had. He was still the same person who'd gone out of his way to comfort and help her. He was still the same man whose touch turned her insides to jelly, but whose voice calmed her fears and made her heart pound for different reasons.

He was still Austin Allen, a man who knew and saw more than most people would in their entire lives. And though he was going along with this business for her sake, she would soon become one of the things he turned off, closed out, refused to see.

She'd bet anything that he wouldn't come to her bed that night. Or any night again.

She was going to have to learn to tune out things, too.

"Seen Austin?" Shaine asked Marge, sliding a pan of bread pudding into the oven.

"Saw him carrying boxes into your office," the woman replied.

Shaine crossed the wood-floored dining room. Outside

the room that served as her workspace, several large boxes and their packing materials were stacked against the wall.

"What are these?" she asked, entering.

"I'll get those in a minute." He looked up from a computer.

"Austin!"

"Look at this. I've loaded everything you're going to need to keep your records. This will make your work so much easier. Wait till you see."

She stood beside him and gestured helplessly with both hands. "Austin, what are you doing? Where did this come from?"

"I picked it up today. I thought it would be great for your business. You can use this program to keep your checking account. You can even pay your bills with it. It'll transfer money from your account and keep the balance."

"If I had the money it took to buy this, I would have had some chimney work done so we can use the fireplace in the dining room this winter. That was next in our budget plans. With all the recent travel, I can't pay for this."

His hand paused on the mouse, and he glanced up at her. "I bought it. Don't worry about it."

"Don't worry about it? These things cost a couple thousand dollars. I know that much."

"It's no big deal, Shaine. I bought it. I wanted to buy it. Enough about that, all right?"

"No, it's not all right. You should have asked me."

He looked away, the enthusiasm gone from his expression.

Minutes ticked past. The room held the unfamiliar smell of the new equipment. Shaine glanced from his face to the screen, and couldn't help a little curiosity about what he'd wanted her to see.

"I'm sorry," he said finally. "You're right. I should have asked before I brought it in."

"I can't afford it," she said lamely. "And I can't accept such an expensive gift."

He turned and took stock of her expression. "Why not?"

She looked into his flint-colored eyes. Confusion littered her thoughts. What was happening? What did he expect of her? Things between them had deteriorated to the point where she didn't know how to act or what to say. He'd gone out often the last two days and fallen asleep on the sofa at night. And now he brought her a computer worth as much or more than she made in a month.

She ran a hand through her hair and turned away, stepping to the window and idly looking out into the side yard. "Because it's too much. You've given me enough already. There's so much I can't repay."

"I don't want to be repaid."

"But this—" she gestured limply "—this isn't the kind of gift friends give one another."

The word *friends* hung in the room like an accusation, and that hadn't been how she'd meant it. She'd meant that an expensive gift intimated more of a commitment than they shared. When placed beside his emotional and physical withdrawal, his generosity bewildered her.

"I've never had friends, so I don't know what they give one another," he said, his measured voice possessing a tightness that brought an unwanted lump to her throat. "I have no family, either. I have more money than I can spend on myself, and I didn't see anything earth-shattering about spending a little on someone I—care for."

His matter-of-fact tone fell flat.

Shaine closed her eyes and tried to assimilate his words with the way he'd been behaving. To him, it really was no big deal. To him, everything they'd had together was no big deal. She resented that, and she hated herself for her irritable attitude.

She'd barged into his life and demanded he teach her to understand her dreams so that she could find Toby. He'd done the best he could, and once they'd discovered she couldn't do it fast enough on her own, he'd made a sacrifice for her. How could she take more than that? She already owed him so much.

And a computer, something so symbolic of Austin, would be a hurtful reminder after he was gone.

Shaine bit her lip. Was that it? Was that really it? Or was the real issue the fact that she didn't want material things from him? She wanted more. She wanted him, and that was something that wasn't so easy for him to bestow.

She wasn't just being foolish, was she? He'd just admitted his lack of friends and family to shower with gifts.

That admission made her wonder about something he'd never told her, and a change of subject suited her. "How did your mother die, Austin?"

He hesitated. "A car wreck," he said finally.

"How old were you?"

"Eighteen."

"That's tough."

"Yeah. She and a friend were both killed."

She turned back to the room. "There's something you're not saying, isn't there? I can hear it."

His subdued voice was unfamiliar. "I knew the exact hour she would be pronounced dead. I knew the description of her injuries."

Shaine walked back and leaned against the old desk. "That must have been terrible for you."

He clicked the mouse a couple of times and turned off the power. "What I couldn't see was the day. It could have been far into the future or the next day—I didn't know."

"How did you get the vision?"

He met her eyes. "In a dream."

Her heart caught in her throat. He'd hinted at precognitive dreams like hers, but he'd never shared any of them with her. She understood the terror of that particular vision.

"At first I wouldn't let her go anywhere. I was terrified of what I knew was going to happen. But that's illogical, of course. Everyone is destined to die eventually. I had no date or exact place. If I'd known it would happen in a certain city, I'd have kept her from there, but it wasn't like that."

"Where did it happen?"

"Pittsburgh. We had a town house there. She'd gotten tired of the isolation, and swore she'd be careful. And she was. It wasn't her fault. A truck ran a red light."

"And then you only had Tom."

"Yes. I stayed with him and his wife for a while, and then I went to college. By then I was all the more determined that I didn't want to see the past or the future. It was all out of my control, and I hated the powerlessness."

"You've done good for so many people, Austin."

"But at what expense? Sometimes it's important to take care of *yourself.* That's what I learned the hard way."

She placed her hand over his on the arm of the chair. "I do understand."

A pulsing low ring sounded nearby.

Pulling his hand from beneath hers, he leaned forward and moved aside a pile of instruction booklets and CD Rom cases to pick up his phone. He flipped it open. "Allen here."

Shaine leaned back and listened to his side of the conversation.

"Where at? Yeah. Did you tell 'em you had the car?... What about Rossi?... She's okay. We're both a little impatient... Yeah." He hung up.

"What's happening?"

"They have the Holbrooks in custody. Ken told them this Rossi person was ready to testify that they had pulled the jobs on their own."

"They found Rossi?"

"Not yet. That's just a tactic. It worked. The Holbrooks got a lawyer, and they're about to spill their guts."

Chapter 16

"Let's go to Arizona," Shaine suggested later that evening as they picked at their dinner in her tiny kitchen.

"What for?"

"Go to that Holbrook place. Look around, get a feel for the kids."

He understood her desire, but he'd dismissed the same idea. "Shaine, do you have any idea how many impressions would be in a place like that? It's been a year since Toby and the Cutter baby were there. A dozen or a hundred kids could have come and gone. I'm sure they didn't keep mementos of the children they hocked on the black market."

"Don't say it like that!" She shivered. "That gives me visions of dark wharves and boats to China."

He shrugged.

"I can't stand this waiting!" She laid her fork down, giving up the pretense of eating. "I feel so helpless!"

The dark smudges beneath her eyes said as much as her words. Austin, too, felt the strain of the last week. "How long do you have until Audrey has her baby?"

She thought for a second. "Four days."

"We could make a trip to Kansas and back by then."

She examined his expression. "Kansas?"

"Amy Cutter's mother."

Her chin dropped. "What—do you think that would do any good?"

"I don't know. She might have something more we could use to go on. We've gone through all of Toby's and Maggie's things."

She shoved her chair back and stood. "Let's go."

"Mind if I hook the modem up to your phone line long enough to check for flights?"

She waved him off. "Go."

By eleven the next morning, Shaine looked almost green as they hurried off a windy runway toward the taxi stand. "I'll never take another small-engine plane," she swore.

"It was a little rough," he agreed.

"A little? I lost *tomorrow's* breakfast back there."

He grinned. "But I got you here fast, didn't I?"

They caught a cab and found the address. Samantha Cutter looked like the nineteen-year-old she was, with a section of her long straight auburn hair braided and hanging against her cheek. Having been expecting them, she opened the door and ushered them in. "Can I get you guys a Coke?" she asked.

"No, thank you," Shaine answered.

"That sounds good," Austin replied, knowing the girl would be more relaxed if he let her serve him.

She brought him a glass of ice and a chilled can of soda, and their fingers brushed. Austin met her eyes, and something in his chest dipped and swayed. He knew this girl. He knew her anguish at the loss of her baby. He'd experienced her every emotion as if it were his own. An experience like that created an incomprehensible connection to another human being.

And she didn't know him from the man in the moon.

"On the phone you said this was about Amy," she said,

her voice shaky. She had wide hazel eyes, and a full figure packed into jeans and a long T-shirt.

"That's right," he returned.

"One of the detectives I keep in touch with said they're checking out a new lead, and then a Detective McKade called me. Are you some of the FBI people?"

Austin shook his head. "No. We're working with Detective McKade, but actually, we're looking for Shaine's nephew. He's been missing since the day after Amy disappeared."

"Really? Is the FBI handling your case?"

"They are now." He exchanged a look with Shaine. How would this girl take the truth? He decided to tell her straight out. "We've seen Amy."

Her face paled, and he realized he'd said it all wrong. "Not seen her, like *seen* her, but seen her, like in a vision."

It was a lame way to explain it, but the only way that someone who didn't have the ability could understand. "The FBI had one of Amy's shoes and Shaine and I held it."

"I saw a lady do that on 'Montel,'" she said skeptically. "You mean you guys can really see things like that?"

Shaine broke into the conversation with "Sometimes we can. Austin has helped the agency find a lot of missing people. I'm a little newer at it."

"Well, what did you see?"

"Austin saw the people who took her."

"He did?" Her eyes widened. "Is this the new lead they told me about?"

"You should let the detective assigned to Amy's case tell you the details," Austin said. "I do know they're getting close to pressing charges."

She nodded blankly.

"And Shaine here saw Amy as she is now or as she will be."

Austin could tell the teen wanted to believe with all her heart, but he knew, too, that a lot of quacks approached police and family members when a case like this hit the press. "And where was she?" she asked.

"I don't know," Shaine admitted. "But she's all right."

The girl's eyes expressed her emotions wavering between hope and skepticism. "My mother would have a fit if she knew I was even talking to you guys," she said. "She blames me for Amy being missing. She always said I wouldn't be able to take care of her."

Anger welled up in Shaine's chest, and she reached for the girl's hand. "What happened was not because you weren't a good mother, Samantha. These people are monsters. They select the children before they take them. They murdered my sister to get to my nephew."

Samantha's hazel eyes rounded in sympathy. "Well, tell me," she said after a few minutes. "Tell me what both of you saw."

They took a few minutes to explain the difference in their perceptions and then the visions themselves.

"Walking?" she said to Shaine, with tears welling in her eyes. "She's walking? Yes, she's so much older now. I've missed so much. I miss her so bad."

"We didn't come here to upset you," Austin interrupted.

The girl visibly composed herself.

"We were hoping maybe you had something else of Amy's," Shaine said, trying to keep the meeting focused and wanting to spare the girl as much unpleasantness as possible. "Something we could use to—get another look."

"You mean something that belonged to her? Like a toy? Clothes?"

"Something that would hold impressions," Shaine supplied. "I know she's just a baby, but something that meant a lot to her."

"I have everything," Samantha said, standing. "Back here." She led the way through the small house with its obviously secondhand furnishings to a bedroom that held a double bed and a crib. The crib was filled with bags and boxes.

She gave an apologetic little wave toward the beds. "We shared this room."

"These are her things?" Shaine asked.

She nodded. "And the bear," she said, gesturing to a stuffed animal lying on her bed. She gave a foolish shrug. "I sleep with it now."

Cosmetics and cheap jewelry littered an old dresser, a teddy bear calendar hung on the wall. Samantha Cutter was just a kid herself.

"You want to touch her things?" she asked, gesturing to the crib.

Shaine nodded. "May we?"

"Sure, but..."

"What?"

"Would it bother you if I stayed and watched?"

Shaine glanced at Austin for his reaction. He shook his head as though it didn't matter to him.

"Okay."

The girl moved to arrange the cartons, dismissing sheets and clothing, and going immediately to the toys and personal items. She placed a box on the floor and showed them a soft-bristled hairbrush and a jar holding barrettes and tiny rubber bands. "She has pretty hair."

She lowered her face quickly. Shaine knew the pain of looking at these things, and made a point to listen with her heart each time the girl spoke of where something had come from and how Amy had liked it.

One by one they went through the items, taking turns, getting impressions similar to the ones they'd already seen. Austin had several views of Amy with Samantha, and after he related them, she cried brokenheartedly.

"I can't do this to her," he whispered aside to Shaine.

"No, please don't stop," the teen said, overhearing. "Now I know you're exactly what you say you are. I trust you. Go on."

Shaine held a bulbous rattle with a red-and-white-striped tube that swirled around inside.

"That was her favorite," Samantha whispered just as the spark of electricity shot up Shaine's arm.

"The day care has one like this," Shaine said.

"What?"

"She's seeing," Austin told Samantha quietly.

The girl brought shaky fingers to her lips.

"She cried and stomped her feet, but they wouldn't let her take it home." Shaine was seeing the same facility she'd seen before. The surroundings were a little sharper this time. "The mother picks her up just after juice time every day. She carries her across the parking lot to the car."

"This is it." Austin mentally nudged her forward with an insistent note. "Turn and look back at the building."

"The van," she said. "It's silver."

"Who are you seeing it through?" he asked.

"I don't know...I just see it."

"You don't know cars—can you see plates?"

"No."

"Damn! The building—turn and look back at the building."

"Tender Care Center," she said. "Tender Loving Care For Your Little Ones."

"That's one smart baby if you're reading through her viewpoint," Austin mumbled.

"There's a car seat in the back. It's upholstered in gray," she went on. "A pile of mail on the front seat."

Austin's breath touched her ear. "Addresses?"

Shaine's hands were so cold, she started to shake. He took them between his and buffed them. A throbbing heat centered in her chest and spread through her upper arms as she painstakingly centered her attention on the envelopes. "A postmark," she said weakly, and squinted at the round stamp mark.

No one breathed.

The ink swirled and came into focus. "Springfield...Illinois."

"Perfect, baby," Austin breathed. "Take it from her."

Shaine felt the toy pulled from her grasp, heard the rattle of tiny balls inside the plastic.

"Hold her hands," he told Samantha.

"Oh, they're like ice."

He flipped his phone open and punched in a number. A pause. "Allen here. Call me immediately."

The room came into focus, and Shaine became aware of the white-faced teenage girl who held her hands.

"I've never seen anything like that before," Samantha said in amazement. "How can you do that?"

Shaine shook her head more to clear it than to answer the question. The heat that had encased her chest dwindled to a dull ache that made her feel as though she'd been running for miles and couldn't catch her breath. "I'll take that drink now."

Samantha shot up and returned with a diet cola. "This okay?"

Shaine sipped it, her pulse sluggish.

Austin's phone sounded, and he answered it before it finished the first ring. "Allen... Yeah, Ken, we've got the Cutter baby. A Springfield, Illinois, postmark and a day care called Tender Care Center. The sign says Tender Loving Care for Your Little Ones."

"Don't forget they call her Amanda," Shaine prompted.

He repeated her reminder, answered a few questions and hung up.

Shaine yawned.

"She needs to sleep," he said.

Samantha tugged her worn bedspread down. "You can lie right here."

He raised his brows questioningly at Shaine.

They'd come straight here from the airport and hadn't planned any further.

"Okay," she said, leaning back, and feeling the residual effects of the draining experience.

"How about you?" Samantha asked.

Austin shook his head and Shaine couldn't help a grin.

"No, I'll be awake for a while," he replied. "But can you tell me if there's a gym in this town?"

Austin's phone woke Shaine. She opened her eyes and listened to him fumble in the dark. "Allen."

While he spoke in his usual terse phone manner, she blinked, trying to orient herself. She'd gone to bed in so many different places over the last couple of weeks, remembering where she slept challenged her. In the gray darkness, she made out the bars of the crib, and the room came into balance. *Samantha's.*

He switched the phone off. "You awake?"

"What time is it?"

"About five."

"In the morning?"

"Yeah."

"That was Ken?"

"The Tender Care Center has an Amanda Bryant enrolled. She's the right age, fits the description to a T. Ken's sending someone to the Bryants' house in about an hour to print her."

Shaine came fully alert and sat up.

Samantha, who'd obviously been roused by the call, appeared in the dimness of the doorway. "They think it's her?"

"How do you suppose the Bryants got her?" Shaine asked.

Light flooded the room. Austin leaned back from turning the table lamp on. "Either they worked something out with this Rossi, or they thought the proceeding was legal. Which I doubt." He nodded at Samantha. "Yes, they think it's Amy."

Samantha staggered to the edge of the bed. "All this time," she said in a hoarse groan. "All this time she's been gone, and now—just like that, you find her?"

"It's not 'just like that,'" Shaine told her gently. "We've been all over the country looking for Toby."

Samantha's body trembled and she hugged herself. "I can't believe it's her. I've prayed for this for so long. And now I'm praying that this is not some cruel joke."

"We can't promise you anything," Austin said, leaning back against the cluttered bookcase headboard. "But it's no joke."

"Of course not," Shaine said, glancing at her wrinkled clothes. She crawled to the end of the bed and put her arms around the teen's shoulders.

A tear splashed the back of her hand. Her heart went out to the young mother who obviously had no support from her family. She didn't know Samantha's situation, but there didn't seem to be a father in the picture. Maybe, like Maggie, she'd made a few mistakes, but she loved her baby and had been though hell the last year.

"I should call my mom," the girl said finally, pulling back and wiping a sleeve across her face. "You'll stay with me?"

Austin looked at Shaine. "We have three days left," he said.

"We'll stay a while longer," Shaine promised.

Two hours later they got the call. Amanda Bryant was Amy Cutter. Samantha nearly fainted, and Austin helped Shaine lay her on the couch. He got her a glass of water, and watched Shaine rub her wrists and talk to her. The young girl cried, huge racking sobs that drained the energy from all of them.

"Can she meet us at the airport in Kansas City in the morning?" Ken asked.

"I'll have her there," Austin promised.

The following morning he and Shaine observed the joyous reunion of mother and child in the bustling terminal.

"The Bryants paid big bucks for that kid," Ken said. "They claim they weren't in on the operation, but they bought a baby that turned up out of thin air."

Plump little Amy cried at the handling of strangers and the tearful kisses Samantha rained over her rosy cheeks.

Shaine felt sorry for mother and child. Even though she'd been found and returned, it had been an entire year since the baby had been with her real mother. The adjustment would be an enormous one for both of them, and it wouldn't be easy.

She had to wonder how Toby would react to seeing her again after all this time. Children were amazingly resilient and adapted to changes far better than adults. Or was that just a fallacy created by adults to justify the changes they forced on the children?

Ken led Austin and Shaine a short distance from the noisy reunion. "The Bryants are being formally charged today. We also have one Antonio Rossi, alias Tony Reames, alias Tim Bradford in custody. He's the top dog. And the Holbrooks have already given their statements incriminating him."

"What about Toby?"

Ken turned to her. "Rossi has a lot of kids to account for, Shaine. It's going to take a while to go over the missing-persons data and connect them with this guy. We're doing everything we can."

She nodded and turned away. Across the lobby, Samantha and her mother comforted the dark-haired toddler. After several minutes Samantha noticed her, said something to her mother and the three of them approached.

"Mom, this is Shaine. The one I told you about. She found Amy for me."

The woman looked like an older version of Samantha, her hair tinted a deeper auburn shade. "Samantha says she'll never be able to repay you," the woman said. "I never set much store by your psychic stuff, but Amy is here with us, and I'm grateful for that."

Shaine assumed that was an expression of appreciation. "Samantha doesn't owe me anything. I'm just grateful that the FBI was willing to work with us. They helped as much as Austin and I did. And Austin's the one who showed me how."

"Well, to all of you, then," Samantha said. "Thanks." Impulsively, with Amy on her hip, she leaned forward and caught Shaine in an awkward hug. Shaine returned the embrace, touched the little girl's soft dark hair once and didn't let herself talk.

"We'll keep in touch," Samantha promised. "I'll send you pictures and I'll call."

"I'd like that," Shaine replied.

Austin came next. Shaine's throat tightened when Samantha pressed herself against his chest, and one of his hands cupped the baby's head.

Then Ken, who shot a hand out before Samantha could hug him. She shook it, giving him a watery smile.

Shaine followed Austin toward the baggage claim.

"We have about an hour," Austin said, looking at his watch. "Let's grab a drink before our flight back to Omaha. Want to join us, Ken?"

"No, thanks. I want to be there when they start questioning Rossi."

"Let us know as soon as you hear anything," Shaine said needlessly.

They waved him off and found a bar in the airport. A listless feeling of melancholy swept down on Shaine as they settled themselves and ordered.

Trying to relax, Shaine found Austin studying her. She looked into his dark, concerned eyes. For not spending much time around people most of his life, he displayed acute perception. Did that go with the gift?

"This is it, Shaine," he said, as though reading her mind, which he swore he couldn't do. "Don't give up now."

"You heard him," she said, tucking her hair behind her ear without thought. "The number of children who went through that place will astound all of us. It's not like they kept records to incriminate themselves, you know. How will they know where Toby is?"

He'd told her from the beginning. Hope was what a person conjured up when they wanted something badly enough. But it wasn't enough to make that something happen. Fate had a way of controlling that, and fate had a way of, more often than not, being cruel.

It was entirely possible that she might come away from this with nothing. Without Toby.

And without Austin.

Chapter 17

Shaine paced the inn's kitchen floor on Thursday morning. "Feel anything yet?"

Audrey looked up from the newspaper and her cup of tea. "For the tenth time, I feel like a blimp."

"I mean pains, twinges, you know," Shaine said in irritation.

"Look, hon, Nick stayed home like you insisted. I'm not going anywhere. I haven't gone anywhere except to the doctor's office in three weeks because I can't get my shoes on. You can go about your business. A watched pot never boils."

Since she was obviously getting on Audrey's nerves, she cleaned and aired the guest rooms, then straightened her office. Austin hadn't returned the computer, nor had he mentioned it again. She'd seen him in here the night before. Curiosity got the best of her, and she sat in her squeaky swivel chair.

The action brought to mind the afternoon they'd put his aquarium together, and he'd sat before his computer. They had never found anyone to send him fish. His generous kisses, his inflaming touches were a sad-sweet memory.

She understood why he'd closed that door between them. He was protecting them both from the pain of their inevitable parting. He couldn't know she would rather have had every moment with him until that day came. This way was harder for her. This way was cheating her of his time and his body and the glorious hours of comfort and closeness.

Had she overreacted about the computer? He'd seemed to think he'd done something perfectly simple. The cost didn't mean as much to him as it did to her. Thinking back over the last several days with the remote, the phone, and now this, was he perhaps unconsciously making her environment more like his so he didn't feel quite so out of place?

She noticed what she assumed to be the power button and pushed it in. The quiet whine of the machine surprised her. The monitor made a fizzling sound and the screen popped on. Little boxes appeared. Cool.

She'd seen him do it enough times; it had something to do with the mouse. She moved the gadget and an arrow zigzagged across the screen.

"You have to double-click on one of those icons."

She jumped a foot. Austin entered the room and leaned a hip against her desk.

"You scared me half to death."

"Sorry. Got caught showing an interest, did you?"

"Shut up."

He chuckled.

She grinned.

He moved a stack of folders from a battered straight-backed chair, pulled the chair beside hers and tapped the screen. "Click on that one."

"This one?"

"Yeah." After a minute he said, "That's a menu. You can try a couple of the games to get a feel for the mouse and the keyboard."

He found her a matching game in which she had to hold the mouse button down, align a row of rocks so that they fit into the puzzle and then release it to get them to stay. The first time she let go too soon, and the speakers made a funny sound. She jumped back, thinking she'd broken something.

He laughed again. "It's supposed to do that. Those are the sound effects."

He prompted her to try a few more of the features, and she didn't want to disappoint him, but her baffled responses had him laughing so hard, he had tears in his eyes. The sound touched her, and she was glad she'd been the one to reach him after so many years. Surely he knew he meant more to her than just being the man who could help her find Toby. She wished she could tell him, but she didn't want to lay any additional pressure on him.

Nothing either of them had given the other had come with strings attached. And that's the way it should stay.

He leaned forward to point at the screen, and she turned her head to look at him.

Slowly he met her eyes.

She hadn't admitted it before. Not really. Not like this. Not like the soul-deep knowledge that rose up inside her now and set her heart on a wild unsteady beat.

She loved him.

She loved Austin Allen. This all-consuming emotion wasn't gratitude, though she recognized she felt that toward him, too. It wasn't simply desire, though she desired him in a completely earnest and elemental way.

This was love. "I'll-want-you-till-I-die, I'll-never-get-enough, I-need-to-have-your-heart-and-soul" kind of love. The emotion filled her with joy, and the knowledge that he didn't want her love stole it away again.

He looked at her like he wanted to kiss her.

She wanted to touch him.

She wanted to keep him.

"Shaine!" Audrey appeared in the doorway, one hand

beneath her swollen belly. "Shaine, it's time. Go find Nick!"

"I'll get him." Austin stood, and Audrey stepped aside so he could leave.

"Oh, God, this is it," she said in a quavering voice.

Shaine hurried to her side. "You're going to be just fine. And you're going to have this over with in a snap." She glanced at her watch. "Six hours. That's great for a first baby."

"Six hours! Easy for you to say!"

Shaine led her toward the back door. "Get in the car. I'll get your bag."

Six and a half hours later, she and Austin sat in the fathers' waiting room, the television droning from a corner of the ceiling. "We should have heard by now," Shaine said.

Austin nodded and glanced at his watch.

"I know what time I saw on that card," she said, as if assuring herself.

He tried to read last week's issue of *Time*.

The double doors opened and Nick came through, beaming. "You can see him in a little while," he told Shaine. "It'll be about an hour before they move her to her room."

"She's okay?"

"She's a champ," he replied, his face flushed. "It was great!" He started to leave, then turned back. "Oh, and I won the baby pool."

Rain gusted against the multipaned window. The darkness outside was relieved only by an occasional spear of lightning. A lonely man's sharply etched features were reflected in the glass.

He knew he was being watched.

Wind howled beneath the eaves. He turned his head and found her.

Lightning flashed, momentarily defining his rugged features.

Austin.

She wanted to touch him, to ease his pain.

"You can't," he said, though she hadn't spoken a word.

And he was right. She couldn't absorb all the pain and hurt like she wanted to. She would only add to his burden.

She'd never wanted that.

A small figure appeared at his side. Shaine squinted through the darkness and made out the fair-haired child. "Toby," she whispered.

"I been waiting for you," he said, his childish voice piercing her soul. "I want Bear."

"I have him," she promised.

"Get him now."

She didn't want to leave. He wouldn't be here when she returned.

"Please?"

Torn between denying Toby's request and losing him altogether, she cast Austin an anguished look.

"I'll take care of him," he promised.

Shaine awoke, the oppressive silence of her apartment closing in on her. The dream's gloominess weighed on her heart. The beginning of the dream had been familiar, but the rest had confused her. Selfishly, she wished Austin had been there to wake her. Usually he heard, even from the other room, and came to gently rouse her.

An odd intuition pulled insistently until she got up and tiptoed to the other room. The streetlight filtering through the blinds striped the empty sofa.

Shaine switched on the lamp.

He was gone.

Chapter 18

Austin called as she prepared breakfast for the two couples from Minneapolis. At his voice, Shaine's heart jolted.

"Ken called," he explained. "He wanted me to join him down here in New Mexico."

"I thought you said there wasn't anything at the farm that would be valuable."

He didn't reply right away.

After thinking, she said, "You were protecting me, weren't you?"

"Yeah. That, and the hunch I had about Samantha."

"Damn you, Austin! How could you go off without telling me?"

"I knew you'd want to come."

"Darn right I would have. This is more my concern than it is yours!"

"In case you've forgotten, you made it my concern."

She didn't have a reply for that one. She rolled the spiral phone cord around her finger and bit her lower lip.

"Besides, you have to take care of things there for a few days, don't you?"

Disappointment washed through her, easing her initial anger. "You know I do."

"Trust me to take care of things and to look out for Toby's best interests."

Instantly his words brought her recent dream to mind. *I'll take care of him,* he'd promised. "But I'm the one who saw where to find Amy," she argued reasonably.

"You were. If there's anything I think can be better solved using you, I'll tell Ken and we'll work around it until you can get here."

She released the cord and held her hair back. "That will be at least a day or two. Audrey will probably come home tomorrow. Her mother is arriving this afternoon, and she'll help with the baby. Nick has the rest of the week off. He and Marge can handle the inn."

"Take my number and Ken's down. Call if you need anything."

She jotted the numbers on a piece of paper.

"Call me," she said, and then hated herself for sounding so needy. She was not like her sister, and she would not make a fool of herself over a man.

"I'll call you tonight," he promised.

Shaine hung up and blinked back tears. This was only the beginning of missing him.

That night he called as promised. Shaine had been reading in bed, and reached over to grab the phone.

"What were you doing?" he asked.

"I've read the last two pages of the same book about ten times."

"Want to sleep? Try the program manuals."

"Thanks, I might do that."

"Ken got leads on a couple more kids today," he said. "He contacted parents and they're overnighting us something I can use."

"You need me for that," she said. "They already have the criminals in hand, they need to see where the kids are now."

"We know," he said. "And it's a hundred percent sure we'll want you here as soon as you can make it."

She could set things in order tomorrow and leave the following day. "I'll fly in Sunday evening."

"I'll book you a flight."

"Can you do it from there?"

"This is the FBI, remember?"

"Right."

She knew they both wanted to say more. She wanted to tell him she missed him and that she wanted to be with him forever. She wanted to tell him she loved him.

"I'll call you with the flight information."

"Okay."

"Good night."

Shaine hung up. An hour later she trudged upstairs for the manuals.

"How's the baby?"

"He's a doll." She slid into the car and plucked her damp blouse away from her skin. "Whew! Good thing I packed some summer clothes. Whose car?"

"Ken's," he replied, pulling away from the curb. "He's meeting us tomorrow morning."

"How's it going?"

"They've located two more kids."

"That's wonderful."

"Not through anything I did. The Holbrooks seem to remember nearly all the kids and where they delivered them. Some they remember on their own. Some of them Rossi volunteers. It's going to boil down to the department coming up with every file for a child missing over about a two-year period, and showing them the photos. We're basically at their mercy, but they don't realize it yet and they're talking to save their own butts."

"What about the man and woman who actually took them?"

"They've been identified, but so far no luck in trying to find them." He spoke as he maneuvered through the evening traffic. "Ken has had to assign people to stay in the homes where the children have been returned. They can't take the chance of this getting out to the press before those two are caught."

"What a nightmare." She looked over at him thoughtfully. "What about you? You were in that guy's head. Can you get anything on him?"

"I've been working on it."

Fatigue was evident in the clear-cut lines around his mouth. "Have you been running?"

He shook his head.

"There a gym at the hotel?"

"He's got me in a motel."

"Is there a pool?"

He glanced over. "You afraid I'll get out of shape?"

"Hardly. I think you need to keep up as much of your routine as you can. It's been hard on you being away from your home."

"I'm a big boy," he said. His hands tensed on the steering wheel. "I take trips. I'm not agoraphobic, you know."

"I know. You take trips, but you don't expose yourself to all this other stuff. You hadn't used your ability for years until you met me. And I can see why."

"Yeah, well, now I have, and I'm handling it."

"I don't want to argue with you, I just care about you."

The words hung uncomfortably in the air between them, and Shaine wished she could snatch them back.

He switched lanes and signaled for a turn. Pulling smoothly into a parking slot, he got out and retrieved her bag from the trunk.

She followed him into the building and down a hall. He unlocked the door to his room and held the door open for her.

Two queen-size beds, a desk and a television cabinet made up the ordinary-looking room. Shaine forced her gaze from the beds with the teal spreads.

"Did you bring a bathing suit?"

She always left one in her suitcase. She nodded.

He lifted her bag to the luggage rack. "Let's go for a swim, then we'll clean up and grab a meal somewhere."

And avoid being here in this room with the two beds until as late as possible. Suddenly she resented the fact that he was putting this awkward distance between them. She unzipped her suitcase and went through the motions of getting ready.

They were the only swimmers in the pool. It extended beneath a Plexiglas divider, which they swam under, and they enjoyed the cooling air outdoors as the sun set. Shaine could tell the exercise had invigorated Austin by the way he seemed to relax.

"I have an idea," she said, as they towel-dried their hair on the way to the room. "Why don't we have a pizza delivered and watch a movie?"

"Really?"

"I wouldn't have to do more than wash my hair, and I'm pretty tired from all the flights."

He agreed and made the call while she showered.

The pizza came while he took his turn showering. He'd thought to order soft drinks and plenty of napkins, so they had a picnic on the bed closest to the TV.

The only movies the pay-TV channel had were old titles, so they chose *Young Frankenstein* and laughed at the same ridiculous antics they had before.

"I love this part," he said as he leaned back against the headboard and crossed his ankles.

She lay on her stomach and plumped a pillow beneath her breasts. Shaine's attention wavered from the screen to his legs beside her, up to the loose sweatshirt and finally to his relaxed face.

A minute later he caught her staring, and turned the volume down. "Thanks."

"For what?"

"Offering to stay in."

"I was tired."

He lifted a skeptical brow. "Okay. But you suggested it for my benefit."

She shrugged and traced the pattern on the spread with one finger.

"And I appreciate it."

"In that case, you're welcome."

His mild gaze studied her face and the hair she hadn't taken time to dry into place, moved calmly to her bottom beneath the nightshirt and traveled the length of her bare legs, which were close enough for him to reach over and stroke. Her skin tingled as though he'd touched her in all those places.

"It would be okay," she said softly.

Her voice brought Austin's attention back to her lips. Up to her tawny eyes. "What would?"

"If you touched me. If you kissed me."

He wanted to. He'd learned something important while he'd been here the last two nights: There were a lot of people in this world he could do without. But he didn't think Shaine Richards was one of them.

He moved his hand to her calf, brushed the silky-soft skin and ran his palm up her thigh as far as he could reach without leaning forward.

What kind of relationship could they have with him living the way he did? Would she come to visit?

He sat up and filled his hand with her firm bottom.

"I've missed you," she said, and rolled to her side, her nightshirt riding up her shapely thighs.

No man could have resisted. This one didn't want to.

He pulled the cotton up, revealing white bikinis, and pressed a kiss on her stomach.

Her fingers threaded through his hair, sending a shiver

of keen longing through his body. He worked the pajama up and kissed her breasts, tugged it off and suckled her neck. Her gratified sigh of pleasure brought his lips to hers.

She kissed him greedily, and he rediscovered the rapture of her pliant lips and the warm recesses of her mouth. The feel of her silky soft skin beneath his hands escalated his all-consuming need for her. Her sighs praised him. Her eager hands encouraged him. He disposed of their clothing, and her soft, ready flesh welcomed him.

Her pleasure crested immediately, giving him blissful time to build his own with slow measured strokes while she kissed him and whispered delicious words of esteem against his mouth.

Minutes later, Austin lay at her side, exhaustion creeping across his body and mind. He dismissed the slender thread of fear that tried to weave itself into his consciousness. He'd held his guard in place, even in his sleep—though not as strongly—for years. Staying on the fringes of deep sleep prevented him from seeing anything he didn't want to see.

He didn't want to see their future.

Sleep crept in around the edges of his mind, and as it did, his inner man gave him counsel. *You can't love her. You don't want to love someone and then know things about them that you're helpless to prevent.*

He feared they didn't have a future. That's what he really didn't want to see.

Chapter 19

"Weather report said there were snow flurries in the Rockies," Austin said to her the next morning. They sat in a booth eating an early breakfast at a pancake restaurant near the motel.

Shaine sipped her coffee. "Have you called to check on Daisy?"

"Yeah, she's fine."

She leaned her chin on her palm and studied him, thinking how handsome he was. The remembrance of their night together brought a flutter to her stomach.

"Can I get you anything else?" the waitress drawled from beside Austin.

Unpleasantly drawn from her ruminations, Shaine reached for the thermal coffee pitcher.

"We're fine, thanks," Austin replied.

"All right. Holler if I can get ya anything else."

Shaine set the pot down with a start. The girl's voice rang in her head.

Austin laid his fork down. "What's wrong?"

"Her accent! *Her accent!*"

"What about it?"

She straightened in her chair. "The woman in my dream had an accent like that. Not exactly, but close."

"The dream about Toby and the woman?"

"Yes!"

"Miss!" Austin flagged the young woman down. She wound her way through the tables and gave him a thousand-watt smile. "Would you mind telling us where you're from?" he asked.

"Lived in eastern Kansas my whole life," she said. "Moved out here about a year ago to help take care of my father-in-law."

"Thanks." After she moved away, he turned to Shaine. "Not exactly like that?"

She shook her head in frustration. "Not exactly. But I think if I heard the exact accent I'd know it. Those words and that voice are permanently recorded in my head."

"We'll tell Ken about this. I'm sure it'll help."

They finished their coffee and Austin drove to the offices where Ken had been working.

"You need to hear accents?" Ken said, scratching his jaw. "Well, that shouldn't be difficult. I'll sit you down here with one of the office people, and they can hook you up with our offices around the country. You can talk to the secretaries or the agents."

Shaine readily agreed, and Ken called a friendly middle-aged woman over to help. Barbara Maddux located offices through the central states, and Shaine spoke with one or two people at each location.

It took about ten tries to hear the sound she wanted.

"Missouri," she told Ken confidently.

"You sure?"

"Without a doubt. There's something about that not-quite drawl that's distinctive."

"Okay. I'll question the Holbrooks right away, and I'll get back to you."

Shaine accepted the plan with an impatient nod. "You have something for us to do here today, right?"

"We have several items from missing children whose MO is the same. You up to a session? I can give you a man to work with you while I go to the jail."

She nodded. Anything to pass the time until he returned.

"Do you have someone who's worked like this before?" Austin asked.

"All of my people are already on this case," Ken replied. "I have agents working 'round the clock to turn these kids up and process them. You can take one of the local guys or wait for me."

Austin met Shaine's apprehensive gaze. "We'll take our chances."

Brett Baldwin was a jerk. Austin knew it the moment he laid eyes on him. The man swaggered into the office, didn't bother to shake Austin's hand and gave Shaine the once-over. "So you two are gonna go into a trance or something, huh? What am I supposed to do—polish your crystal ball?" He snickered. "Read an incantation?"

He was afraid of them. Austin sensed it in his offensive attitude. "Don't worry," he said. "You don't have to do anything except keep the proceeding official."

"Official? In order to do that, we'd need a real witness. And I don't see any. This is about as official as calling the psychic hotline for a lead."

"We don't have to do this." Shaine picked up her purse and stood.

Austin caught her wrist. "No. We don't. If you don't want to, you don't have to. I'll do it alone, or we can sit out in the lobby and wait for Ken."

Resignation replaced the irritation on her face. She sat back down. "Okay."

Austin turned to the detective. "I know you've been briefed on how to conduct this and yourself. Sit there. Check the evidence, keep the recorder going, take notes and keep your mouth shut."

Baldwin stared him in the eye, a muscle ticking in his cheek. He'd obviously been given orders from someone with more authority than Austin, because he folded himself into the chair behind the desk and checked the tape, starting the recorder.

He opened one of the envelopes that he'd brought with him and reached inside.

"Don't touch it."

His provoked gaze flew to Austin's.

"Just hand the envelope over or dump it out on the desk."

Baldwin looked inside, then spilled a small doll onto the desktop.

Austin got only a few hazy impressions from the doll. The name Catherine kept coming to him, and he wondered if that was the child's name.

Shaine did better, getting a clear sighting of a small-town grocery store. She got the name of the store and read the captions from a row of candy and gum machines.

The next envelope held a small thin blanket. Austin had an immediate impression of the kidnapper, the same one who'd taken Toby. The broadening vision showed a vicious assault on the child's mother. Her purse lay on the cement, its contents spilled into a heap. A credit card lay in plain view. Austin read the name and numbers.

Shaine couldn't get an impression from the blanket, but she didn't look frustrated. He'd tried to teach her she couldn't pick up a channel on everything, and apparently she understood that better now.

They continued through the remainder of the envelopes, until they'd held all of the objects hopeful parents had sent.

Austin signaled for Baldwin to shut off the recorder, and he complied. Baldwin placed the envelopes back in the box they'd been in, closed his notebook and stood. "Thanks for the show."

Austin didn't bother to watch him leave. He turned right to Shaine. "We've done everything we can now."

She nodded, then looked aside briefly and pointed toward the door. "Are you used to that?"

"I don't know if you ever get *used* to it. I was prepared for it. What we can see makes a lot of people nervous."

She shook her head in disgust.

"He was probably cheating on his wife or something," he said lightly. "Didn't want me to read his mind and expose him."

She grinned. "You're terrible."

"Well? I'm not too optimistic about most people's character anymore."

"There are a lot of great people in the world," she argued. "You've just seen more than your share of the rotten ones."

"So, you're a great person. Who else?"

"Ken. Audrey. Nick. Samantha."

"Don't exactly need a calculator to count 'em, do you?"

She covered a yawn with the back of her hand. "Well, don't count them out."

"Okay. You win. You gonna fall asleep?"

She shook her head. "I'll make it."

"I'll get us coffee."

A half hour later Ken poked his head through the doorway. "I have something, but I have to run a couple of checks on it. Sit tight."

It was another thirty minutes before he returned with news. "They delivered a blond boy fitting Toby's description to a couple in Columbia."

Shaine's stomach hit rock bottom. "South America?"

"No, Missouri."

"Oh." Feeling foolish, but relieved, she sat forward.

"Apparently this couple had tried to adopt by conventional means, but the woman has a history of alcoholism. She'd cleaned up her act, but none of the agencies would take a chance on her."

"This is just incredible," Shaine said, exasperation lacing her tone. "So what do these people do to get a stolen baby? Advertise in the personals? Ask around at the mall? If I wanted to buy a baby, I wouldn't have the least idea how to go about it.''

"Of course *you* don't," Ken answered. "But if you were desperate enough, you'd find a way."

"They should all be locked up," she said fiercely. "They're just as much to blame for Maggie's death as the man who pushed her car into the river!"

"Rossi had a real slick operation going here," Ken said. "He preyed upon young single mothers, poor, without family support, so they wouldn't have the means to hire private investigators or continue a search for long."

"He's scum," Shaine said scornfully.

Austin reached over and placed his hand on her arm. "I think you need some rest."

"What about this boy in Missouri?" she asked Ken.

"You gave me Toby's birth certificate," he said. "I entered his footprints into the computer. I'm having someone go to the house, make sure the child is there and take the boy into protective custody to process him. Just like we did with the Cutter baby. There's a lot of red tape."

"I should be there," she said, sliding to the edge of her chair as if ready to leap up and run out.

"You can't be there," he said calmly. "If and when he is identified as your nephew, then you can have custody of him."

"How long will that take?"

"Just as long as it takes the agency to find him, take him into custody and print him."

"Today?"

"I can't tell you that, Shaine."

"What would they do with him overnight? I should go there."

"Baby," Austin said persuasively in her ear, "nobody's going to do anything to frighten him any more than he's already been frightened. If this is him, you'll be the first one notified."

He wrapped his arm around her shoulder and guided her out of the chair. "Let's wait at the motel. Or take a drive."

She knew staying here wouldn't make the time pass any faster. Nor would it hurry the events taking place three states away. She just felt closer to the investigation here. She felt closer to Toby.

But she didn't want to hinder Ken or his work. He would call as soon as he had something. She gathered her composure. "Let's go for a run," she said to Austin.

He stopped and stared in surprise. *A run?*

Shaine lay on her stomach in total exhaustion, her cheek pressed against the spread of one of the beds. "Why didn't you warn me it would be so hot?"

"This *is* Arizona," he replied dryly, toweling his hair.

"I don't have the energy to shower."

"You'll feel like a new person."

"You said that before we ran."

He chuckled.

He had run, sprinting ahead, and then coming back to wait for her time and again. She had huffed and puffed and cursed him for encouraging her insanity.

"I can't get up."

He gripped her arms, hauled her to her feet and left her in the bathroom doorway. "I'm going for ice."

"Good idea, bring enough to fill the tub." After her shower, she padded to her suitcase, a towel wrapped around her. He hadn't returned.

The red light on the phone blinked.

Shaine scanned the directions, buzzed the desk and got a message to call Ken. She hung up in frustration. She didn't know the number.

She finished dressing just as Austin let himself in.

"Ken called while I was in the shower," she said. "What's the number?"

He told her and she called.

"That's his pager, so he'll call you right back," he added.

She replaced the receiver and stared at it.

Austin carried a cup of hot water and a tea bag he'd brought from the lobby and set them on the nightstand beside her.

She dunked the tea bag idly.

The phone rang and she snatched up the receiver. "Yes?"

"Shaine? Ken."

"Well?"

"Are you sitting down?"

Her heart did a back flip in her chest. She groped for Austin's hand and squeezed it unthinkingly. "Yes."

"The prints match."

Her heart stopped. An enormous swell of emotion rose up inside her like a tidal wave. This was what she'd yearned for, prayed for, begged for. Her self-protective shields raised and gave her a moment's doubt. "Are you sure?"

"We're sure. They took a Polaroid and faxed it to me. He looks just like the picture you gave me. Older. The footprints match, the description matches, the blood type matches. We're a hundred percent sure this is your nephew."

Exhilaration and relief pressed up in her throat. She grew light-headed.

"Shaine?" Austin said, when she swayed where she sat. In shock, she thrust the phone at him.

Austin exchanged a few words with Ken and hung up.

Promptly she burst into tears.

"Hey," he said, scooting beside her. He cupped her face in a palm and rubbed her back.

Shaine leaned against his chest. "When—when can we go? I didn't ask."

"It looks like we're going to Kansas City again," he said.

Shaine leaned back and looked up at him. Wiping her face, she got up and hurried over to her suitcase.

In its hiding place in a pocket, she found what she was looking for and pulled it to her chest.

Bear.

Chapter 20

Ken McKade had double-checked and assured her a dozen times that the identification was positive. The child the agency was bringing to her was Toby. Her self-preservation instincts wouldn't let her get her hopes too high until she saw him for herself. There had been too many obstacles and delays already. Another would devastate her.

Unwilling to miss the events taking place, Ken met them in the Kansas City airport restaurant that morning. "How are you doing?" he asked Shaine.

"I'm okay."

"She's a wreck," Austin corrected.

Ken reached inside his suit jacket and pulled out a Polaroid.

Shaine accepted the photograph, awe and elation mixing with a healthy dose of trepidation in the pit of her stomach. The blond-haired boy in the picture stared at the camera. His hair was cut shorter than it had been a year ago. He had Maggie's familiar eyes and the Richardses' look around his mouth and chin. He was older, of course, but he looked like Toby.

Was she just wishing so hard that she saw what she wanted?

No. No, everything had been verified. This was Maggie's son. And he would be here within the hour.

"Can you tell us anything more?" she asked shakily.

"As a matter of fact I can. We've taken the Missouri couple into custody. They're Dave and Pauline Gilbert."

"That's right," Shaine interrupted. "I'd forgotten all about it, but I heard her say that name. In my dream she told Toby that Dave left because Toby was a bad boy."

"Dave left because she was a drunk." Ken went on to explain. "We've questioned family and neighbors. It seems Pauline has had a drinking problem since before anyone can remember. Their marriage was on the rocks about two years ago, and she went to a clinic and dried out.

"That's when they started looking for a baby. After being denied a child through the agencies, they obviously found a corrupt way to get one. Apparently it was a last-ditch effort on Pauline's part to save the marriage. They told everyone they'd adopted this little boy they called Brandon."

"He must be so confused," Shaine said, thinking of the year the child had been away. But there was more she had to know. "Was he abused?"

"No. He's been examined, and there's no sign of abuse. He's well nourished and physically healthy."

"Thank God."

"Of course, buying a child wasn't enough to save the marriage. Dave moved out and filed for divorce about two weeks ago. Last week Pauline started drinking again."

It sounded like a story on one of those prime-time news shows. Shaine would no doubt be approached for her input on a movie of the week. She stared at Ken. "Will the media hear about this?"

"I'm sure they will eventually. We've kept a tight lid

on it, but as soon as our men are out of the homes we've been guarding, the story will be out and the press will follow a trail straight to you. We'll do our best to keep it quiet as long as we can, but I can't make you any promises.''

''I know. I'll deal with that when the time comes.'' She sat with her chin in her hand, her elbow on the table, piecing together all this information with her dreams. A waitress refilled Austin and Ken's cups, and for the first time she noticed the coffee in front of her.

''So the dreams I had about Toby, the really bad ones, those events haven't happened yet.''

''I don't believe they have,'' Austin confirmed. ''Everything you saw about Toby, Amy Cutter, the other children, that was all in the future. Some of those sightings, like the woman picking up Amy Cutter from the day care, were in the near future. That could have happened the same day. Others, like the dreams of Toby and Daisy, were in the more distant future. Your visions of the woman at the cemetery and the man at the piano could be either, because they're such normal everyday events.''

Austin gave her a look she couldn't read. ''One of the reasons I had to get away from this,'' he said, ''was because I couldn't change anything I'd seen. I saw so much horrible stuff in the past.''

''I know that,'' she assured him. ''I've seen what it does to you, and I understand now.''

''But you *changed* things, Shaine. Because of you, all these children are being returned to their parents and their homes.''

''Not just because of me. You helped.''

''I helped, but it was your intuition that led us in the first place.''

''My motivation was selfish.''

''You two make a great team,'' Ken inserted, reminding Shaine he'd been listening to their exchange. ''Think you might want to do a little part-time work with me after this is over?''

She met Austin's eyes and knew his thoughts because she knew him so well. He'd only done this for her. She'd shown him hope in this case, but he'd extended himself as far as he was able.

"No." Austin gave Ken a serious look. "My stand hasn't changed.

"Yeah, well, I knew that, but I figured it couldn't hurt to ask. You?" he asked, turning to Shaine.

"I don't think so," she answered with a shake of her head. There were still many more nuances of the gift she could learn from Austin, among them the ability to turn it on and off at will. She had questions for him, but this was neither the time nor the place.

Their conversation had momentarily steered her thoughts away from the plane they awaited, but once again, she found herself looking at her watch.

The plane ended up being twenty minutes late. Austin and Ken sat in the molded plastic chairs in the waiting area, but Shaine paced before the floor-to-ceiling glass, watching, praying.

At long last a plane landed and taxied to the terminal. The men in jumpsuits took forever to stretch the ramp out and secure it.

Shaine stood at the front of a small crowd awaiting the passengers. Austin and Ken stood to her right. She met Austin's eyes, and he gave her a smile of encouragement. A million butterflies danced in her stomach.

The door opened and a man in a gray suit carrying a briefcase walked past. Two women with canvas bags followed. An older woman appeared and a man and woman greeted her.

Several more men filed past. A young girl whose parents hugged her.

Where *were* they?

The crowd around them had thinned. A few more passengers came through the doorway.

Austin's hand touched her waist.

Shaine's heart pounded. They had the right flight, didn't they? She almost turned to ask Ken, when a dark-haired woman stepped through the doorway. In her arms she held a little boy with blond hair.

Eagerness surged in Shaine's chest. *Is it him? Is it him? Is it him?*

The woman looked toward them and Ken moved forward, flashing his badge. She met him, took papers from a slim case and handed them over.

The boy was looking over her shoulder and Shaine couldn't see his face. He wore tiny jeans, a red turtleneck shirt and a miniature pair of suede boots.

Ken said something to the woman and she replied.

The child turned around, bringing a finger to his mouth, and wide blue eyes assessed Ken, then flickered to Austin and finally Shaine.

It was him.

Oh, dear God in heaven, it was him! Uncontainable joy bubbled up inside and Shaine covered her mouth with her fingertips to keep from blubbering. Toby! This was Toby!

Ken and the female agent had finished their confirmations, and Ken stood back expectantly.

Legs trembling, Shaine stepped forward, afraid to frighten her nephew any more than he'd already been frightened. She'd imagined this moment a hundred times since the day before, and still she didn't know what to do or how to act.

"Toby?" she said softly.

His enormous eyes looked from her to the woman holding him and back. The finger remained securely between his bow-shaped lips.

"He doesn't remember me," she said, and glanced at the woman for the first time.

She wore a pitying look for both of them. "He's a good boy," she said, patting him on the arm. "He took a nap on the big airplane. Didn't you?"

He nodded somberly.

"This is the lady I told you about. This is your aunt Shaine." She shifted and unhooked a bag from her shoulder. "His diapers are in here."

Shaine reached for the bag, but Austin took it.

"Hi, Toby," Shaine said tentatively. "Are you ready to come with me?"

Those enormous blue eyes blinked.

He didn't know her.

Over the PA system, the echoing voice of a woman announced a departure, and he glanced around wonderingly.

Shaine opened the small bag she'd brought and pulled out the worn terry-cloth toy. "Look, Toby. Look what I brought. Do you remember this?"

His eyes locked on the bear. The finger popped out of his mouth. "Bear!"

Jubilant relief flooded Shaine. "That's right. Bear. I've been keeping him for you until you got home."

He reached out.

The dark-haired woman used the opportunity to place him in Shaine's arms. Oh, but he was big!

He snatched the bear and held it tightly.

That heart-stopping gaze lifted shyly to Shaine's, now mere inches away. "I'm going to take care of you, Toby," she promised and kissed his round cheek. "I've missed you so much."

She couldn't resist hugging his little body closely. *Oh, Maggie.* Remembering the pandemonium at Samantha and Amy's reunion, she used all her determination and restraint to keep from crying. The last thing she wanted to do was upset him.

With a lump the size of Denver in his throat, Austin watched Shaine hug the child. He glanced over at Ken, relieved to note he wasn't the only one trying to keep his cool.

Shaine kissed Toby's cheek and he clung to the bear. He did look like the photographs she'd shown him. His mouth, with the pronounced dip in his upper lip, looked just like Shaine's. A cute kid.

Shaine had her nephew. Her family.

She would be eager to take him home and rebuild their life.

Austin watched the reunion with a bittersweet satisfaction. He'd helped her. Together they'd assisted Ken in finding half a dozen children so far. And another dozen would follow.

And after that, he'd return to his mountain, not at all the same man he'd been a few weeks ago.

Toby seemed comfortable in the small room he'd shared with Maggie for a few months before the "accident." After he'd been missing for about six months, Shaine had taken the crib down, realizing he would be too big for it by then. Maggie's narrow bed was still there and, sleeping on it, he looked tiny and helpless.

"I can't believe you really found him after all this time," Audrey said. She tiptoed away from the doorway and sat beside her sleeping infant on the sofa.

"Neither can I. This ordeal since Maggie's death has taken so long. Sometimes I didn't think I'd get through it."

Audrey gave her a strained smile. "But you did."

"I'm going to have to buy him clothes," Shaine said, thinking aloud. "And when Austin and I unpacked the toys, I realized they're all baby toys. Well, he liked the cars, but he'll need things to play with."

"Shaine?"

Audrey's serious tone interrupted her ruminations.

"I want to apologize for doubting you."

"You don't need to apologize."

"Yes, I do. I wasn't as supportive as I could have been, I know that now. I was just so worried about you."

"It's okay, really. Any sane person would have had their doubts about my obsession with finding Toby."

"What are you going to do now?"

Shaine flattened her palms on her jean-clad knees. "Ken—that's Austin's FBI friend—wants us available until the rest of the kids are found. He thinks that will only take a couple more weeks. I told him I wasn't going anywhere. I won't take Toby traipsing across the country and I won't leave him."

"What did he say?"

"He said he'd use express mail or send someone to me."

Beside her, the baby squirmed, and Audrey patted his back. "What about Austin? What's happening there?"

"On the flight home he mentioned he'd be leaving. Maybe tomorrow. Maybe tonight, I don't know."

Audrey gave her an uncertain look. "Are you okay with that?"

"What do you mean?"

"You know what I mean. You've fallen for this guy. Now it's over? Just like that?"

"I don't have a whole lot of choices, Audrey. I went to him for help. He warned me from the beginning that he'd—"

"He'd what?"

That he'd take me to bed. "That if I wanted a commitment, he wasn't the man. He never pretended anything more than what this was. An interlude. I accepted the conditions."

"I can't believe this is you talking."

"Why not?"

"You're not an 'interlude' kind of person, Shaine. We both know that. When you love somebody, you love them forever."

Her words brought the sting of tears to Shaine's eyes, but she blinked them away quickly and stood. "I have a lot of laundry to catch up on." She emptied her suitcase into a basket and carried it to the appliances in her kitchen. She twisted a knob and scooped in detergent.

These unfolding events all boiled down to the fact that she'd gained one person she loved, but was losing another.

"I didn't mean to make it worse," Audrey said from behind her.

"You didn't," she replied, shoving clothes in the washer. "You couldn't."

"Well, I won't bring it up again unless you want to talk about it."

"Deal." Shaine turned around.

"I'm so happy for you that you found Toby. What am I saying? I'm so happy for him!"

Shaine stepped into her impulsive hug. "Thanks."

"What have we here?" Nick came through the door, followed by Austin.

"Where'd you guys go?" Audrey asked.

"We thought we needed to celebrate," her husband replied, and held up a bottle of champagne.

"I can't drink that," Audrey said with a pout.

"Sure you can," he replied. "I thought of that." He displayed the label specifying nonalcoholic.

"Not near as much fun, but that's okay," she said, and turned to Shaine. "Glasses?"

Shaine rinsed stemmed glasses that hadn't been used since she could remember, and they toasted the arrival of their boys.

The Pruitts left shortly after, and Shaine checked on Toby.

Austin entered the tiny bedroom behind her. She sat gingerly on the bed's edge and stroked her nephew's hair back from his forehead.

At her hesitant touches and cautious manner, Austin realized that Toby's return still hadn't struck her as reality yet. He wished he could see her with him in the coming days and weeks. He wished their worlds weren't so very different and far apart. He wished he could be certain he had the capability to let someone into his life without seeing when they'd be taken away from him.

"He needs new toys," she said softly. "Maybe you could help me pick out little-boy things."

There was no way to say it except to say it. "I'll be leaving in the morning, Shaine."

She brought the hand caressing Toby's hair to her lap. Slowly she stood and stepped past Austin. Once he followed her, she closed the door gently. "Do you need something washed for tomorrow?"

She headed for the kitchen.

He came up behind her and caught her arm.

She tried to pull away. "I can throw your jeans in with mine."

He held fast and pulled her back to him. "Shaine, talk to me."

She looked him in the eye. "What's to talk about?"

That stumped him. Indeed. What was there to talk about? How miserable he'd be without her? She didn't need to hear that. How much he wished things were different, so he could be the kind of man she needed and deserved? That would serve no purpose.

What else was there to say? *Goodbye?* He didn't think he could handle that. He released her arm.

She stared at him.

A sick, cheated feeling convulsed in his belly. He couldn't stay here until morning. He couldn't prolong the torture. He wanted to possess her so badly, the desperate desire scared him.

He had to go now. Before he spoiled everything they'd had up until tonight. Now. While he still had his fast-failing dignity.

"I'm leaving now."

In the dim light from the hallway, he thought her face drained of color. "Where will you go?"

He moved past her. "The airport."

He found his phone in his jacket pocket and called a cab.

Shaine moved into her living room like a zombie. Austin's suitcase still sat by the door; he hadn't unpacked since they'd come back that afternoon.

He went into her bedroom and returned with a smaller

bag. ''I think I have everything. If I didn't have it in my suitcase, I don't need it.''

His impatience and the finality implied stung. Shaine watched him with her heart aching.

''We'll keep in touch,'' he said without looking at her. He hadn't looked at her since he'd said he was leaving. ''We'll still be working with Ken for a while, so we'll talk.''

She didn't have anything to say. If she tried to talk, she'd break into a million pieces.

''I'll want to know how Toby's doing,'' he said, pulling on his jacket.

Finally he looked at her.

Their eyes met and held.

Shaine's chest felt like he was taking her heart with him.

He broke their locked gaze, tucked one bag under his arm and picked up the other.

Without another word he turned and left.

Shaine commanded her feet to carry her to her bedroom window. In the dark, Austin strode to the end of the drive and dropped his bags onto the concrete. He paced the street in front of the inn a few times. Finally he sat at the curb.

The buzzer on her dryer went off, but she paid it no attention. She wanted to cry. She wanted to throw up. She gripped her stomach and wanted to run down to the end of her drive and throw herself at his feet.

Miserable, Shaine tore herself from the window. She looked in on Toby once again, almost afraid she'd only dreamed him up, too.

How bitterly unfair that in finding him, she'd found and lost the only man who'd ever meant anything to her.

Returning to the window, she caught sight of red tail-lights disappearing in the distance. A morose sadness fell upon her. He was gone.

She paced the apartment. Sat on the sofa. Picked up the unfamiliar remote and set it back down. She'd bet his tapes were still in her player. If she turned it on, she'd hear

Frankie Valli or The Belmonts or The Drifters singing something that painfully reminded her of him.

If she went to her bed she'd smell him.

If she lived to be a hundred she'd want him.

An hour later, she lay down beside Toby on the narrow bed, touched his baby-soft face and breathed in his childlike scent.

She would not cry. She would not subject Toby to her internal trauma. He'd been through too much. He needed a secure home and a stable caregiver. He needed her.

And she intended to be strong. For him.

Chapter 21

"Mama?" Toby repeated, pointing to the photograph of Maggie that Shaine held.

"That's right, sweetie. Do you remember her?"

He nodded his head, but she'd discovered Toby nodded yes to everything, whether he understood what she meant or not. She smiled and kissed his forehead.

"I play pickups," he said, turning back to his favorite toys, a set of die-cast monster trucks that Austin had sent him.

"Okay, you play pickups. I'll play with you as soon as I put the macaroni and cheese in the oven."

She'd also discovered his favorites foods were hot dogs and macaroni and cheese, and after a month of boxed dinners, she'd been experimenting with casserole dishes he would like.

The phone rang, and her heart skipped a beat the way it always did. She'd spoken with Austin several times as the kidnapping cases were concluded. He'd given her guidance just as he always had, coaxing her to see more on her own than she would have been able to without him.

The man who'd pushed Maggie in her car into the river had been found and charged. Of course, Shaine had no part in the upcoming trial, but the evidence all pointed in his direction. He already had so many counts of kidnapping against him, the murder conviction would be the icing on the cake.

Though emotion was evident in the long pauses, she and Austin never spoke of their feelings for one another, or their separation, and that exclusion left her aching.

She grabbed it on the third ring. "Hello?"

"Shaine, this is Sam."

Instantly she recognized Samantha Cutter's voice. "Hey, how are you? I haven't talked to you for at least, gee, two days!"

The girl giggled. "I had to tell you my good news. I got accepted at the university!"

"That's great! Congratulations."

"Thanks. My mom is going to help me with Amy."

"I knew she'd come around."

"Shaine, he paid for an entire year's tuition, can you believe it?"

"He who?"

"Mr. Allen. I got a call from the credit office. I had a million apps in for student loans, and anyway, they said I got a grant. When I pushed, the guy confessed it was an anonymous gift in my name. I know it was Austin."

Shaine knew it, too.

"He's already done so much. Every week something is delivered for Amy. She has the biggest rocking horse you've ever seen, a collection of Disney videos and more dolls than a little girl could play with in a lifetime."

"He's never had anyone to shower with gifts, Sam. He's enjoying doing it as much as Amy is enjoying getting them. And I know what you mean. I can't walk in this apartment without tripping over cars and trucks." She glanced around the crowded space, seeing Austin's gifts everywhere.

Just then the doorbell rang.

"I'll have to let you go, Sam. I'll talk to you soon. Congratulations on your acceptance. Bye!"

A familiar brown-uniformed deliveryman stood outside her door, an enormous box on the ground beside him, and a clipboard in his hand. "Hey, Miss Richards. Another delivery for Toby."

She shook her head and signed the invoice. "Thanks. Just leave it here."

"What's zat?" Toby stood behind her.

"I don't know. Something else from Austin, it looks like."

"Open it?"

She grabbed a pair of kitchen scissors and slit the packing tape. Beneath a mountain of bubble wrap, she discovered a hand-made wooden rocking horse. She wrestled it from the carton and carried it into the living room.

"It's for Toby?" he asked, pointing at the beautifully crafted toy.

"It's for Toby," she said. "Aunt Shaine would look a little silly on it. Want to ride it?"

He nodded solemnly.

She lifted him on and showed him how to rock.

Shaine backed to the edge of the sofa and sat, watching him. She wondered if Austin had ordered it on his computer, and a smile tugged her lips upward.

A sense of familiarity nagged at her. She'd seen the horse before. She focused on remembering. It had been in one of her visions of Toby. She'd seen him sleeping in what looked like a loft bedroom, and this rocking horse had sat under the eaves.

At the time, she'd been afraid that Toby would never be returned to her, and that she may have to resign herself to the fact that he was okay, but that he wasn't with her.

Her prophetic dreams could come true. Or they could be

changed by circumstances. She recalled the dream of Toby
and the dark-haired toddler playing in the sandbox. The
man who'd come home was the dark-haired baby's father.

So...if Toby was with her now, and Toby had a little
brother, the brother would be her child.

She couldn't really draw any comfort from that.

Her dreams didn't have to come to pass. Finding Toby
in time had prevented the awful images she'd seen. She'd
been able to take action to change the outcome. Thank God.

Her dream of Toby with the brother and the man who
hugged him didn't have to happen, either. She might do
something to prevent it.

Shaine checked on her casserole in the oven and stood
in the doorway watching Toby.

The realization hit her like lightning.

*She'd already done something to prevent that dream
from happening.*

By allowing Austin to pass out of her life, she'd stopped
the chain of events that led to that moment in time.

She would never want to marry anyone else. He had been
the one.

But he hadn't wanted a commitment, she reminded herself.

"I think our supper's ready, Toby," she said.

He stopped his energetic rocking and looked skeptically
at the floor. "Me want down."

"You got it, buckaroo." She swung him off the horse
and into the air. He laughed, and the sound eased her heavy
heart. She kissed his cheek soundly and sat him at the table.

"We have to blow on this. It's hot." She got him a
second glass of milk after he spilled the first, and ate her
macaroni and cheese happily because he enjoyed it so.

He hadn't wanted a commitment.

Her feelings had been so raw, she'd taken that as the
truth. But the truth crystallized before her like a divine
revelation.

Austin Allen was the king of self-preservation.

He'd been shutting out people and tuning out feelings for so many years, it would take a lot more than a determined woman on his doorstep to crack his protective barrier and get him to place himself at risk.

It would take...

Love.

He wouldn't come to her. He couldn't. She understood it and she understood why. If she had the power, she was going to see to it that her dream of Austin as a lonely, haunted man didn't come true. And at the same time see another dream turn to reality.

"Toby?"

"Hmm?"

"You liked the big airplane, didn't you?"

He nodded. "I fwied in the big airpwane."

"Would you like to fly in an airplane again?"

His blond head nodded.

She picked up their plates, already planning. "We're going to take a trip."

Austin stared at the array of colorful fish in his aquarium. He wished *she* could see them. It had never bothered him before that he was the only one to enjoy his mountain home and all the things in it. He'd always been alone.

But he'd never been lonely.

Until now. Until Shaine Richards had impressed her image on his brain and his body and his home. He could see her everywhere. He could smell her in the shower, hear her in the kitchen, feel her beneath his hands. She'd become a ruthless attack on his senses.

He'd always been an outsider. But he'd never resented the cruel sentence of his unearthly uniqueness until now. If, for even a short time, he could be like any other man, he would leave the confines of this place and go to her.

He'd thought of it many times.

He'd dreamed of it many times.

But he'd tried living like other people. And he knew he couldn't. His place was here.

Austin tugged his gaze from the mesmerizing fish and ambled back to his desk. He'd only gotten a couple of good hours of work accomplished this day, but he'd wait until later and try again. He needed his run and his workout to get him in sync.

The music transported him while he used the weights. He slipped into sweats, grabbed a stocking cap and took off through the woods, Daisy at his heels.

Daisy deserted him sometime later, but she often chased a rabbit or a squirrel, so he didn't take the abandonment personally.

The sky hung heavy and gray, a sure sign of threatening weather, though the temperature seemed oddly warm.

He returned by his usual route, breaking into the clearing, and slowing as he approached the house. He opened the door and stared at Daisy in confusion. How had the dog gotten in?

His gaze traveled to a familiar battered suitcase against the wall, the sight piercing him with a covert thrill he quickly tamped down. The smell of cooking stabbed him with bewilderment.

He tugged off his cap and hooded sweatshirt, unconsciously running a hand through his hair.

A familiar blond-haired boy sat between the two sofas, running trucks along the floor and making accompanying noises. A delightful rush of warmth spread through Austin at the sight of the child.

Austin turned to the kitchen, and she stood on the other side of the divider, a hesitant smile on her flushed face.

"We let ourselves in," she said. "I knew where you were. I hope you don't mind."

"No—of course not," he choked out.

"I'd have felt pretty silly, if you'd have had someone else here," she said.

"No one else has ever been here," he replied.

"I'm fixing us some dinner. You didn't have anything started."

"Great."

"It's macaroni and cheese."

"I haven't had that for a while," he replied.

She shrugged. "It's Toby's favorite. Toby, remember Austin?" Shaine walked into the living room.

God, she looked great. She wore faded jeans with a slit in the knee, and that innocuous patch of skin gave him a pathetic thrill.

She perched on the edge of the sofa and rested her elbows on her knees.

Toby looked up at Austin.

"Hey, bud," Austin said.

"You give-ded me these trucks?" Toby asked.

Austin glanced at the trucks and recognized the collector set he'd ordered from an on-line shopping site. "Yeah. Do you like 'em?"

Toby nodded.

"They're his favorite toys." Characteristically, she tucked her hair behind her ear. "Those and Bear."

"Bear's in dat suitcase," Toby clarified, stopping his play long enough to point. "Aunt Shaine will get him out in a minute."

She rolled her eyes. "Everything's 'in a minute' now. I didn't realize I answered him that way so often until he started saying it all the time."

Austin grinned at her obvious pleasure in her nephew. He couldn't help his curiosity at her unannounced appearance. Why had she come? Did she plan to continue seeing him occasionally? "What day is this? Friday? Isn't the inn busy?"

"Audrey and Marge are taking care of the inn," she replied simply. Her unhurried gaze moved over him.

Self-consciously he looked down at his damp undershirt. "I'm going to go—"

"Grab a shower," she finished for him. "Supper will be ready when you are."

He hurried through his shower, disbelieving she'd come. What was she thinking? They couldn't continue a weekend affair, her bringing Toby along as he got older. He couldn't turn her down. He loved her.

They ate, Shaine sharing stories about Toby, bringing Austin up-to-date on the Pruitts and their new son. Ignoring the dishes, Austin showed Toby the fish.

Shaine peered into the tank, the bright blue background reflected in her eyes. "Did you order these from the home computer shopping network?"

He hunkered down beside Toby and grinned. "No, I got them in Colorado Springs."

She raised her winged brows. "You went shopping?"

"I have a friend who does woodcraft, and I wanted to pick out a couple of things."

"A couple of things being two rocking horses?"

"You talked to Sam."

"Yeah. She was so excited about getting into the university. Did she tell you someone paid a year's tuition for her?"

"Really? Look at that big orange one, Toby."

"Yeah. An anonymous grant."

"That's nice." He turned and found her face inches from his.

"Mmm-hmm. It would take someone really generous to do that."

"Think so?"

"Or someone who doesn't have a family or friends to spend his money on and wants to spend it on people he— cares for."

"Anything wrong with that?"

"Not a thing."

"It's not about the money. She'll be able to get a good job and take care of Amy," he told her.

"It was an admirable thing you did for her, Austin."

Her hair smelled wonderful. He wanted to reach for a handful and bury his face in it.

As if reading his thoughts, she straightened and moved to sit on his leather sofa.

Austin showed Toby Daisy's tricks of begging and rolling over. Toby laughed delightedly.

"I think Toby had a dream the other night," Shaine said, as they watched the boy and the dog play tug-of-war with an old sock.

Austin looked up to see the concern on her face. "A nightmare? You said he was adjusting really well, and you've had him to a psychologist, right?"

"Yes. She said he's going to be untrusting for a while. He lost his mother and has been passed from stranger to stranger. I have to show him he can trust me. We're going to wait on toilet training until he acts like he's ready. She doesn't think I should expect much of him right away. Then again, he could surprise us."

"You sounded like this dream was disturbing."

"Not to him." She glanced at the boy and back. "He woke up in the morning and told me about his big doggie."

"Did they have a dog where he was staying?"

She shook her head. "He talked about it several times, then not again until we got here. When we drove up, he saw Daisy, and shouted 'My big doggie!' like he'd seen her before."

Austin stared at her. "Do you think he dreamed of Daisy? Had you told him about her? Did you tell him you were coming?"

She shook his head. "I didn't decide to come until yesterday, and I never mentioned the dog."

They shared an amazed look. "Do you think he has the ability?" Austin asked.

"I don't know. You said you remember things from when you were very young. I'm almost afraid for him," she admitted.

Austin mulled over the probability. "It's very possible," he said at last.

Toby rubbed his eyes. Shaine changed him into his pajamas and helped him brush his teeth. He fell asleep on her lap before the fireplace. She placed him on the sofa and covered him.

Austin sat on the hearth. "It's great to see the two of you together."

"Sometimes I'm afraid it's not real," she said.

"It's real," he assured her.

"I suppose I should do the dishes."

"I did them while you were getting him ready for bed."

"Oh."

She sat at the other end of the hearth, the firelight flickering across her shiny hair.

He'd never have a better opportunity. "Shaine, why are you here?"

She looked up at him, her heart stuck in her throat, and wondered if she had the courage to say the words. He could turn her down. He could laugh at her silly hopes. But somehow she didn't think he would.

She was tired of losing the people she loved. She'd fought for Toby, and she would fight for Austin, too, even if it meant losing. At least she'd know she'd tried. "You made a promise to me," she said.

He frowned. "What promise?"

"That you'd teach me to turn this thing off."

His expression softened. "And that's what you want?"

She nodded.

"Okay," he said. "I'll teach you."

Shaine nodded her satisfaction at his agreement. There would be time for him to see their love wasn't a threat. She wouldn't let it threaten him. If he'd thought it odd that she'd come, bringing Toby, he didn't say so.

"Okay, then," she said. "We'll be staying awhile."

His expression revealed nothing and her resolve quivered.

"Have you been all right?" he asked.

"Yes. Having Toby with me is…well, I can't even describe how happy it makes me."

"Good," he said softly. "I always want you to be happy."

Then kiss me, she thought desperately. *Take me in your arms and let me know how much you want me.*

"How are the Pruitts and the new baby?" he asked.

Shaine changed mental gears. "They're doing great. Nick is so crazy about that kid. It's fun to watch them together."

"I like Nick," Austin said. "Both of them. Your friends are good people."

"Yeah." She moved to get comfortable on the sofa beside Toby. She'd been up late the night before, getting ready for the flight. Waiting in terminals with Toby and hauling all his accessories around had worn her out.

Austin brought her up to date on his interaction with Ken and the progress of recovering the children. He noticed when her eyelids grew heavy, and she snuggled down by her nephew.

By the time he went for a pillow and returned, he had to raise her head and tuck the pillow beneath. His fingers lingered in her silky hair, stroking it back from her temples, and he admired the sweep of lashes against her cheek, the delicate bow of her kissable lips.

Seeing her with Toby gave him great pleasure. She did seem happy. But she'd come back. Perhaps her new life still wasn't complete.

He didn't dare let himself think it.

He unfolded the lap robes and spread the blankets over the woman and child who made his log house seem like a home. Kneeling, he unlaced Shaine's boots and gently tugged them off. Her brows rose, and she burrowed more comfortably into the covers, but she didn't awaken.

Austin ambled into his office and tried to work for a while, but couldn't concentrate, not with her so close.

Thunder rumbled overhead, peculiar for this late in the year. He shut down his computer and added a log to the fire to keep the living room warm. He watched Shaine sleep until Daisy wanted out, then he let the dog out and dried her coat off when she returned.

Rain came down in earnest, now, pummeling the roof and the window panes. The wind gusted. If this turned to ice, Shaine would be trapped here for a while.

The thought didn't disturb him in the least.

He had unperishables in the storage room downstairs, firewood to last, and a back-up generator. He'd been snowed in many times.

But then he'd been alone.

Austin walked to the window and looked out at the threatening weather. This time he wasn't alone.

Even the word gave him pause. *Alone.*

It was the price he'd paid for putting distance between himself and everything, everyone.

He'd been an oddity his whole life. His own mother had treated him like a circus act. He had volumes of legitimate excuses for his reclusive life. Tom Stempson understood. Ken understood. Shaine understood.

All his reasons for protecting himself—avoiding the torture of being inside the victim's heads; being repulsed by the thoughts of the perpetrators; fear of seeing and knowing when someone he grew to love would die—all those rationales were real.

He now had the fairly reliable capability of turning off his psychometric skills. It was rare that he got an unwanted impression from an object, but it was a possibility.

Predicting someone's death was a possibility rather than a probability, too. Just because he'd seen his mother's death, didn't mean he'd see anyone else's.

He'd even wondered whether or not he'd be a good role model for Toby. Money certainly didn't make someone a father. That took love and caring and commitment. He could certainly love the child and commit to him, but Austin had never had an example. Would he make mistakes as the boy got older?

Or would he rather not take the chance at all?

Was he cutting himself off because of *possibilities?*

Which would he rather risk? An occasional ugly vision…a mistake here and there…or the certainty of the pain of being alone?

Which would hurt more? A disturbing premonition, righting a wrong, or living the rest of his life without Shaine?

These past weeks had shown him just how much he needed her. He'd thought he could return and pick up his life where he'd left off before she'd come, but he couldn't.

Maybe he was nothing but a big hypocrite. Maybe he did need to see the future to assure himself he wasn't taking any risks. How pathetic. Nobody ever got to see how their choices were going to turn out, what kind of partner or parent they'd be. His unwillingness to take a risk only added to making him different.

Shaine had become everything important to him. He remembered her bungling attempts at erecting her tent, her determination, her pride. He thought of the times they'd spent together, the sharing, the laughing, the loving. He envied her unshakable love for Toby and her sister, admired her relationship with her friends. She was far more courageous than he. She'd been willing to do anything it took to find and claim the child she loved, even if it meant looking like a fool…making mistakes…or failing.

And he'd been a coward.

A leaf blew against the window and clung tenaciously for a moment before the wind carried it off. Suddenly the security and privacy of the log house made it seem more like a prison than a sanctuary.

He would forever be alone if he wasn't willing to take the risks and ask Shaine to marry him.

There was nothing he wanted more. Not privacy. Not a painless existence. He couldn't quite picture himself living in the bed and breakfast in Omaha, but surely there was a compromise they could reach. He would do it. Whatever it took.

When should he ask her? In the morning? After lunch? While Toby was napping?

Nervousness skittered through him at the prospect. And something else…something more. A warmth seeped across his chest and settled in his abdomen…the strangest feeling. Not like a vision, but….

Shaine.

He turned and found her standing a few feet from him, one of the blankets wrapped around her shoulders.

"Austin?" she said, her voice gravelly from sleep. "Is everything all right?"

He'd known she was there, had felt her watching him. "Weather's turning bad," he said. "Looks like this rain will turn to ice and snow."

She wore a strange expression.

"What's wrong?" he asked.

"You at the window. That was my dream, the dream I had before I ever knew about you. You were in such torment. I could feel your anguish. I'd hoped I had prevented that dream. I never wanted to bring you pain."

"You haven't brought me pain," he replied, even though the rock in his belly denied those words.

"No?"

"No."

"Getting you to teach me isn't really the reason I came," she confessed.

He'd wondered. But he'd been too glad to see her to care why she'd come.

Shaine admired his chiseled features in the scant light from the window. She hadn't traveled all this way to chicken out.

"There's something else I want, too." Her heart hammered against her ribs.

"Something I can give you?"

"You can. I just don't know if you'll want to."

"What is it?"

Shaine stiffened her spine and looked him in the eye. "I want you."

His expression flattened with surprise, then slowly, his brows lowered in confusion. "What do you mean?"

"I mean I want to marry you. I want you to marry me. I want us to be together. Always."

"But—" He looked hopeful and wary at the same time. "But you know I won't leave here," he said. "I can't live like you do."

"I know that. It doesn't matter."

"But your inn, your friends…"

"My inn is a job, Austin. It's a place, a house full of things. My friends are my friends, but they'd be my friends if I lived somewhere else, too. Toby is the only person I have to have with me. And you. And you're here."

"You mean you'd be willing to live here?"

She nodded. "I loved it here. I didn't miss anything while I was gone. Except pizza."

He ignored her jest. "I told myself I wouldn't love you, that I wouldn't love anyone, because I couldn't bear to love and know when something awful was going to happen."

"Because you saw your mother's death in advance?"

He nodded.

"You loved her, even though she exploited you, and you suffered when she died. Everyone feels guilty and responsible when a loved one dies. Remember how horrible I felt about Jimmy Deets? And I didn't even know him. You showed me I wasn't responsible, and you weren't responsible for your mother's death, either. Austin you're not God."

He shook his head sadly. "When I left you in Omaha I hadn't realized that yet. Being me—being like we are—I tend to forget that I'm not entirely different from everyone else, and everyone loses people they love, too. You lost

Maggie. I had a lot of time to think this last month. And I figured out that the only real certainty in life is death.''

She braced her palm on the stones and leaned toward him. ''Nobody ever knows how much time they'll have together,'' she said. ''The important thing is what we do with the time we have between now and then. Do you want to waste what happiness we could have together worrying about something in the distant future that's out of your control?''

He shook his head. ''No.'' He moved to kneel in front of her. ''Are you serious about living here? You'd leave people behind and come live with me? How can I ask that of you?''

''You didn't ask it of me. You big jerk. I asked you. Besides, you go out occasionally, right? We'd take trips, visit friends?''

''What about school for Toby?''

''They send buses from Gunnison, don't they? If you don't trust 'em in bad weather, we can take him on the snowmobile. Or I can homeschool him.''

''Shaine, you want to marry me?''

Seeing the hope and joy in his eyes, she nodded, her heart close to bursting. ''I love you,'' she whispered.

He took her hands, brought her fingers to his lips and kissed them. ''And I love you.'' He pulled her against his chest and hugged her fiercely. ''Oh, I love you, too.''

He buried his fingers in her hair and held her close. He kissed her, and she knew she'd done the right thing, the only thing. Getting to the truth had been her challenge from the beginning: the truth about Maggie and Toby; the truth about Austin, about their feelings for one another.

The kiss grew as warm as the fire at her back. She pulled away enough to ask, ''S'pose it's started snowing yet?''

''I don't know. Want to go see?''

She checked on Toby and ran up the stairs ahead of Austin.

Sometime later, she lay in his arms, gazing at the snow flurrying across the mountain sky. He stroked her bare shoulder.

"You know," he said thoughtfully. "We could always build a bigger place."

"We'll need one," she said. "We're going to have another little boy in a year or so."

His hand stilled. "Really?"

She nodded.

"What will he look like?"

"Dark hair like yours. Adorably cute and chubby."

"Wow." His hand moved again. "I was thinking about a bed-and-breakfast retreat. Like a hotel."

She pushed up to look at his face. "Really?"

"All new, of course," he said. "No antiques."

"No," she agreed. "Nothing with impressions." She ran her finger over his lips.

"If Toby and our other children have the gift, we'll teach them early," he said. "They'll never have to use it if they don't want to."

"And they can use it without feeling like a freak if they do choose to," she added.

He hugged her tightly, as though he never wanted to let her go.

"We're going to have a wonderful life together," she said.

He held her head and kissed her nose. "How can you tell?"

Beneath her palms his heart beat steadily, the heart of the man she was going to spend the rest of her life loving. "I have the gift, remember?"

* * * * *

Take 4 bestselling love stories FREE

Plus get a FREE surprise gift!

Special Limited-time Offer

Mail to Silhouette Reader Service™

3010 Walden Avenue
P.O. Box 1867
Buffalo, N.Y. 14240-1867

YES! Please send me 4 free Silhouette Intimate Moments® novels and my free surprise gift. Then send me 6 brand-new novels every month, which I will receive months before they appear in bookstores. Bill me at the low price of $3.34 each plus 25¢ delivery and applicable sales tax, if any.* That's the complete price and a savings of over 10% off the cover prices—quite a bargain! I understand that accepting the books and gift places me under no obligation ever to buy any books. I can always return a shipment and cancel at any time. Even if I never buy another book from Silhouette, the 4 free books and the surprise gift are mine to keep forever.

245 BPA A3UW

Name	(PLEASE PRINT)
Address	Apt. No.
City	State	Zip

This offer is limited to one order per household and not valid to present Silhouette Intimate Moments® subscribers. *Terms and prices are subject to change without notice. Sales tax applicable in N.Y.

UMOM-696   ©1990 Harlequin Enterprises Limited

SILHOUETTE WOMEN KNOW ROMANCE WHEN THEY SEE IT.

And they'll see it on **ROMANCE CLASSICS**, the new 24-hour TV channel devoted to romantic movies and original programs like the special **Romantically Speaking-Harlequin® Goes Prime Time.**

Romantically Speaking-Harlequin® Goes Prime Time introduces you to many of your favorite romance authors in a program developed exclusively for Harlequin® and Silhouette® readers.

Watch for **Romantically Speaking-Harlequin® Goes Prime Time** beginning in the summer of 1997.

If you're not receiving ROMANCE CLASSICS, call your local cable operator or satellite provider and ask for it today!

ROMANCE CLASSICS

Escape to the network of your dreams.